AGE OF SECRETS

BOOK EIGHT IN
THE DRUID'S BROOCH SERIES

CHRISTY NICHOLAS

GREEN DRAGON PUBLISHING

Irish pronunciation is very different than English, despite using a similar alphabet. See the first pages for a pronunciation guide and glossary for Irish names and terms.

There is also a link in the back for a family tree of all the characters in this trilogy. Be warned, there may be spoilers!

Table of Contents

Dedication

As always, I want to thank my husband, Jason, and my author group for all their help, support, and friendship. My beta readers, Ian Erik Morris and Mattea Orr, your feedback was invaluable.

We get to choose our friends, but not our family. Sometimes you have to remove yourself from those you are related to for your own well-being. I dedicate this to all those people who must choose between their health and their relations.

Pronunciation Guide

People
Adhna — Eye-na
Aebh — Ayv
Airiu — AY-ru
Bodach — Bud-ukh
Bres — Bresh
Caicher — KAY-kher
Cailleach — CAL-yukh: The hag goddess
Creidne Cerd — KRED-ne KURD
Elatha — eh-LA-tha
Fionn ma Cumhaill — FINN mack cool: Legendary leader of the Fianna
Goibniu — GOB-noo
Grian — GREE-ahn
Guaire — GAY-reh
Luchta — LUKH-tah
Manannán — Ma-na-NAAN
Míl — Meel: Leader of the Celts who came to Ireland from Spain
Onchú — AHN-khu
Pádraig — PAD-rig
Rúadán — ROO-dan
Tuireann — TOO-reen

Places
An Ruirthech — an ROOR-thekh: The River Liffey
Hy Brasil — Hee Brass-el: A mystical land to the west of Ireland
Imleach — IM-leekh
Tír na nÓg — Cheer nah Nohg: Land of the Ever Young

Other
Dearbhfhine — jarv-INAH: Related by having a shared grandparent
Fomoire — Foe-MORE-eh: Ancient race in Ireland before the Túatha Dé Danaan
Géis — gesh: A curse or requirement
Léine/Léinte — Lay-na (singular)/Layn-tah(plural): A long belted tunic
Murdúchann — MUR-doo-khan: mermaid or merrow
Túath — Twah: Medieval extended household
Túatha Dé Danaan — TWAH-ha day DAH-nan: Fairies or people in Ireland before the Sons of Mil

Chapter One

Fingin flung the fishing net with all his might. The circular sieve spun wide and nestled onto the surface of the gently flowing *An Ruirthech* River. The weights on the edge sank slowly to the rocky floor, and with gentle tugs, Fingin pulled the handline and tightened his snare.

A few times, the edge caught on stones, but a slight twitch freed the twine. Once he hauled it to shore, he scowled at the paltry three small salmon and one young pike he'd caught.

Typically, he did much better at this time of evening, as the sun kissed the edge of the dusky horizon. Nevertheless, he had plenty to eat and more for the morning market.

Since Fingin had left home seven winters before, he'd learned to balance his work and his needs pretty well.

Perhaps just one more cast would be wise. He secured his catch, sniffed the fresh wind for any hint of rain, and waded back into the water.

The river narrowed at a sharp bend, making the current run swift and strong, and corralling the fish into a smaller area. Fingin whispered, urging the fish to come closer. His voice flowed out through the air and into the water.

Sometimes, the fish listened, but more often, they fled. Fish were wary of any fisherman, despite his ability to talk to them. Just because they understood him didn't mean he could command them.

He didn't like speaking with fish. Even with magic, his voice was distorted by water. He preferred talking with larger animals, as they had more interesting conversation. But sometimes he could persuade fish to swim closer toward his net.

A ripple upriver caught his eye, glinting in the setting sun. Fingin squinted as it grew closer. Something large swam beneath the surface, a fish too big for his net.

Hastily, Fingin yanked his net in, but it caught on a rock. With frantic hands, he tried to untie the handline from his wrist, but the water-soaked knot stuck fast.

His heart raced as he yelled, "No, no, no! Go away! Go around!"

The huge salmon ignored his shouting and hummed a sprightly tune as it leapt, cutting the river's surface with a glint of silver and pink, before barreling into the net.

Fingin held on for dear life as the fish plowed through, snapping braided horsehair and vine like a rotten bit of thatch, but the main part of the net held. The force pulled Fingin well into the center of the river, spluttering and gasping for breath like the fish he often tossed on shore.

The water roared above him and into his lungs, forcing his breath out. His panic rose as the current slammed him into a jagged rock. Pain shot through his midriff.

When his face reached the surface, he sucked in a deep breath and coughed. The water snatched him away from blessed air. He gasped again, but water flooded his mouth. His lungs burned as he sunk under again.

The handline cut deep into his wrist, digging through his soaked skin. He clawed at it as the water and the salmon swept him downriver, then wriggled through two more bends in the bank as Fingin's sight turned to gray.

His arms wrenched as the huge salmon finally tore through the net. Fingin fought back to the surface. He rasped a huge breath, drawing sweet, fresh air into his lungs, then drifted downriver, his tattered net trailing behind him.

When he finally made it to the riverbank, Fingin retrieved the shredded remains of his net and slogged back to the shore.

He clenched his jaw at the damaged net, pulling the now useless thing onto the bank, squelching through the river mud and reeds to dry land. After he wrapped it into a ball, he considered throwing it back into the river as a just reward for its betrayal.

With a deep sigh, Fingin tucked the awkward, sopping bundle under his arm and walked upriver. The net hadn't been at fault. A salmon that size had no business being this far up *An Ruirthech*. He was leagues away from the sea, and only the smaller salmon ever made it this far past the weirs and the rapids.

The river wound through the countryside, but walking overland to his hut was fairly quick.

Fingin didn't live in high style. The rough hut wouldn't last more than a winter or two, but he never bothered with building a permanent home. Not anymore.

His current home stood in a clearing nestled within a riverbend. A beach allowed easy access to the water, with a flat rock next to the hut. This rock allowed Fingin to spread his net out when it needed repairs, or to clean his catch.

Fingin preferred the simple life, and while he craved friends, he didn't dare seek people out. He spoke to birds and squirrels, but they only talked of sweet, simple things, like food and rain and mating.

From his flat rock, he stopped repairing the net to watch the meandering river, wiggling his hands to keep them from aching. Then he bent back to his task, determined to fix at least half the damage before dusk. Occasionally, he'd glance up at a sound or to stretch his back.

That salmon must have been a cursed fish, or maybe some faerie conjuration. His net never had a chance. Still, he jerked the strands with frustration as he knotted vines and braided new strands.

Fingin rose to fetch more rope from his hut. Although the ball of rope was hefty, repair on this scale would use most of it up, so he'd need to make more.

When he sat again, he let out a deep sigh. He'd forgotten to stoke the fire. While he'd banked it that morning, if he didn't start it now, it would be dark before he cooked his meal.

He stood again, watching the water as a log swung lazily along the current, with something round and furry in the middle. Fingin squinted to see the object between the glints of the setting sun.

The thing lifted its head, and Fingin realized it was a scraggly wolfhound, soaked and scrambling to stay on the branch.

Without a thought, Fingin rushed to the far end of the river bend. He scurried down to the beach and dove into the water, swimming with powerful strokes to reach the log. He almost got a handhold before it spun away.

With a spluttered curse, he yelled at the dog, "Come! Swim to me! I'll take you to shore!"

The dog lifted his head up. Fingin had seen that expression on animals before. He'd never have heard anyone speak to him in words he understood.

After a heart-breakingly long moment, the dog leapt from the dubious safety of the soaked log and paddled toward Fingin. The enormous dog draped his huge paws on his shoulders, almost dunking him, but Fingin rolled on his stomach, asking the dog to lie on Fingin's shoulders. "I'll bring us back to shore. Just keep your head above water."

He crawled to the beach and dropped onto the sand, trying to catch his breath. The dog did the same, his pink tongue flopping out of his mouth.

When Fingin could breathe again, he sat cross-legged across from the beast. The poor thing looked half-starved and half-drowned. The silver-gray fur looked matted and patchy, and his ribs showed through the skin.

He patted the poor dog a few times. "Stay here just a few moments, dog. I'll be back with food, water, and a nice cloth to dry you. When you're fed, I'll take you up to the fire and get you warm, aye?"

The wolfhound opened his eyes once and closed them again, still exhausted. Fingin took that as agreement and climbed the rough stairs he'd built into the hillside. He gathered fish from the day's catch, turnips left over from yesterday's stew, and a skin of water. On the way out, he grabbed his blanket and returned to the beach.

The dog hadn't moved so much as a paw but was breathing easily now. Fingin spied a gash on the dog's leg, and he daubed it with river water. The dog whimpered but let him work.

With some urging, Fingin convinced the hound to sit up to drink and eat. He took a little fish but wouldn't touch the turnip. Fingin let out a chuckle. He didn't care for plain turnips either, and he lived too far from the ocean to spice it with salt.

"What's your name, boy? I'm Fingin."

The hound turned his head and Fingin heard his words within his mind. "Why can I understand you? I never understand humans."

Fingin gave a shrug. "My grandmother gave me a faerie gift when she left me."

The dog shook his head, as if the last bit didn't make sense. Fingin supposed it wouldn't, to a dog.

The hound let out a single woof. "I'm Bran. At least, that's what my friend called me."

Bran. One of the two famous hounds of *Fionn ma Cumhaill*, the legendary leader of the Fianna. A worthy name for an enormous wolfhound.

Putting a hand on Bran's shoulder, Fingin asked, "Do you want to be called Bran? If you'd rather another name, I'll call you something else."

Bran's tongue lolled out. "Bran is good. I'll remember Bran. I don't remember things very well. That's why my friend sent me away." He ducked his head as if ashamed.

Fingin put a hand under Bran's chin and lifted until he gazed into the dog's eyes. "Hey! That was a mean thing for him to do. Would you like to be my friend? I promise I won't make you go away."

The dog's tail thumped three times on the sand before he gave a cautious, "Yes, I would like that very much. Do you have more fish? My leg hurts."

With a grin, Fingin nodded. "I have fish up at my hut, and a warm fire. I'll wrap up your leg so it can heal. Here, let me dry you off first."

Fingin rubbed the wiry gray fur hard with the blanket, and Bran squirmed under him, the tail now wagging so hard it bruised Fingin's arms. "Settle down, Bran! Settle down. We'll be done here in a moment."

Once Bran's coat was fluffy and dry, Fingin led him up the hillside. Bran didn't like the steps but made it to the top after several whines. When he spied the fire, he rushed next to it and lay down, "This is warm. I really like warm. Will you let me stay near the warm for a while?"

With a chuckle, Fingin said, "You can stay next to the warm all night if you like. I'll be there, too. The sun's going down. Let me put more fish in the pot for my meal, and I'll give you the rest."

He glanced over at the still ripped net and sighed. He'd have to repair it in the morning. Keeping the hound warm and fed was more important just now than the net.

Fingin woke the next morning with a warm body next to his, all along his back. He panicked, not remembering meeting anyone. He hadn't talked with another person in a long time, much less been comfortable enough to fall asleep next to them.

With cautious movements, he twisted around. In the dim light of the growing dawn, he made out the gray, furry form of Bran, stretched out almost as long as him, snoring slightly.

Yesterday's events came rushing back, from the massive salmon to the nearly drowned dog, and he grinned.

Fingin once had a dog when he was eight, a puppy who'd loved him like no other. The dog had lived with them before Fingin could talk to animals, and before his grandmother had disappeared.

The puppy had been a mixed hound from across the sea. At least, that's what his grandmother had told him. He'd always believed her tales. His father would tell lies all the time, just to make himself more important or impressive, but his grandmother had never lied to him.

Fingin gulped back the memories, rose from the warmth of the dog, and stoked the banked fire back to life. He poured water into the tin kettle for tea and stepped outside to greet the day.

His parents had been fanatics of the new Roman religion, but his grandmother had taught him the proper way to honor the dawn. Fingin faced the east and sat cross-legged on the outcropping overlooking the river. As he waited for the sun's first rays to peek out from behind the hills and across the countryside, he closed his eyes. When the sun touched his skin, he smiled at the warmth, then sang.

The song had no words, at least none he recognized. He'd learned it by rote, some old language his grandmother had known. Or perhaps she didn't know the meaning either.

It didn't matter. They'd called to the sun as the sun now called to him. He drew in the power of the morning, energizing his body and his soul with the promise of the new day.

When the shimmering orb cleared the hill, his voice faded to blend into the song of the surrounding birds. The power within him tumbled into the earth below, curling away like a heavy smoke from a smoldering fire. Once he'd released the strength back into the soil, his body and soul were refreshed and ready for what lay before him.

Fingin strode back to the hut where Bran still lay sleeping, now curled into a ball next to the flickering flames of the hearth fire.

He needed more fish for breakfast. Yesterday's catch had been enough to feed himself for two days, but not himself and a starving wolfhound.

But to get more fish, he needed to repair his net.

With a determined stride, he fetched his abandoned project and bent to his task. He pulled a length of thin rope, braided with horsehair, thin vines, and reed stalks. Fingin tied knots to one side of the enormous gap left from yesterday's fiasco and tied the other end to the opposite side of the gap. Then he tied parallel lines across the gap until he'd connected each strand in that direction.

Now for the hard part. He added rope cross-ways, tying new knots at every juncture. This step took much longer than the first pass, and he had to get up often to stretch his legs and back.

The hound still slept. Fingin smiled every time he glanced at his hut. He hoped Bran would want to stay. It would be nice to have a friend.

Just as he tied the last knot of the main gap, a loud yawn came from the hut. Bran stretched and rolled over but didn't wake.

Fingin held up his repaired net, searching for gaps. There, that knot didn't look secure. He re-tied it and tested the fastness of the net as a whole, tugging and pushing each section.

A sloppy job now meant empty bellies later. If Bran stayed, he had two bellies to fill, and failure wouldn't mean just his own hunger.

"What's that for?"

Fingin just about jumped out of his skin. He spun to find Bran staring at the net with a cocked head.

After he calmed his heart, Fingin explained, "It's a net. I throw it in the water to catch fish."

At the mention of fish, Bran's ears perked up and his tongue fell out of his mouth. "Fish? More fish?"

"In a little while, Bran. I have to catch them first. Do you want to come watch?"

"Fish!" Bran twisted crosswise and nibbled at the bandage on his leg.

Fingin tapped his nose away. "Don't eat that, Bran. It will help your leg heal."

Bran stared at him, then at the bandage. With a pout, the dog left the cloth alone.

Together, they walked down to the river. Fingin waded out to his normal perch, a flat stone in the middle of the river. He cast his net, letting the weights pull the edges down to the riverbed. When he tugged, he watched for any unusually large salmon, but none appeared to ruin his net this time.

A few expert tugs and he almost had the net drawn in. Bran bounded into the water and yanked the net, his teeth latched onto one edge. "Bran, no, no, you'll tear it. It's only designed for one person to pull."

Bran bowed his head and shrunk away with a whine.

Fingin hadn't wanted to hurt his new friend's feelings. "It's all right, Bran. I'm glad you wanted to help. But I've made my net so I can work alone."

Fingin tugged and pulled at the net. He pulled in a decent haul, at least a dozen trout and a pike. One little salmon wiggled through a hole in the net, and Bran leapt after the tiny fish, losing it in the splashes.

One paw stepped on the net as Fingin was still struggling to pull it to shore. Soon, both paws were twisted in the net and he yipped, trying to get free. His eyes grew wide with panic and he yipped again.

"Bran! Stop moving. I'll get you out."

Fingin waded back out into the river and patiently extricated Bran from his freshly repaired net. "Now, stay clear of the net. It's easy to get tangled."

When Bran returned to shore, he tried to nibble on the cloth again.

"Stop that, Bran. It won't heal if you don't stop bothering it."

Bran bowed his head, his wet fur dripping on the shore. "I'm sorry. It itches."

"Don't be sorry. Just learn." Fingin grinned to take the sting from his words. "I'm glad to have you as a friend."

Bran's tail wagged so hard that droplets splattered them both.

As Fingin cleaned their catch on the rock next to the hut, Bran's tongue lolled out of one side of his mouth. "Can I eat this one yet?"

"Not yet. I have to clean it. I don't want you choking on a fish bone."

"What about this one?"

Fingin shut his eyes for a moment, wondering if he'd been this eager as a child. "No. Wait a few minutes and I'll have this one cleaned. Then you can have it. But eat slowly, because I have to clean all these fish, and no, you don't get to eat them all."

Bran settled down and placed his head over his crossed front paws, the very picture of patience and virtue. Fingin stifled a chuckle and set to cleaning the first fish.

It had been quite a struggle to drag the net up the steps with Bran's all-too-willing help. Just as he reached the halfway point, the dog had let out a volley of furious barks, making him slip two steps and lose his grip on the net.

Once the squirrel who had caused that mishap disappeared, he'd trodden on Bran's paw, causing the hound to yip and whine.

Finally, Fingin wrestled the net full of fish to the clearing. Now he had to clean each one. With fourteen—no, fifteen—fish, most decent-sized, he could give two to Bran, two to himself, and have eleven for market.

Fingin glanced at the sun to judge the day. He'd woken early and the sun hadn't reached its zenith yet. With luck, he'd still have time.

The market was less than a half day's walk through the woods to a valley. Ten families lived in a cluster and met every ten days to trade when the weather was bright. And today was a fantastic day, full of sunlight and singing birds. Everyone would be out just to enjoy the warmth.

Fingin hated going to market, but he needed to trade his fish to get things he couldn't catch or make. He talked well enough to Bran and other animals, but his ability to speak with humans left much to be desired.

His voice always stumbled and halted, making him sound like an idiot. No matter how much he practiced or tried, he barely got words out, much less whole sentences. Each word was like pushing against a riverbank.

He'd often wondered how much of this difficulty was because of his grandmother. Before she left, he'd talked like anyone else to humans, and not at all to animals. At least, when he spoke to dogs then, they hadn't answered back.

But when she left, she took his human voice and left his animal voice. This left him unsuited to living with other folks. Invariably, the locals chased him away after a few seasons.

He'd grown used to moving on every two or three winters to a new place, which is why he didn't keep many things. He had to carry everything he owned on his back too often.

While Bran gleefully munched the growing pile of fish guts, Fingin gutted and cleaned each one. When he'd finished, he stretched his arms behind his head and let out a long, low groan. His back ached from hunching over.

Bran looked up from his meal, slime dripping from one side of his mouth. "Is my friend hurt?"

"Not hurt, just aching. I sat in one place too long. I shouldn't do that."

Fingin cracked his neck to each side, then cleaned his gutting knife. After wrapping the cleaned fish in bark and tying it with string, he placed it inside.

"No more fish?"

"You've had two. No more now. I have to cook some for myself."

"Cook?"

"Make it hot with fire."

Bran cocked his head. "My other friend did that. Why?"

"It tastes better. I'll let you try a bite when I'm done."

Bran pouted again. "He never let me taste any."

Sending a silent curse to whoever had been Bran's *friend,* Fingin poked the fire with a stick. He skewered the two fish on another and placed it over the fire, across two Y-shaped sticks staked into the ground.

Just then, he realized he'd eaten nothing since yesterday afternoon, and it was already midday. The sizzling fish made his mouth water.

He poked the flesh a few times to gauge the cooking. When he judged the fish ready, he pulled it from the flame.

"More fish now?"

"Wait until it cools, Bran. Otherwise, you'll burn your mouth, and that'll hurt."

Again, Bran pouted with impatient eyes. When Fingin pulled the cooked flesh of the fish apart with his knife, Bran perked up and his tail pounded against the ground in delighted anticipation.

Fingin placed a big chunk of cooked fish on the ground near Bran. The dog sniffed at it several times before he licked the treat. He nibbled the edge and then devoured the whole thing in less time than Fingin took to blink.

With a chuckle, he said, "I suppose that means you like the cooked fish?"

Bran let out a yip. "I do. More?"

"Not just now, Bran. I have to finish my meal. Then I need to go to market with the rest of the fish. Would you like to come along? Or would you rather stay here and guard our home?"

"Home?"

"This place, where we sleep. It's our home, yours and mine."

His tongue lolled to one sided. "I like our home, but if you leave, I want to go with you."

The simple answer made Fingin smile.

Why had he never had a dog since he realized he could speak with animals? His grandmother had left fifteen winters ago. In all that time, he'd *seen* dogs, but usually they were working on someone else's farm.

He'd talked to a cat once, but when he moved away, she didn't want to follow. She'd been far too independent to attach herself to any human, no matter how nicely he talked.

Birds, squirrels, rabbits, even the occasional deer, had spoken with him, but the simpler the animal, the simpler the speech. While he barely understood bees and beetles, the bits he did understand centered around food and survival. And their conversation didn't help his loneliness.

Bran, however, might become a true companion, someone to help him through the long, lonely nights. Someone to watch his back while he slept on the road. Someone to share the things he did and saw and thought.

He ruffled the dog's head until the gray, wiry fur stood on end. With a grin, he rose and gathered his wares, wrapping the fish to sell in a woven reed mat he'd made.

Birds filled the woods with song and swooped across the path as Fingin and Bran walked along the trail. His new friend bounded after partridge and rabbits, delighting in the adventure. The distance seemed shorter with Bran at his side.

Once, after burrowing into a rabbit's hole, Bran raised his head and Fingin had to laugh out loud. A ring of dirt and clover surrounded the hound's snout. After a sneeze and a violent shake of his head, Bran trotted next to him in quiet dignity, as if nothing had happened. Fingin continued to chuckle every few minutes.

They passed a derelict roundhouse in the next glade. The place had been empty for a while. Fingin had even considered moving in, but something about the place made him wary. Besides, the thatched roof needed lots of repair, difficult for one person.

They passed another bend in the river, the huge badger hole in the hillside, and a stand of enormous oak trees. He spied a burdock bush and paused to harvest several large leaves to wrap his fish in.

Then Fingin had to call Bran away from investigating the badger hole. He didn't want his new friend to suffer a nasty bite on the nose.

Beyond the oaks was a circle of three ancient standing stones. Fingin shivered as they passed. Even in the bright sunlight, the circle gave off a sense of danger, a feeling of being watched. He never went there.

After they rounded a tall hill, the village came into sight. Five farms clustered in the middle, with five more on the outskirts. Folks gathered in a center space for fairs, harvest celebrations, and markets.

The largest roundhouse held a family of seven and rose two stories. The smallest was almost the size of Fingin's home. Farms with fields of turnips, wheat, cabbage, barley, and rye radiated out from the roundhouses in a random pattern, like a broken wagon wheel. Smaller kitchen gardens grew herbs such as rosemary, onions, garlic, and chervil, things he could smell as he walked by. Fingin wished he could afford some of the fancier herbs.

Mid-summer meant the first fast-growing vegetables would be harvested and offered in trade. Fingin spied several people he knew by name. They knew him, but rarely offered any friendliness.

He'd moved into his hut only a winter ago, and so would still be considered a stranger, even if his speech hadn't been broken.

Twenty people gathered in the village center. Several sat behind benches, blankets, or trestle tables to show their wares. A few had a lean-to set up for shade. Summer dust rose from the trampled ground and tickled his nose until he sneezed. Bran echoed his sneeze and shook his head.

The first bench held the tanner's goods. Sometimes Fingin caught a deer or rabbits and traded with the tanner, but today he only had fish.

He continued past the baker, the weaver, the chandler, and took the space at the end, next to folks selling vegetables and fruit.

Bran examined each person, sniffing them and their wares. The tanner shooed him away, but the baker gave him a small treat, much to his delight. After that, Fingin called him back, but he wouldn't listen, not with the possibility of food.

Unfurling his blanket, Fingin put down his pack and unrolled his fish. Bran settled down on the blanket behind him.

"I want to go sniff more people. The woman with the blankets smells like sheep."

Fingin murmured, keeping his lips still. "Stay behind me until the fish are gone. Maybe she'll come to us."

A few minutes passed before anyone approached them. A young mother, toddler on her hip, strolled up and peered at his offerings. She lifted a pot and raised her eyebrows. "I have honey. How many fish would you trade?"

Fingin hadn't had honey in moons. His mouth watered at the memory of the sweet treat. He licked his lips and counted his fish. He'd never been good at adding, but his grandmother had taught him numbers.

A fair trade demanded at least four of his catch. He'd caught fifteen fish. Bran had eaten two and he'd cooked two. Another two remained at his hut for tonight's meal, the smaller ones. That left him nine to trade.

If he gave four of the nine to this woman, he'd only had five left. There were lots of other things he should trade for instead. He craved bread, he needed a blanket for Bran, and he'd love some potatoes. Maybe the honey woman would bargain. He held up three fingers and raised his eyebrows.

The woman frowned and examined the fish with a narrowed gaze. She pointed at the three largest. He nodded and wrapped them in a burdock leaf. She put down her child and handed him the pot of honey. Then she stowed her fish into a bag over her back, hiked her child back onto her hip, and strode away.

As the sun dipped lower in the sky and no one else had stopped, Fingin gathered his remaining six fish and told Bran to wait for him on the blanket. Bran whined and wagged his tail, but stayed as he walked to the weaver.

The portly woman scowled as he approached. Fingin assessed the items on her trestle bench. Three thick blankets, a léine, and two hats. The thickest blanket had been dyed a lovely, vibrant green. He wanted something thick for Bran for cold nights. However, the vibrant dye would cost more fish than he had. He pointed to the gray one and held up his fish.

She narrowed her eyes. "What's the matter, boy? Can't you ask like a human? Or have the Fae stolen your tongue?"

They'd encountered each other before. She knew quite well that he had trouble speaking. He set his jaw and repeated the gesture.

She waved him away. "I don't sell to mutes. Prove you're human."

He closed his eyes and swallowed, willing his voice to cooperate, just this once. "F-f-f-four fish… gray blank…et?" His voice scratched out, barely audible.

She let out a nasty, mocking laugh, and gestured over the baker. "Come, listen to him try to talk, Máire."

The baker waved the weaver off. "You've heard it a dozen times, Nuala. When are you going to tire from the sport? The man just wants a blanket, for Danu's sake."

With a scowl at her friend's betrayal, Nuala shoved the blanket in his face and put her hand out for the fish. "There, you're done. Now go."

Fingin rolled the blanket like a snail's shell and tucked it under his arm. He had wanted to get some turnips with the remaining fish, but he felt he owed the baker some custom for her unexpected support. After placing the blanket next to Bran, he approached her table.

She wrapped three loaves into a thin cloth. "Here. Take these and welcome. No, I won't take your fish, young man. You deserve better than such treatment. Save that fish for something else."

Tears pricked his eyes at the kindness, and he bowed his head in thanks, putting one hand over his heart. With a shy smile, he left her and went to the vegetable table.

When he completed the last trade, he grabbed both blankets and the bread. He stowed them and they walked out of the clearing, giving another shy smile to the baker. She waved at him and turned to her own child, murmuring something to the girl.

He hadn't even walked halfway to the first hill when the baker's girl ran up to him. She held something in her hand. "What's your dog's name? Can I give him a piece of bread?"

Another prickle of tears threatened him as he nodded. He squeaked out the name, "Bran," as the child petted the hound with a clumsy hand. For his part, Bran wagged his tail with great enthusiasm and slobbered all over the girl.

She gave him a final pat and a grin and ran back to her mother's bench.

"What do you think, Bran? Was it worth the long walk?"

Bran's tail thumped. "Can we come back tomorrow?"

Chapter Two

Bran's leg healed over the next few days, and he bugged Fingin every morning, asking if it was time for the market yet.

After the third morning, Fingin gave a sigh and told Bran to watch him. He grabbed a stick and marked a line in the sand. "That's one line. You know what *one* means, right?"

Bran nodded eagerly. "I have one friend!"

Fingin couldn't help but smile. "Yes, you do! So do I. Now, if I make another line, that's two."

He did so, and Bran gave a hesitant nod. "Two. Like there are two of us."

"Right. Now if I draw a third line, that's three."

Now, Bran cocked his head but didn't say anything.

Fingin drew a fourth line. "This means four. One, two, three, and four." He pointed to each one in turn.

Bran gave a yip and pawed the ground. "That's a lot of lines. More than two. Many lines."

"Now I can draw a fifth and a sixth line. That's how many days until we can go to market again."

The dog shook his head and barked. "That's just lots. I don't understand!"

Fingin took a deep breath, erased his lines, and tried again. But after explaining three more times to no effect, Fingin gave up. So, Bran asked each morning. And each morning, Fingin had to say no.

When he was finally able to say *yes* to Bran's daily question, the dog leapt around the clearing, barking and spinning like a child with a toy.

Luckily, Fingin had not only caught several dozen fish this week and dried half so they'd keep much longer. Fresh fish tasted better but dried fish would last into the cold winter, if kept well. But he would keep those, as he had two mouths to feed now.

Even with only the fresh fish, he had twenty to trade, which should get bread, vegetables, and maybe meat for Bran. A diet of all fish and bread might not appeal to a dog. Fingin had grown used to such fare himself, but he was human.

As he cleaned the last of that morning's catch, a sound to one side caught his attention. Bran stood to the other side, his nose deep in the fish entrails, happily munching. Then Bran's head popped up, alert and wary. Fingin gripped his knife tightly and scanned the trees.

A branch snapped. Bigger than a rabbit. A deer might have ventured close. Fingin wished he had skill with a bow, as a deer would last them a long time. He'd never learned how to shoot, though, and his snares were too small for deer.

Bran let out a low growl, a menacing warning to whatever threatened their glade. Fingin held up a hand to signal him into silence. He listened again, trying to find the sound, the intruder, or whatever lurked in the shadowy trees.

No birds sang. No wind rustled the leaves. The low buzz of a few bees filtered through the bushes and the ever-present murmur of the river gurgled behind him.

Another twig snapped. There, behind the ash tree. A flash of blue where none should be. Something curled up at the base of the tree, almost hidden by a rowan bush.

Then came a piteous sob and a sniffle. He lowered his knife hand and glanced at the dog. "That doesn't sound like an animal, Bran. What do you sense?"

Bran snuffled at the still air. "Human, definitely human. Wet? He's wet. In several places."

Fingin wrinkled his brow, unsure what Bran meant by that. Had they fallen into the river? If they were sitting under a tree, they weren't drowning. With a painful grip on his knife, he crept toward them.

As he drew closer, their sobs grew louder. A child's sobs, full of anger and despair. The boy looked up, perhaps eight winters old, younger than Fingin had been when his grandmother disappeared.

The child huddled under the tree, his blue *léine* sleeve torn ragged. His bare, dirt-smeared feet poked out from under his arms, beneath a mass of messy brown hair.

"Hey, n-now, are you hurt?"

The boy jerked his head up, his eyes wide and darting back and forth. He shrank away from Fingin's outstretched arm.

"It's f-fine. I won't hurt you."

Bran had stepped up behind him and the child's eyes grew even wider. Fingin glanced down and put a hand on the gray hound's head. "Bran won't hurt you. He's f-fond of children."

Fingin didn't know if Bran had a fondness for of children at all, but this child needed comfort and friendliness.

Long ago, in his own childhood, he'd run off on his own and cried until his throat burned raw with pain. No one had come for him. No one had comforted his own anguish.

Bran lay down and inched forward, his nose near to the ground. As he got closer, his tail thumped the ground and his butt wiggled. His antics elicited a high-pitched giggle from the boy, cutting through his sobs.

Fingin extended his hand to the child. "C-c-come with us? I have f-fish stew, if you're hungry. What's your name?"

The boy sniffed mightily and rubbed his ripped sleeve back and forth under his nose, smearing dirt and snot rather than cleaning it. "I'm Lorcan."

With a half-smile, Fingin took the boy's hand and they walked to his clearing. He led the boy to a log. "Sit here. B-bran will stay with you."

Bran said, "He's still wet on the other end. He can't lick himself, can he?"

Fingin realized what the other *wet* meant. The boy had pissed himself. He must have been so frightened, he lost control.

"Would you like to swim in the river? You can be c-clean."

The child backed away, shaking his head, bumping into Bran. "No, not the river! I don't like the river."

Bran let out a woof at the child's distress and shoved his head under the boy's hand. Surprised, Lorcan petted the hound while Fingin thought fast.

Something bad must have happened in the river. But if the child didn't care about his wet clothing, Fingin wouldn't force him to wash or change.

Fingin stoked his fire circle, then sat on one of the surrounding logs. The boy scooted on the ground on the opposite side of the fire and Bran curled around him, forming a protective circle. Fingin smiled, pleased he had been right about Bran liking children.

"W-w-wait here. I'll get the… stew."

After Fingin stuffed both dog and child with fish stew, Lorcan curled up against Bran's flank and promptly fell asleep. Fingin gazed down with a wistful smile. He would have enjoyed having a family. Once he'd dreamed of finding a lovely girl with a nice farm and raising his own family full of laughing children.

However, being unable to speak to a girl without tripping over his own tongue made wooing difficult.

After swallowing down a sudden tight throat, Fingin let out a deep sigh, grabbed a length of stout canvas, and escaped into the woods. He'd gather more deadfall for their evening fire while the two slept. Bran would take good care of the boy.

The whisper of undergrowth as he walked turned into a tune, a wild song of the forest, raucous and strong. A sudden exclamation of surprise came in his mind as a rabbit fled to the left.

"Don't worry, bun. I'm not after you."

The rabbit stopped and turned, twitching his ear a few times. Then it bounded off, not trusting this human, despite his words.

Fingin chuckled. He'd lived in this glade for a full turn of the seasons, but smaller animals had fleeting memories. He'd spoken to that rabbit at least a hundred times, and he still didn't trust Fingin.

A bird swooped at him, warbling madly. He glanced up into the branches and spied the nest. With a respectful nod, he moved away from the tree and the bird's precious eggs.

Fingin gathered several large branches, fallen from the last summer windstorm. After scratching his arm on one, he stopped to pick off the entwined thorny vine. After he added an armful of smaller branches and some kindling to the canvas sling, and he headed back to the glade.

Lorcan was still sleeping, but Bran eyed Fingin and whined. He wagged his tail with three solid thumps on the ground. "I need to pee, but the boy is happy where he is."

Fingin chuckled. "I'm sure he'll forgive you."

Bran wiggled away from Lorcan, inching to keep from waking the boy. Lorcan moaned once when his head shifted to the ground, but Bran pulled away without waking him. He bounded to the edge of the glade and watered a tree.

When he returned, he was stepping high, then he cocked his head at the sleeping child. "Are we keeping him as well? He doesn't smell good, but he is gentle."

"I don't think we can keep him, Bran. He'll have a family, and we should find them and return him. They'll be very worried about him."

"Do you think my first friend worries about me?"

Fingin frowned. "I don't know, Bran. But from what you've said, he doesn't sound like the sort to worry about anyone but himself."

Bran nodded. "That's him."

He wondered if he knew the man. "What did your friend look like? What did other people call him?"

"They called him Guaire. He had thinning gray hair and stood very tall. He used his switch a lot."

Fingin's blood grew hot at the mention of a switch. "He hit you?"

Bran ducked his head and his tail. "I was a bad dog."

In an instant, Fingin was hugging the dog's huge head. "You were *not* a bad dog. He was a bad friend. I promise I will never whip you, never ever."

The tail thumped twice. Bran licked Fingin's face, making him laugh. "Stop that! It tickles!"

A giggle from behind him made him turn. Lorcan had risen and watched them with a grin.

Without urging, Bran bound to the boy and licked his face. This made Lorcan throw up his hands in mock defense and roll on his back, which gave Bran more room to lick the child. Fingin couldn't hold in his laughter, and they all laughed until his side hurt.

As the laughter died, Fingin offered the child a bucket of water and a cloth. "Go into the… hut and c-c-clean. We'll be at the river." He pointed to the steps down to the beach, and the boy nodded, a hint of uncertainty in his eyes.

"Take as long… as you n-need."

Once the boy disappeared, Fingin grabbed his net and led Bran down the bank. Every moment, Lorcan's eyes had darted from side to side, as if expecting a sneak attack. He'd only relaxed around Bran.

Fingin had been no stranger to bullying or abuse. He'd had more than his fair share when his grandmother stole his voice away. His own older brother had been the worst, dancing around him with cruel disdain, yelling, "Finny-fin-fing can't say a thing! Come on, push the words out like a calving cow!"

Such taunts often came with punches, kicks, or even red-hot sticks poked into his arm. But crying to Ma or Pa did no good. Pa would tell him a warrior never complains about pain, though he'd been a farmer, not a warrior. Ma would just click her tongue and shake her head.

Each memory of taunting, bullying, and cruelty crashed in after the first, like a tale with a series of challenges. First, his brother. After he'd been bullied too many times, Fingin had run away the first time. Then he found a new place, settled into a new community, gotten bullied again, and run away again.

One after the other, his slices of life fanned out before him, a glimpse into a life barely survived and rarely cherished.

By this time, he'd waded to the middle of the river. Bran watched from the beach as he used his angry memories to fuel his throw. The net flew from his fingers with a spin, kissing the waves and sinking below the sparkling surface.

Each time Fingin cast his net, calm surrounded him, quieting his fear, settling his mind, and salving his soul. Casting the net perfectly was intensely satisfying, proving that he could do something well. Every day, he strove to grasp a small sliver of peace as the swirling waters of the wide river caressed him with loving tendrils.

Gurgling water was soothing music as the faint chatter of fish below the surface crowded in his mind like a chorus.

Even pulling in the net required no mental effort, a series of actions his muscles remembered while his mind wandered.

A voice above him interrupted this meditation. He glanced up, expecting Lorcan. Instead, a woman with dark hair stood on the cliff, hands on her hips, glaring down at him.

His calm shattered and he stumbled, his hands unable to work the net he knew so well.

He finished pulling in his fifteen medium salmon and three trout, dragging the bounty to the beach. He left it there, tied to a rock to keep the fish from flopping back into the water. Next, he ascended the steps to meet the angry-looking woman.

She waited until he'd reached the top of the cliff before she spoke in a strident tone. "Who are you? How dare you take off with my son? What are your intentions toward him?"

Beside him, Bran growled, his hackles rising. "What does she say, Fingin? I don't like her. She smells of hate."

"I... I... wouldn't... I..." Fingin took a deep breath and tried again, struggling to use simple words. They wouldn't cooperate and leave his mouth.

She glanced back to the clearing, where Lorcan hovered near the tree line. He looked both miserable and worried. The boy shuffled forward, his head low. "Don't be mad at him, Ma. He helped me. He gave me food and let me pet his dog."

The sparking anger in her eyes faded and Fingin let out a breath of relief.

Fingin waved as the mother, Aideen, led Lorcan away from his glade. The boy had rescued him from further speech, for which his gratitude soared.

He hoped the child would be safe, but surely the mother wouldn't be the bully. She seemed much too cheerful for such cruelty. She'd relaxed after Lorcan explained and even invited Fingin to supper the next day, in thanks for his help. Fingin nodded, but he knew he'd never take her up on the offer.

As they disappeared into the woods, Fingin wondered if he should leave again. Aideen mentioned they'd moved into a roundhouse up the river, at the next bend.

Having neighbors that close had always resulted in pain and fear. Life would be easier if he left before it got to that point. Lorcan had been a sweet boy and Fingin would hate if being his friend made the child's life harder.

With a pat to Bran's shoulder, he glanced around his clearing, trying to remember what he'd been doing. He peered down to the beach at his full net. *Curse the crows.*

He climbed down to retrieve it. He'd lost two fish who'd wriggled out of the sieve and re-entered the water. The rest would need to be cleaned, so he wrestled it up the hill and bent to his task.

As he tossed the last of the fish guts to Bran, who attacked the mess with wild abandoned, a few raindrops hit his head.

With a deep sigh, Fingin gathered his cleaned catch, his net, and anything else that he wanted to keep dry and carried them inside. The rain grew heavy, and the odors of the forest rose in a green, humid fragrance. He took a deep breath, reveling in the lush scent.

Fingin loved the rain almost as much as he loved the sunrise. The intensity of sound, odor, and air made his spirit soar, as long as he had shelter. Despite getting caught in freezing winter rains, he still loved summer showers.

Pounding drops made a song, a rhythmic tattoo he hummed with, swaying as the sound swept him into another world, another time, and another life.

His grandmother had taught him to treasure these moments. She swore every part of the world held innate magic. "Pay attention to the music in the wind as it whistles and moans, the rain as it drums, butterfly wings as they fly, and sparkling stars in the midnight sky. Each one has a different song for those who listen. Each one can impart wisdom to those who pay attention. The Gods will never forgive us for wasting the dawn."

Only the cold nose of his hound recalled him to the present. He glanced down at Bran, a string of fish gut still hanging from the dog's mouth. Fingin grinned at his friend and pulled it free, then stoked the fire back into cheery warmth. He needed to cook those fish before he slept.

He counted his fish. Sixteen left, despite those who'd escaped, which was a good haul. Luckily, he wouldn't need to make a second cast.

Glancing out at the rain, he wondered if he'd lost track of the day. Was it a market day? He tried to count back to the last one. Eight days? No, market wouldn't be for another two. He'd have time to dry the rest of his fish.

He roasted four for him and Bran and stewed four more for tomorrow. The rest, he placed on a drying rack on the edge of the fire, near the one window. He'd much rather do the drying outside, but the rain made that impossible. Luckily, his thatched roof kept them dry while still allowing the smoke to dry the fish. Still, he and Bran would have to sleep near the entrance.

He pulled several green branches from his supply and placed them on the side of the fire near the drying rack. Once they caught, they made lots of smoke.

He coughed several times, a cough echoed by Bran. "Why did the fire do that? It hurts my throat."

"I know. But we need the smoke to dry the fish. That way, they don't spoil, and I can sell them at market."

Bran coughed again, shaking his head and then his entire body. "I'm going outside. I don't like it."

"Don't get caught in the mud."

As Bran left, his head drooped and his ears twitched as the rain pounded on his head. He shook a couple times, ears still twitching, before padding meekly back into the hut.

He shook again, spraying Fingin with water. "Hey!"

Bran lay down, resting his head on his crossed paws. "Maybe that smoke stuff isn't so bad."

The next day, the rain had eased, but clouds still covered the sky, so Fingin didn't perform his morning ceremony. It made him feel strange when he couldn't start his day that way. But he'd learned that trying to greet the dawn without being able to see the sun made it worse.

The sunburst of a clear morning had more power than any other dawn. Perhaps he only harnessed that power when it shone strong, and any other time it was twisted, lessened. His grandmother had never explained, and he didn't know how the magic worked.

The clouds spit sprinkles on his head as he moved the smoking fire to the doorstep, making sure to move each bundle of burning branches with care. His hut's thatched roof had an overhang that kept the light rain from dousing the fire. The few drips that got through only increased the smoke.

He shouldn't leave until the fish had dried. Even the short time he'd need to cast another net would be enough for the hut to catch fire. That would leave them both without a home and wasn't worth the risk.

Crunching sounds behind him made him whirl, expecting Bran to return from his morning patrol. A flash of gray through the trees reassured him. The dog often came back empty-mouthed, or with a squirrel or baby rabbit.

Fingin welcomed the occasional bounty Bran caught. He'd skin the catch and give the meat to the dog, who deserved the treat. He wasn't an expert tanner, but he did well enough. In just the few days since he found Bran, they'd gotten enough rabbit skins to make a nice lining for a winter coat. He should make one for Bran as a surprise, since the hound had caught most of the skins.

Today would be a good day to twist more twine. He should have enough material on hand. After he gathered his supplies, he sat on the stool near the door for the best light. But the smoke made his eyes water, so he moved next to the window.

Spreading out his supplies, he separated individual filaments into even sections. Though he didn't have many fresh thin vines, he could braid the former together for a strong string.

Fingin unrolled the remaining twine and hooked it on a nail in the wall post. Then he braided new material, grafting it onto the old.

After he finished grafting, he tugged it a few times to test its strength, then settled into the mesmerizing task. In and out, he pulled the sides to the center over and over again. His world faded away as he repeated the task without thought.

One, two, three. One, two, three. In and around and down. In and around and down. The twine grew as he braided and twisted, forming the thread which would become his net, the tool that allowed him to catch fish and eat every day.

One, two, three. In and around and down. One, two…

"Hallo! Hallo, are you there, today?"

The female voice crashed into his meditative bliss, making his heart race as he dropped his twine. His vision had blurred, and he grew dizzy with the magic he'd woven into his work.

Fingin stood, using the wall post to steady his knees. When he glanced out into the muzzy morning, he narrowed his gaze at a form in the mist. A single bark from the left told him Bran had returned.

The voice sounded like Lorcan's mother, but why would she come back? Had Lorcan gone missing again?

He waved into the mist. "I'm… here."

"Oh, thank the good God. I hoped I'd find you home. I wanted to thank you again for caring for my son. He's such a silly boy, always running off on his own. I didn't worry so much when he ran off *before* our move, as we knew the area so well. I knew his haunts and could find him quickly. But this new place has hidden spaces. It will take me *seasons* to find them all! Well, I wanted to bring some things by for you. You seem too young to be all alone. Do your parents live in the village?"

He blinked at the barrage of words and had to steady himself again. People didn't talk to him like this once they realized he had trouble talking himself. They assumed him to be either stupid or dangerous, and he couldn't argue against their assumptions.

What's the mother's name? Aideen, that's it. As she took a few steps closer, out of the misty drizzle, he spied a large bundle wrapped in cloth. Fingin narrowed his eyes. He didn't need charity from anyone. He had enough skill to feed himself and his hound.

She patted the bundle. "These are some leftovers from our meal yesterday. My husband, Faelan, decided he hates garlic, and I made this bread with garlic, so now it's all banned from the household. Lorcan suggested you might like it. And I added some clothing my eldest has outgrown. I'm afraid it's not in the best of shape, but it should be useful enough, even if there are a few spots which need mending."

She paused again for breath, but Fingin didn't know how to answer, or if he'd even get a word in edge-wise once she started in again. He satisfied himself with a quick nod.

"Well, I must be off before the rain returns. I hope you'll come to our roundhouse tomorrow night, as we agreed yesterday. I'll make a grand feast for us all! See you at midday! We're around the next river bend, remember!"

As she left, Fingin was able to breathe again. He stared at the bag as if it would bite him. Bran lumbered up and sniffed at the package, nosing open the fabric. "Something smells strong in here! A good strong, though. Like in the village."

He didn't want to touch the bag, but the thought of fresh bread, really, anything but fish, was too tempting. He grabbed the bag, pulling it into the house and out of the rain.

Inside, he found three sturdy, threadbare *léinte*, and two huge loaves of bread, each with cloves of garlic studded in the top. In addition, he found a package of fresh wild garlic and rosemary.

With delighted relish, he broke a generous chunk from one loaf and offered it to Bran. The dog sniffed the treat, backed up, sneezed, then pushed it around with his nose before licking it.

Finally, the dog ate the chunk and chewed noisily, the gummy bread turning into an unappetizing mess before he swallowed. "That tastes warm. Spicy."

Fingin inhaled the aroma of his own chunk of bread, savoring the rich scent and warmth. He took a bite, enjoying the garlic, salt, and rosemary flavors. He chewed each mouthful slowly, wanting to prolong the treat.

Bran hiccupped and wagged his tail. "She talks a lot, but she brings food. I didn't like her at first, but now I do."

Fingin nodded in agreement. Someone who talks so much might be pleasant to be around, because she wouldn't expect him to talk as much. Perhaps he *would* join them for a meal tomorrow, after all.

He glanced over at his drying fish and remembered tomorrow was market day.

Chapter Three

Fingin argued himself into going a dozen times that day. And a dozen times, he argued himself back out. Bran, on the other hand, enthusiastically supported a venture to Lorcan's home.

The dog had woken feeling somewhat ill, but the nausea soon went away. Fingin was almost sorry Bran felt better, as the illness would have given him an excuse to turn down Aideen's offer. Fingin's natural wariness around other humans kept him from settling on a decision.

Instead of deciding, he made more twine. Far more than he needed, to be fair. Within a few hours, he'd braided three large balls, enough to create a whole new net.

When he ran out of horsehair, he patrolled the outside of his hut, searching for spots to repair. However, he was good at keeping his home in good order, so no glaring spots cried out for his attention.

Bran, who'd been lounging on the flat rock while Fingin made his rounds, perked his head up. Fingin turned to see what had alerted the hound. Someone was crashing through the brush and a female voice cursed with a creative flair.

With a quick check to make certain his *léine* looked presentable, he stood next to Bran as Aideen's soft, round form broke through the branches, brushing a stray leaf from her sleeve.

She stumbled as she peered into the sun-bright glade, shading her eyes. "Ah, there you are! Lorcan begged me to come fetch you, as he pointed out you might not be able to find our house. Are you both ready?"

The decision had been taken out of his hands. Fingin masked his sigh and gave her a nod, his hand on Bran's flank.

Sometime later, Fingin felt relief at how far away they lived. He'd been imagining a throng of noisy, rowdy children invading his quiet solitude every afternoon. However, they were far enough from his place to keep visits blessedly infrequent.

Strange how he'd craved human companionship when young, but when he no longer fit in, he treasured his peace above all company. Well, not all company. Bran was a true friend. He glanced at the hound, who explored every side path and strange hummock along the trail.

Once, he'd stuck his snout into a rabbit hole and pulled out just as quickly. From his yelp and reddened nose, he must have learned that rabbits have powerful back legs for a reason. Fingin muffled a chuckle as the dog ran to catch up.

While Aideen chattered the entire trip, he'd stopped listening after the first few sentences. She didn't seem to require any response other than an encouraging nod or grunt now and then.

Now, however, she began listing names, so he paid attention. "Now, Lorcan, he's my youngest. The baby of the family, without a doubt. He gets grief from his older brothers, of course, but so do most children. Lugaid is three winters older than him and sometimes sticks up for him against the others. Ségán, he's the eldest. He's about to marry his sweetheart, and her father's set up a farm for them already. I'll miss him dearly, but one less mouth to feed is a blessing, make no mistake about *that*. She's a sweet girl, but not very bright. Still, she's got nice, healthy hips, so I expect lots of grandchildren from her."

She paused for a breath. "Now, Faelan, he's my husband, he won't talk much. But never you mind that. He's got a sharp mind. Sometimes a sharp tongue, as well, but you're not his son, so pay no attention to his words. We don't have a dog around the farm for your hound to play with, but he should be happy lying in the sun outside the door, won't he? Faelan doesn't care for animals inside, you see."

Fingin glanced at Bran. He didn't want to talk in front of her, but he'd make sure Bran behaved. Aideen hadn't made fun of his speech, but the fewer reminders of his difference, the better.

"I do hope you like lamb stew. We slaughtered two of our lambs last week, as our ewes birthed too many this season. The meat has just aged to perfection. Luckily, we got a huge load of salt on Faelan's last trip to the coast. He makes a trip once every few moons to a large town right on the river mouth with people who do nothing but trade. Can you imagine that? They grow no crops and raise no kine. These people don't even sail any ships! They just trade fish and salt with farmers. Such a strange world we live in. Last trip, Faelan said he even met someone from Rome!"

Rome, the eternal city, and according to his parents, the cradle of all civilized manners. His grandmother hadn't been of the same mind, but she didn't contradict them where they could hear. Their fervent belief in the new religion came from Rome, and they refused to hear any criticism of it.

Rome brought images of short, stocky, dark men in loose-wrapped robes, with skin darkened by a strong southern sun. Cities thronging with hundreds of people, maybe even thousands. Fingin couldn't imagine being so close to so many people, living each day shoulder to shoulder with all those strangers. He couldn't suppress a shiver, despite the warm day.

"Wouldn't it be something to travel to Rome? To see temples to the Gods, the Forum, all those foreigners in one place? Faelan heard tales of people with skin as black as tar! So exotic. I asked him if we could go with him to the shore when he traded, but he got a bit upset. After that, it seemed best not to mention it."

She fell silent for the first time, her eyes pinched in a pensive expression. Fingin wondered if Faelan's version of *a bit upset* looked anything like his own father's version. If so, he didn't blame Aideen for avoiding an argument.

His father had rarely struck either him or his mother. Fingin's grandmother wouldn't have stood for such abuse. However, his words had cut deeply enough for Fingin to avoid him, even when he could still speak well. The few times he'd been beaten, it hurt hard enough for him to avoid another at all costs.

For a panicked moment, Fingin frowned. He couldn't remember his grandmother's name. His father was Rumann, and his mother's Mugain. *What was my grandmother's name?*

He wracked his brain, trying to remember what his mother had called her. *Something with a C. Clooadh? Clodagh? Something like that.*

"Ah, here we are! See the house on the hill? That's where our brood lives. The field to the left is all rye, and the one on the right has turnips and cabbage. I have my herb garden, of course. Would you trade some of your fish with me? I really have too many herbs to use this winter, even with drying."

Lorcan must have mentioned how bland his own stew tasted, but he didn't mind. If he could trade without braving the market and Nuala's nasty taunting, he felt glad the boy had said something.

Perhaps he would enjoy visiting this family, despite himself.

A shrill scream cut across the countryside as they approached the two-story roundhouse. A thin, blond boy of about twelve winters darted out the front door toward them, followed by an older boy with heavier shoulders and red hair.

The younger boy swerved left and right, evading the other's grasp with easy agility. Another shout drew Fingin's attention back to the doorway, where a third young man with brown curls stood with his hands on his hips.

He shouted again, but this time Fingin understood his words. "Get back here, both of you! Ma will be back soon, and the table's not set!"

They meandered back toward the building as their chase continued. Soon, they barreled past the older boy and back through the doorway.

The momentary silence made Aideen grin. "Those were my three eldest, Niall, Muirchu, and Ségán. You'll meet Lugaid inside. He's almost as quiet as Lorcan, but my baby is still the sweetest."

She stopped and put a hand on his shoulder, her expression suddenly serious. "I want to thank you again for helping him that day. We couldn't figure where he'd run off to. The boys had all been playing in the river, collecting deadfall for the fire. Ségán said he just ran away without a word. He's usually so biddable."

After Lorcan's violent reaction to the suggestion that he wash in the river, Fingin doubted that he *ran away* with no reason. In fact, he suspected the older boys had been too rough in the water. Regardless, he wanted to protect the lad. Fingin liked the child, especially as Bran had already adopted the boy as another friend, and he trusted Bran's judgment.

As they got close to the house, Aideen waved at Ségán, who peeked out the door again. He waved back and disappeared into the house.

"They'll have food ready for us. Ready? Don't worry about speaking. Lorcan said you had trouble with some words. I speak enough for all of us!"

He let out a chuckle, thrilled at her understanding. Fingin crouched next to Bran and whispered. "You stay outside, Bran. I'll be out with food for you later. Understand?"

"Of course, I understand. Why are you speaking so softly?"

"Because other humans don't know you can understand my words."

Bran cocked his head in confusion.

"Just stay here."

The hound cocked his head to the other side, but he stayed put as Fingin entered the roundhouse.

The bright daylight dimmed to darkness inside. He blinked several times to adjust his vision. He'd never been inside a two-story roundhouse before. No peaked thatched roof here, but a flat ceiling of wooden planks forming the floor of the upper story and changing the shape of the great room below. In the center, a hearth burned. A long, wooden table creaked under a wealth of food.

A gaggle of people resolved into two distinct groups. The younger three boys, including Lorcan, stood to the left of the table. The tall blond man must be Aideen's husband, Faelan.

She brought Fingin forward. "This is Fingin, the young man who found our Lorcan the other day. Please, Fingin, be welcome in our home. May you have both bread and salt. May you never thirst and never starve."

The eldest son, Ségán, offered a wooden tray with a chunk of bread and a mug of milk. Fingin accepted it with a nod of thanks, and took a token bite of the bread, washing it down with a sip of the milk. The ceremony complete, Aideen introduced her family.

She stood next to the two boys. "Lorcan, you know, of course, and this young lad is Lugaid. They were born but a winter apart."

Next, she put her hands on the heads of two blond twins. One had been the boy screaming earlier. "These are Niall and Muirchu. Never mind if you can't tell them apart. Neither can they, most of the time."

The redhead came next. "This tall man is my eldest, Ségán. And then Faelan, my husband."

The tall burly man with long blond hair regarded Fingin with a hooded gaze. His warrior's braids looked ragged, and his paunch belied a life of fighting. Still, no man would dare wear the braids of the Fianna without earning them. He must have once been one of the famous warriors. As such, a man to be wary of, no matter what shape he had.

Fingin bowed to the father. The man grunted and shuffled off to sit at the head of the table.

Once he sat on his stool, the others all found their places on the benches. Faelan took a ladle of lamb stew for himself and passed it to Ségán.

After the family passed the bowl of stew, then came vegetables, bread, and a fruit tart. Fingin stared at the pile of food and hoped he could eat it all. He didn't dare insult his hosts, but he hadn't eaten a meal so huge since he'd left home.

Fingin ate slowly, trying to savor each bite. Aideen certainly cooked better than he did and used herbs from her garden. He shut his eyes when he crunched a clove of roasted garlic, the spicy tang flooding his tastebuds. The lamb melted in his mouth and crunchy bits of roasted turnip rounded out the flavors.

Fingin took a drink of cool spring water from his mug. His stomach was already bulging, but he wanted to taste everything. The berry tart glistened with strawberries covered in honey, catching his attention. Even with his recent acquisition of a jar of honey, this sweet was a luxurious treat.

"The man in there smells bad. But the food smells delicious. When do I get some?"

Fingin smiled at Bran's mental nudge. He'd already palmed a big chunk of lamb and wrapped it in a piece of cloth.

Conversations among the family flowed around him. He'd expected more curiosity about himself, but maybe Aideen had warned her children not to ask him questions.

Once he'd mopped up every savory drop from his plate, he picked up the tart, examining its glistening beauty in the dim afternoon light streaming through a window.

Aideen had sliced the pale red berries, arranged in an overlapping circle, covered in a glaze of golden honey, and hemmed in the confection with a crunchy wheat crust.

In an ecstasy of indulgence, Fingin bit into the tart, careful not to let a drop of the honey escape. He licked his fingers and lips, chewing each sweet bite with relish.

Fingin often found berries in the woods as he foraged. He might even beat the birds to them. But wild berries were more tart than sweet, unless served with honey. Something this sweet was a rare delight.

His head buzzed and his skin felt itchy, like he needed to rub it away. He shifted on his bench and realized everyone was watching him. Fingin grew self-conscious, bowing his head over his half-eaten tart.

Aideen laughed. "No need to feel shame, young man. Seldom has any cook received such obvious praise for her efforts. Enjoy the tart and welcome. There's even a second one for you, if you saved room for it. Ségán, pass down the tray, will you? The boy must be half-starved for sweets."

Faelan scowled but said nothing. Ségán passed the tray, with three more tarts, to his end of the table.

Should he finish the first tart before taking a second one? He wanted to take his time eating it and not bolt it down. He glanced back and forth between the half-eaten one in his hand and the one on the tray. With a mischievous grin, Lorcan placed a new tart directly on his plate, forestalling his indecision.

He winked at the boy in thanks for his conspiracy and took another bite of his first tart, savoring anew the wonderful taste.

When he emerged from this tasty bliss, he opened his eyes to find Aideen grinning, while Faelan scowled. The boys were all concentrating on their own sweets except Lorcan, who wore a half-smile. "You're funny, Fingin."

Fingin didn't mind being funny. Being funny had much fewer dangers than being feared or hated. He glanced at Faelan, but the older man no longer sat at the head of the table. He'd gone to the sideboard to pour himself a mug.

His own father used to drink ale all day long. Fingin wondered if Faelan did the same.

Aideen shooed all the boys out, including Fingin. "Go outside, now. I've plenty of work to clean up after you lot. Go, now!"

Ségán led them outside to the side yard, where he set three of them to work mucking out the stables. "You, Fingin, and Lorcan, come with me."

He glanced at his new young friend, but the younger boy had cast his gaze to his feet. Fingin shrugged and followed Ségán. Bran trotted behind, his tongue lolling.

"That was a long time! Did you bring anything for me?"

Surreptitiously, Fingin slipped Bran the chunk of lamb he'd tucked into his hand. The hound gobbled it up and licked Fingin's fingers as they walked.

The eldest son stood taller than Fingin by at least a handspan and had broader shoulders. However, from what Aideen had said, Fingin was several winters older. Still, age was one thing, and physical strength was another.

Ségán stopped next to the pigpen and grinned. It wasn't a nice grin. "So, Lorcan's found himself a protector, eh? How good are you at fighting, Fingin?"

Fingin narrowed his eyes at the other young man but said nothing. He clenched his fists until his knuckles turned white, and Bran's growl was low and menacing.

"Now, now, no fair siccing your mutt on me. It's just you and me. Man to man." Ségán put up his fists and settled into a fighting stance.

"I won't f-f-fight you. I'm a g-guest."

"Oho! So, the mute speaks! I heard about you in the village, you know. The mute boy who can't speak. But you can talk! Sort of. Lorcan, couldn't you choose better than this? He isn't even a real man."

Lorcan said, "Leave him alone, Ségán! You can't violate guest-right. Mom will kill you!"

Ségán ignored his brother and brushed his words aside. He circled Fingin, throwing a few test punches his way. Fingin didn't match his stance.

He hated fighting. That didn't mean he didn't know how.

Bran jumped several times. "Can I bite him? He's mean. He's the one who smells bad. He smells like anger. Please, can I bite him? Please?"

When Fingin's back was to the pigsty, Ségán made his move. Bran barked wildly, but Fingin cried out, "stay!"

Ségán let out a bestial yell and barreled forward, but Fingin ducked, not quite in the right place for what he wanted. He whirled around, ready to face the bully again. Ségán pushed himself from the sty fence and circled once more. Again, Fingin positioned himself.

This time, when Ségán growled and rushed him, Fingin grabbed the other man's shirt and crotch, bent his knees so he was lower than his opponent, and flipped Ségán over the fence and into the pig sty.

With a satisfying squish, Ségán landed in the mud and let out a stream of invective. Two pigs nosed him with their snouts, grunting in confusion.

Lorcan and Fingin stared at the muddy mess, then their gazes met, and they darted away. Ségán's shouts and curses followed them as they ran around the roundhouse and out of sight.

"W-w-will that mean t-t-trouble for you later?"

Lorcan giggled while covering his mouth. "It will. But the sight of him with those pigs made it worth it. Can I come to your roundhouse tomorrow? Ma is going to her sister's and when she's gone, they get worse."

Fingin looked down at the boy and nodded. "We can f-fish." He patted Bran on the head as the dog's tail thumped hard on the grass. Giving Lorcan a pat on the shoulder, Fingin headed home, his stomach still full of delicious berry tart.

As he walked home, he recalled a fight his father and his grandmother had. He'd hated when they fought, but hadn't been able to escape or fight back. However, that had encouraged him to learn how to do both.

His grandmother had been acting strange, leaving for entire days with no reason or excuse. She came home late at night, or not at all on others. Every time Rumann asked where she'd been, she ignored him. Even

Fingin's mother couldn't coax an explanation from her. Her eyes had glazed over and Fingin suspected she might have been losing her wits, but she seemed sharp enough.

Fingin's father had been drinking ale all day, which hadn't been unusual. His mother had been sleeping, exhausted from her busy day.

When his grandmother stumbled into the door late after the evening meal with stars in her eyes, Rumann pounced upon her. "There you are! What's your excuse tonight, woman?"

She speared him with a withering look. "I do as I like, Rumann. You aren't my husband."

He threw his mug against the wooden wall, startling Fingin's mother awake. She groaned in complaint but didn't rise. Fingin huddled in his own alcove, afraid to make a noise.

"I'm your son! Not that you ever acted like a mother should. You ought to be sitting by the fire and sewing, not gallivanting off at all times of the night! What do you do, meet some lover? Are you sinning in the dark? Like some animal?"

Her laugh echoed through the roundhouse. "Sin? Who are you to speak of sin? You and your dead god. Keep your artificial morality to yourself, Rumann. I'll have none of it."

Her footsteps rang across the flagstone floor and toward her own alcove.

Rumann grabbed her shoulder and yanked her back. "Don't you walk away from me, harridan! Come back and explain yourself."

She'd scowled at him, pulling her arm from his grasp. "Should I use small words so you can understand them? I went out. I am back. Go away."

"This is my house, old woman, and you'll live by my rules!"

"Your house! Ha! I lived here long before I opened my legs to push your ungrateful self from my loins. I should have left you inside to rot!"

Fingin had tried to cry himself to sleep. He stayed as quiet as he could, but his father had heard him anyhow. The cloth curtain separating his alcove flung open, revealing Rumann's angry red face. "What are you blubbering about? I swear, I don't have a son, I have a sniveling daughter, good for nothing."

His father had jerked him from the alcove into the main room, out the door, and into the stable. Fingin knew better than to argue, but he thought he might have grown big enough to fight back.

He tugged on his father's arm, trying to pull him off balance. While Rumann stumbled, it did nothing to break his iron grip. Instead, he dug his fingers into tender skin, making Fingin whimper.

With silent deliberation, Rumann removed the switch from the stable wall and whipped Fingin. He lost count after ten. Perhaps that's why he'd never learned numbers well.

After that, Fingin had learned to run and hide as soon as noticed trouble brewing.

Back in the present day, Fingin let out a sob. Bran butted him. "What happened? Did someone hurt you? Where are they? Is it that bad-smelling man?"

"No, no one hurt me now, Bran. I was just remembering something which happened long ago. No need to protect me."

"I'll protect you! And Lorcan, too! The bad-smelling man is mean."

"Yes, he's very mean. Lorcan needs protecting more than I do. But you have to be careful. That man is also his brother, his kin. It would be bad to hurt him."

Bran cocked his head. "But he wanted to hurt you! He tried to hurt you. Why can't we hurt him back?"

"Because no one would know he tried to hurt us, and it would be our word against his. He lives there, and I don't. They'd believe him, not me."

Bran sneezed. "I don't understand. That makes no sense. That's not true."

He patted the hound's back. "You're right. It doesn't make sense. But sometimes things make no sense, no matter how much you want them to."

The next day, when bushes snapped behind him, Fingin didn't need to turn around. Bran had already bounded toward the sound, his mental voice cheering for his new friend, Lorcan. "He came! He came! We're going fishing now, right? We'll show him how to fish?"

Remembering Lorcan's unease about the river, Fingin suspected Lorcan would rather watch from the beach while Fingin fished, but still, he'd show the boy. Perhaps he could ease the child's fear of water, without his bully brother around to shove him under the surface.

As Lorcan emerged from the trees, Bran hopped around him like a drunken rabbit. The enormous hound jumped back and forth, making the boy giggle at his antics.

"C-c-come, sit. Would you like to see how I make my net? I'm repairing a worn p-p-place."

With a determined set to his mouth, Lorcan sat next to him and peered at the net.

"See here? The line is f-f-frayed and will b-b-break the next time I p-pull it, or if a larger fish p-pushes against it. I don't want to lose a b-b-big fish, so it's b-better to fix it b-before it breaks."

The boy touched one of the knots. "Where do you get the twine?"

"I make it myself. Here, I've g-got horsehair, flax strands, d-d-dried vines, and c-cattails. Anything strong and thin will work. The t-trick is to have each end start at a d-different place. Each strand is weak, but t-t-together, they're strong."

Lorcan looked down at his hands and fidgeted with his fingernails. "Like my brothers."

Fingin clenched his teeth. "Like your b-brothers. But even something with c-combined strength can be broken."

The boy looked up, entreaty in his eyes. "Can you teach me how to do what you did to Ségán?"

"I can t-t-teach you. But it only works in the right place. I had to move so he ran t-toward the f-fence. Did you notice that?"

He gave a nod, his eyes growing wide. "How did you flip him like that?"

"I crouched d-d-down so I stood lower than him. Th-that way, when he hit me, he t-t-tumbled over me rather than into me. I stayed c-close enough to the fence that falling over me also meant going over the fence. Ségán won't let himself b-b-be in that situation again any t-time soon."

Lorcan bowed his head.

"That doesn't mean you can't fight b-back, just that it takes some p-planning."

He brightened at that. Fingin finished tying his repair and tugged it a few times. "That's b-b-better. See how much stronger it is? Now, let's go t-test this out."

Lorcan followed him and Bran down to the beach, but he stared at the water with cautious eyes. "You don't have t-t-to go in if you don't want to. Would you p-prefer to watch as I cast?"

He talked as he cast, pulled, and hauled his net to shore, explaining each step. The fish didn't swim into his net today, despite his humming, as it was midday and fish preferred dawn and dusk.

Still, a few trout and a sunfish wriggled in his net, making Lorcan laugh. "Do you eat those right away?"

One fish escaped, flopping on the beach. Lorcan jumped and tried to catch it, but it leapt from his fingers and into the water.

Fingin gave him a grin. "Great try, Lorcan! Well done!"

Bran leapt back into the river after the escapee, splashing all of them with a wave. Lorcan shouted in complaint, and even Fingin chastised the eager hound.

In apology, Bran placed both his front paws on Lorcan's shoulders and licked his face, making him giggle and scream for the dog to stop.

However, Bran held him down and gave him a thorough licking. The boy earned a few shallow scratches, but his face glowed with delight.

When they settled, Fingin saw a bird flit by and had an idea. "Lorcan, have you ever held a b-b-bird?"

The boy shook his head, so Fingin said, "Come closer, wee blackbird. I won't hurt you." He held out his hand, sending a mental urging to the bird to alight upon it. The bird cocked his head back and forth. It flew to a closer branch and regarded the trio for a few more moments. After hopping to the ground, it came closer every few moments, jumping in a zigzag until it was just out of reach.

Lorcan froze, entranced by the sight.

"Remember to breathe! Blackbird, will you come to my hand? We won't harm you."

The bird looked between him, Lorcan, and Bran. It hopped on Lorcan's leg. The boy drew in his breath and his eyes grew wide.

"Can the boy pet you, wee bird?" He turned to the lad. "Be gentle, Lorcan. Barely touch him."

Lorcan reached out a hand with tentative eagerness. The bird allowed the touch, bobbing twice, and asked in a tiny voice, "Do you have any seeds?"

Fingin shook his head. "I have no seed today, but I might tomorrow."

"It's so soft and light! No weight at all. It's like an air spirit."

Fingin's grandmother used to speak of the nature spirits. Spirits of the air, the water, the trees, all the wild things around them. "Perhaps that's what he is. Have you ever seen an air spirit b-before?"

A strident voice cried out, "What are you doing! What devilry is this?"

Lorcan's blissful smile turned to horror and the bird flew away in an instant. Bran jumped up and growled, placing himself in front of both Lorcan and Fingin.

Aideen climbed down the stone steps to the beach. She grabbed Lorcan's arm, ignoring Bran's furious barking. "You'll come home this instant, young man. I'll have none of that pagan evil taught to my child! You're not to touch my son, do you understand? You will not speak to him, you will not seek him out, and you will not teach him your evil ways! Begone, devil! Out with you!"

She held up the small wooden fish on a string around her neck. Fingin recognized it. His parents wore symbols just like it.

"It wasn't... evil! Just a b-b-bird! I s-s-s..." He swallowed, trying to get control of his voice. "I swear!"

"Stop! Do not swear at me, devil-man! And call off your hellhound. I'll have none of you! Begone! I banish you!"

She dragged Lorcan up the hillside, though the boy sent an entreating look. Fingin dropped his gaze.

He knew what happened next. Next would be the grumblings, the rumblings of something terrible going on in his glade. Maybe a few villagers would visit next, maybe a mob. They'd come with torches and burly men and force Fingin to leave. The last time, they'd almost caught him. Angry voices and burning torches still haunted his dreams.

Escape before it got to that point would be safer. He'd learned his lesson as a child. No amount of argument, with his forced and horrible voice, had ever changed their minds. He'd vowed to stop trying after the last time.

Once again, he'd have to find a new home.

Chapter Four

Fingin's fishing net took most of the room in his bag. Three blankets, a few tools, two spare *léinte*, some pottery, his cooking pot, dried fish, and his twine took up the rest. He stared at a blanket Aideen had gifted him and swallowed down the tears as he stuffed it on top.

Even that would be heavy enough after the first day of traveling, in his experience. At least he had Bran to keep him company on his journey this time.

Bran jumped all around the small hut, excited and anxious at the same time. "Where will we go? Will we travel far? Will we meet other people? Will we be able to fish?"

"I'm not sure where we're going, or how far we'll travel. We'll surely meet someone, and I won't settle anyplace I can't fish." Fingin turned to the hound. "Would you like to choose our direction?"

Bran's head popped up and he looked left, right, and left again. "Which is the best direction?"

"The best direction is away from here. Just don't go that way." Fingin pointed the direction he'd come from when he moved here.

The dog woofed and shook his head, an action which moved down his body until just his tail was wagging. He sniffed the air in several spots around the glade and finally chose a spot, opposite from the path to Lorcan's home. "This smells like rabbit. Let's go this way. The other way has badgers."

Fingin grinned and patted Bran on the head. "Rabbits sound better. Lead the way, trusty hound!"

He reveled in the familiar freedom of being on the road, but at the same time, dreaded the unknown crowding against his mind. They had enough food for three days, no more, unless they foraged while they walked.

Bran could hunt as they traveled, but Fingin had discovered his hound didn't hunt very well. Perhaps that's why his previous owner had sent him away. Fingin still hadn't forgiven that person for such an act. Dogs are friends, not tools.

Bran dove into a rabbit's warren, burrowing down to find his prize, but the hole seemed empty as Bran came up for air with nothing but dirt on his nose and a laugh in his voice. Fingin didn't care if he never caught game. His dog's joy made him happy. What more could he want in a companion?

Back and forth across the trail, Bran investigated each new scent and sound. Fingin strode at a steady pace, halting only when Bran darted across his path, lest he trip over the tall hound.

Bran spoke as he explored. "I've never been down this road. There's a new scent, something I haven't smelled before. I wonder what it is? It's not rabbit or badger or squirrel or deer or…"

Fingin let out a chuckle. "There are lots of animals in the woods, Bran."

"But this is a new scent! I want to see what the new creature is."

"No, we have to keep moving. I want to find a safe place to sleep tonight. See those clouds? It might rain before night falls."

Bran bowed his head. "I'm sorry. I don't want to sleep in the rain."

"Neither do I, which is why we have to keep moving. Look, the path splits up there. Do you want to choose which branch to take?"

Without a word, Bran bounded to the fork and sniffed in both directions. He didn't hesitate, taking the right-hand path, so Fingin followed.

This path didn't look familiar, and he thought he'd explored most of the surrounding countryside, but he must have missed some. As he got further from his hut, Fingin realized he'd miss this part of his journey.

Fingin's life had been divided into three distinct sections. The first had been his childhood, filled with anger and fear from his parents, but love from his grandmother. Once he'd reached adulthood, his life was divided into the settled times, with fishing, loneliness, and sneers from people in the marketplace, and the traveling times, with uncertain days but the frightening freedom of being bound by nothing.

Some people lived in the same place their entire lives. Their ancestors had worked the same land they worked for hundreds of seasons. Their very blood was part of the dust and dirt they returned to in death.

Others lived on the wind, never staying in one place for more than a few days, dancing on life like a cloud. His was a split life, with change orchestrated by the whims of those around him and his own inabilities to fit in.

Did he want to live in a village? Loneliness was difficult sometimes, but he also treasured his solitude. Being alone meant no one criticized or wanted things from him. Bran demanded nothing but fish and the occasional dig into a rabbit's warren. In return, he gave love and cheer.

He and Bran could be their own village. Would they be able to survive alone? A diet of nothing but fish might pale. Fingin craved other foods and sometimes didn't feel well if he ate only fish. He'd tried that before and once, he'd been so ill that he barely gotten to the market. The onions he'd traded for had tasted so good.

The light was growing dim and Fingin glanced up at dark, swirling clouds. He frowned, looking around for a likely shelter from the coming storm, but finding nothing.

"Bran! Can you watch out for a cave or hut? I'd rather not sleep in the rain."

Bran glanced over his shoulder. "I sensed a hut back a little while ago, but I also smelled people."

"We need a place with no people, if we can."

Bran stopped in his tracks. "No people? But I like people!"

Fingin gave him a pat as he chuckled. "I know you do, Bran, but people don't like me very much. It's easier if I don't live near them."

Bran hung his head and walked beside him for several silent minutes before he raised his head. "What if I find people who like you?"

Fingin knelt beside the dog and hugged him tight. "I already found someone who likes me, and he's enough."

The wind picked up, rustling leaves and blowing their hair around, like Fae playing with their locks. His neck tickled and he rubbed it, wishing he didn't feel the storm in his bones. Dread came over him like a wave, making his eyes dart around for the danger.

Bran would sense any danger before he did, so his wariness didn't make sense. That didn't stop him glancing back every few minutes and into each dark spot beneath the bushes. A bird flew straight at his face. He ducked, throwing his arms up to shield his face.

Fingin didn't like this at all. They needed to find shelter right away. "Bran, can you see any place? The wind is throwing sand in my eyes."

"Just a little farther. Something delicious is ahead."

That didn't reassure Fingin in the slightest. The dog, beloved or not, was a slave to his stomach. A delicious odor could easily distract him from an important task. But, he had few other options than to follow the hound's scent trail, no matter where it might take them.

The forest grew darker. Or perhaps the sky? He could barely see Bran's fluffy tail whipping the brush in front of him as he followed the dog down a dwindling trail. He shoved branches and bracken away from his face as they pushed through.

The wisdom of following a dog through a strange forest in an oncoming storm might be questionable. Still, Bran wouldn't want to drown in a rainstorm any more than he did. He pushed on, catching small scratches from thorns and branches. One whipped into his stomach as Bran passed it, and he gasped as he double over.

Then the trees cleared, opening into a cozy glade. A fat white cow with red ears chewed her cud beside a hut and an old, bent woman pulling a bucket from a well. He glared at Bran for his betrayal, but the dog glanced up with his mouth open and his tongue out, as happy as ever.

Fingin whispered, not wanting to gain the woman's attention. "This isn't an abandoned hut, Bran."

"But this is a person who will like you! You said that's what you want!"

A querulous voice rose over the whisper of the wind. "Make up your mind if you want to come help me with this blasted bucket or stand there and gabble all day."

With a final withering glance at his hound, Fingin approached the woman, who was holding the bucket rope. He leapt to help her lift the thick wooden vessel from the stone pit.

Once she had it in her hands, she scowled at the bucket, glanced at the sky, and sighed. Her iron-gray hair had been tied up in a messy bun, and her short, round figure looked solid in countless layers of woolen shawls. "I suppose I should have just waited for the rain. But I need water if I'm to make some stew for my guests. Come inside now, before the rain hits. Bran can come inside, too."

She strode into her hut, leaving both Fingin and Bran astonished. *How did she know Bran's name?* They exchanged a glance, but Bran just tilted his head.

The shambling roundhouse leaned to one side, the stones around the base haphazardly scattered. The thatch had patchy parts. Cautiously, he ducked into the low door, blinking to adjust his eyes to the darkness.

Once inside, the space felt warm, cozy, and most importantly, dry. A cheerful flame burned in the central hearth. The first heavy drops of rain whipped onto his back and he hastened to shut the door.

The old woman settled onto a well-worn and well-padded bench. She gestured for him to take the only other seat, a wide stool next to the hearth. Bran settled at Fingin's feet and gazed at the woman. "She smells friendly. I like her. Do you think she has any fish?"

Though the dog's voice was in Fingin's mind, the old woman answered. "I have no fish, Bran, but I have some venison. Would you like that? Your young man may also have some, if he likes."

Fingin stared at the woman in growing apprehension. *How can she hear our thoughts?* With clammy palms, Fingin glanced at the door, now closed fast against the furious storm pounding against the daub and wattle walls.

Outside, the wind screamed in a furious gale like few he'd experienced. Yet the danger of staying inside with a clearly supernatural being might be worse. Would he ever see the open sky again? Had he just doomed both of them to a horrible death?

She let out a raspy chuckle. "Have no fear of me, Fingin. I mean you and your hound no harm. Hounds are special to me and have ever been my friend. Besides, this one only came to you because I sent the salmon to distract you."

That nugget of information made his mind spin. Mustering his courage and bracing himself for his broken voice, he pushed out the words, "What's your name?"

The words came as easily as they did for Bran or any other creature of the forest or river. Maybe she was magical. Any Fae creature would require a price for the shelter she provided them. Fingin doubted a few seconds' help with a water bucket would be a proper exchange for such a gift.

She grinned, showing bright teeth. "You may call me Brigit, my dear. You've honored the dawn many times in your life, and I take that as honor to myself. Consider that plenty of payment for a warm place and a meal. Now, I'm glad for your help with the water. May I repay you with a story?"

Brigit. Goddess of the Dawn. Healer, poet, and smith. The devoted goddess for a thousand sacred wells, to cattle and crafts.

She couldn't be, could she?

She raised one eyebrow, waiting for him to come to his conclusion. He cleared his throat and put a hand on Bran's shoulder for comfort. "A story would be lovely, thank you."

The goddess poured liquid into two iron mugs, offering one to Fingin. He took it and peered into the dark vessel. The aroma wafted strong and sweet, so it must be mead.

She poured more into a bowl and placed it in front of Bran, who sniffed it warily. With a glance at Fingin, he lapped it, cocked his head, then lapped more.

Fingin drank half of his own mug down and the warm alcohol suffused his body. His anxious worry slipped away, and he relaxed to listen to her story.

"Long ago, when the *Túatha Dé Danaan* battled the *Fomoire*, they chose one of their men to spy on the battle. They wanted him to spy upon the camp, the soldiers, and the magical prowess of those who opposed them. The man they chose was *Rúadán*, son of *Bres*."

Fingin recognized the tale and the name. While Bres may have been his father, Rúadán's mother was Brigit.

"Rúadán spoke of the things he saw. The ironwork of *Goibniu* the smith, the woodcraft of *Luchta* the craftsman, and the gold work of *Creidne Cerd* the goldsmith. He spoke of the four healers around the Dagda's Well, and how they brought every warrior who'd fallen the previous day to life.

"Bres told him he must go back and destroy Goibniu. But Goibniu had much power and possessed great magic, so Rúadán crafted a plan and returned to the enemy camp."

She paused to refill her own mug and took a long drink. "He requested a boon of each smith. He asked Goibniu for a spearhead, Luchta for the spear shaft, and Creidne Cerd for rivets of gold. Armed with this magically crafted artifact, he whirled and thrust it into Goibniu's stomach, wounding him with grievous violence."

Bran whined and Fingin stroked his head to reassure him.

Brigit folded her hands across her belly. "But Goibniu did not die from his wound. Instead, he yanked the spear from his body and cast it back at Rúadán with such force that the spear plunged through his body and out the other side. Rúadán then died in front of the Fomoire and the Túatha Dé."

She fell silent, mourning her son, the foolish pawn of his father. To Fingin's surprise, she let out an unearthly keening, filling the roundhouse with echoes of pain and longing, the agony of a mother who's lost her son. Bran howled, and Fingin had to cry with them, the grief and sorrow welling inside him. It poured out of his voice and his eyes.

Fingin didn't mourn for Rúadán, though. He mourned for his grandmother, for his childhood. He mourned for the dozen places he'd lived and loved, only to be chased away. And he mourned for the normal life he'd never have.

The three of them cried and keened and wept for time and life. They shared a common grief and would always have this part of each other.

When their sorrow faded and Fingin took a true breath once again, he stared at the cup he'd drunk. Had the mead made him so sad? Despite his sorrow, he felt lighter than he had for many winters, almost as if a great weight had lifted from his shoulders.

When he glanced up, the old woman seemed younger, more like a mature matron, with a strong jaw and crisp, blue eyes.

She peered at him with a knowing smile. "My story has touched you, young Fingin. I'm glad my tales still evoke such strong emotions in the world. Now, will you join me for a meal? I don't eat in any style, just stew and bread. Still, it's better than dried fish, is it not?"

She stood and stirred the pot in the hearth. Fingin didn't remember there being a pot on the hearth, but he was in a magical place with a magical being. He must take nothing for granted here.

Buzzing bees tickled his mind, but he saw none flying around. He glanced at Bran, but the hound had lain across his feet, content with his spot. If the dog sensed no danger, why should Fingin be so cautious?

And yet, tales from his grandmother about the dangers of dealing with the Fae haunted the back corners of his mind, and he resolved to keep wary.

Brigit chuckled as she stirred the pot but said nothing. She must be listening to his thoughts, but he didn't know how to keep his mind quiet. He had no walls to keep her out.

"Indeed. Now, the venison stew is just finished cooking. Fetch two bowls from the shelf, there's a good lad. One for you and one for Bran. No, no, I've already eaten. Your grief fed me well, and I thank you for that."

He found the bowls, expertly fired pottery with a subtle flame design in the outside glaze. She filled both with generous ladles of stew.

A rich aroma permeated the small hut, making his mouth water. The venison had been cooked so tenderly, the meat fell away when he poked it with his spoon, and the chunks of turnip and onion melted in his mouth. He didn't recognize which herbs, but the salty fat seemed to be exactly what his stomach craved.

Fingin had never eaten anything tastier in his life.

The bread he used to sop up the last drops of broth had been well-baked, with flecks of salt and exotic black pepper on the crust.

Once he finished, Fingin offered to clean the bowls.

Brigit waved away the suggestion. "Just place them outside. The wind and the rain will do most of the work for us."

That didn't help pay his debt for her hospitality. He peered into the thatch and noticed some thinner spots. They weren't leaking, but they looked darker, wet from the rain seeping in. "Maybe I can do some repairs for you? I must repay you for letting us stay."

She regarded him for a silent moment. "I suppose you do need to repay me, at that, young man. Let's sleep upon it tonight. In the morning, I'll give you some ideas on how you might help. Not to worry, none of them will be difficult."

Only slightly reassured, Fingin nodded in agreement. She handed him a woolen blanket and a soft pillow to lie upon. He curled around Bran and fell asleep almost as soon as he lay down.

A vivid dream slammed into his unconscious mind like a sudden storm. His grandmother stood in the center of a crowd. He was one of the people watching. She looked younger than he remembered, with midnight hair and milk-pale skin. Wind whipped her hair like dancing feathers as the crowd screamed and shouted. They brandished angry-looking faces and burning torches.

He glanced to either side and didn't recognize anyone. Even their clothing seemed strange. He didn't know the place, either. Some ancient stone circle on a hilltop with a massive cairn covered in turf.

The crowd surged forward, calling his grandmother nasty names. She spat to the side and bared her teeth, gripping a pitchfork with white-knuckled hands.

She protected a man from the crowd, someone who held a carved wooden staff. His eyes grew wide and his simple *léine* had been torn in several places. A scorch mark on the shoulder might have been from one of the torches.

The man had long black hair and beard, with sun-dark skin. The two circled, back-to-back, against the angry mob.

Fingin tried to run to her, to stand by her side, but he couldn't move. A bee buzzed by his face and landed on his nose, making him cross his eyes to see the creature. It tickled his nose and flew away, heading toward the man next to Fingin's grandmother.

The wind grew stronger, making torches sputter and flare. The gale swirled around the circle of anger, so strong it threw them off balance. Fingin stumbled into his neighbor, and he could move now. He took advantage of the freedom to flee to his grandmother.

Her dire straits did nothing to diminish her beauty, and Fingin felt uncomfortably attracted to her. She looked no older than he, a buxom maiden with fire in her eyes.

She glared at him with suspicion. "Who are you? Go away!" She stabbed at him with a bronze, leaf-shaped knife. The wicked blade came close to his stomach and he jumped back.

The man next to her stared at Fingin. He gave a slow nod, as if the man knew Fingin and why he watched. "Go, my child. She doesn't need you in this time. You have other work to do."

A crash behind him forced him to whirl, and he fell into the blackness.

Fingin spun and flipped, his sense of balance vanishing. His hands touched no surface, his eyes saw no light, and his stomach rebelled at the nothingness.

Something squishy lay beneath him, a soft pillow. The tantalizing odor of sizzling bacon awoke his senses. He opened his eyes, then shaded them from sunlight streaming through the window.

Bran licked his face with instant affection, and he shielded himself from further attacks. "Bran! Stop that!"

The sizzling bacon surrounded him, but his bladder needed tending to first. Fingin stumbled out the door to the edge of the woods and relieved himself.

The night before must have exhausted him, for him to miss the dawn. He hadn't greeted the dawn today, and he felt a twinge of regret and guilt.

Jumbled memories of his dream crashed into his waking mind. He tried to sort through the images to make sense, but they refused to cooperate. Fingin shook his head as he returned to the cottage. Fuzziness took over his memories and they drifted away into the darker recesses of his mind, places he rarely peered into.

Brigit raised one eyebrow as he entered. "You had quite a night, young man. Here, you need your strength."

She handed him a plate piled high with eggs, cheese, bread, and bacon. He glanced to ensure Bran had also been served before eating.

By the time he'd sopped up the grease with the last crust of wheaten bread, Brigit was regarding him with a thoughtful expression. She seemed even younger than the night before. Perhaps the harsh light had been unkind to her.

Now, she seemed young to middle-aged, rather than the bent old woman who'd struggled with the well bucket. His grandmother had always said a good night's sleep would cure what ailed you, but this seemed far more than a nice rest.

"Ah, yes, Clíodhna. Quite a woman in her time, you know. Few dared to cross her, and those who dared invariably regretted it. I believe you saw a glimpse of that just last night."

Fingin remembered the dream, and a vague memory of his grandmother's name niggled out of his deep memories. Clíodhna. He'd never called her that, but his mother had. "Did you know my grandmother?"

Brigit chuckled once, then a second time. The third laugh came loud, bouncing around the small hut until she held her side. "Know her? Did I know her? Yes, child, I knew her well."

"I dreamt of her last night, but she looked young."

"She had great beauty then. She's younger now, of course, but that's how it works sometimes."

This made no sense to him. But Brigit didn't give him time to ask questions. "Now, if you've finished your meal, I have another tale to tell you. Would you like to hear it?"

"Yes, please. But can you tell me what you'd like me to repair in payment for your hospitality?"

She pursed her lips. "You can repay me by sitting down and listening to my story, young man. Did I not just tell you?" The steel in her voice made him sit still and listen, his face growing warm.

"Now, many winters ago, when your grandmother was a young woman, we called her Clíodhna. She was a great beauty, with long, flowing, black locks, as dark as the midnight sky. Many men courted her, eager to make her his bride, but she rejected them all."

Fingin didn't doubt she'd be in great demand, from the glimpse he'd had in his dream. She'd had strength in her eyes, a woman not to be trifled with. From what he remembered of her in real life, she'd kept that strength and then some even as an older woman.

"Clíodhna reached the age of five and twenty winters before her father insisted she choose one of her suitors. Until then, he'd indulged her whims, for the riches he might get when she wed. However, when she still gave no sign of accepting a suit, he grew impatient."

Brigit stared out the window for a moment. "At this time, I was studying the new religion in a nearby abbey, vowed to the sacred fire burning inside. I had an intense curiosity, eager to learn new things, despite my own nature. As part of my studies, I'd vowed to eschew the company of men, though I was allowed female visitors."

She gave a smile now. "Clíodhna came often to do charitable work, and we developed a close friendship. I saw fire within her soul and appreciated her ability to temper strength with an uncommon wisdom. I nurtured this desire and even taught her a few tricks."

Fingin grew confused again. What power could an unmarried woman have? She was her father's property until she married, and then she was his. True, some had great influence upon the leaders in a *túath*, but they didn't have influence themselves.

A strong breeze whistled through the thatch, reminding him of the storm in his dream, the wild look in his grandmother's eyes as the gale whirled, surrounding the people. Something clicked in that memory, something about the storm.

Had his grandmother called the wind? Was this the strength of which Brigit spoke? He tried to pull up memories of his grandmother involving the weather, but most were tied to either his own misery or delight, not to his surroundings.

Brigit cleared her throat. "The day that man came to the village, however, everything changed."

Did she mean the same man in his dream? Somehow, he knew deep within his soul, that his dream had been a true memory. "Was he a dark-haired man with a beard?"

She took a sip from her mug and gave him a knowing smile, filled with the wisdom of the world within. "Why yes, young man, that is correct. He came to trade honey, but he left with the sweetest jewel of the land."

Had his grandmother run off with this man? He'd never known his grandfather. Had he died before Fingin's birth? "What was his name?"

She shook her head. "No, I'm afraid his tale is not mine to tell. Now, I'm weary, and must take my rest. An old woman must nap during the heat of the day, to rest her bones, you know. There might be extra thatch in the alcove next to the well, if you insist upon doing some repairs."

With that, she curled up into her own bed and pulled her wool blanket over her head. Within moments, her soft snores grew louder than bees in a glade, and Fingin led Bran outside, lest they disturb their mystical hostess.

Chapter Five

The tale of his grandmother churned up too many memories. Fingin performed the mechanical movements of cutting the straw, binding it to the roof, and tying bundles to the trusses. As he worked, the last time he saw his grandmother flooded into his memory.

Her hair had been black streaked with white, and she wore it in a thick braid around her head. While her face had grown lined with the weight of winters, her eyes were as clear as a summer sky, blue and sparkling. Her voice didn't quaver, but bit with caustic strength.

He'd been mucking out the stable, a job he enjoyed as it kept him from being bullied. His brother disliked horse manure, but Fingin enjoyed the horses' scent. They had a calm presence and always nickered in greeting while he worked the stalls. They'd even rear up when his brother tormented him nearby.

He was singing a low tune in time to his raking motion when his grandmother's voice broke through his woolgathering. "Fingin! Stop that now. I have something for you."

Though he only had eight winters, he knew better than to ignore his grandmother's commands. She had a quick hand and a quicker tongue. Unlike his father, though, she didn't hit to punish, only a sharp slap to command attention.

Fingin followed her down the path away from their farm. The sky shone clear overhead and the sun pounded on his scalp. His curiosity grew strong, but she would tell him in her time and not one moment before.

They climbed up the path, around the rocky outcropping the goats favored, down past the glade where his father was repairing his tools, and through a young oak grove. The trees grew older as they traveled deeper into the forest, more ancient trunks of gnarled bark and thinner undergrowth. The tree canopy blocked out most of the light, leaving the world in shadow and gloom.

Fingin had rarely explored this far at his age. He'd only climbed down to the river to fish, as his father taught him. Once a day, he'd cast his nets, and while some days he caught nothing, other days he contributed to the stewpot and earned a rare smile from both his parents. He'd wished he could bring fish home and earn those smiles every day.

They climbed a low hill now, to the scary place.

Twelve thin, dark stones jutted out around the crown of the hill at an outward angle. Though trees edged the circle, nothing grew within the stones. Dark clouds swirled overhead, and he smelled rain on the wind. The stones loomed black in the stormy world.

Dread swept over Fingin at the sight of them, a dread which screamed at his legs to run far away as fast as he could. But his grandmother had a firm grip on his hand, and her strength was greater than his.

Storm clouds roiled above, and thunder boomed across the hilltop. Vibration buzzed through his feet and his bones. A chilly wind tickled his skin. It was the height of summer, but now he shivered, aching to be anywhere but here.

She drew him into the circle. At the edge, a shock passed through him, making his skin tingle. A few drops of rain fell on his head.

His grandmother stood in front of the westernmost stone. It loomed with dark menace over them, forbidding and dangerous. "Stand here, boy. You must stay here, no matter what happens. Do you understand? I have to do work before the ceremony."

"Ceremony?"

"Shush now! All will be clear shortly."

Fingin stood rooted by terror of disobeying his grandmother, which was even stronger than his fear of the stones. He stared up at the tallest one as she walked around the circle, chanting in archaic words.

Sparks flew from her feet and hands as she marched three times, sunwise, around the stones. Each time, the glints grew stronger, brighter, and crackled in the foggy air.

A breeze swirled with her pace, a slow whirlwind. *Did the wind move her or vice versa?* She gestured on the third pass, the sparks forming arcane shapes before her, like carvings on the fairy stones. Triple swirls and endless curvilinear knots, a serpent forever eating its own tail.

As she completed her third round, lightning struck, the searing light leaving a black spot in the circle's center. Fingin's resolve fled, and he scrambled toward the outer edge, hugging a stone as if the unyielding rock was his own mother's arms.

Thunder muted his sobs of fear and rain drowned his tears.

His grandmother now stood in the charred spot, her arms raised high, chanting at the top of her voice. She called down the weather gods, beseeching them with speech and will to do her bidding.

Mysterious Manannán and Aebh, rulers of the mists.
Shield us with your cloak!
Brilliant Grian and Elatha of the sun and the moon,
Transport us with your silver craft!
Powerful Tuireann of the thunder bolts,
Guard us with your fury!
Honored Cailleach, the ruler of ice and snow,
Keep us in your arms!

The woman standing in the center of the circle was no longer his beloved grandmother. In her place stood a powerful druid, a woman capable of calling the heavens to earth to destroy them all.

Fingin squeezed his eyes shut and prayed to any god who'd listen that he'd wake up from this nightmare, but no divine intervention came. Instead, another flash of lightning forced him to open his eyes just in time to see his grandmother struck. But rather than burning to cinders, she shaped the light. Stars, circles, spears, and other, less recognizable images flew from her fingers.

Afterimages burned into his mind, to live there forever. When the light faded from his sight, his grandmother seemed young again, no longer the tired matron. Now she stood tall and beautiful, with smooth skin and imperious eyes, just like in his dreams.

She turned to him, and again he wanted to flee for his life. "Now, child, are you ready for your legacy?"

Fingin swallowed, unable to speak.

She reached into her bag and extracted a package of white, shimmering fabric. She approached him with an air of ceremony, holding the object before her like a burning ember.

When she was an arm's length away, she unfolded the fabric. First one corner, then a second, a third, and the fourth. She revealed a glowing artifact of gold, silver, and green. Filigree gold and silverwork entwined in animal shapes, a penannular brooch with four green gems, glittering in the dim light with a mystical shine. The emerald light bathed them in a preternatural glow.

Despite the part of his mind that screeched in terror, Fingin reached out to touch one of the gems. He half expected his grandmother to pull the jewelry away, to laugh in cruel jest at his temerity. However, she allowed him to tap the jewel.

Pain flowed through his finger, seizing every muscle in his body in a rictus of agony. A red glow surrounded him. He shrieked through the anguish, his strained voice echoed by the thunder. A metallic scent tickled his nose as he collapsed. His head wouldn't move as the rain splattered his face.

Fingin had one last thought before he lost all sense. His grandmother could have found a much simpler way of killing him.

As this memory faded, Fingin returned to the present, working on Brigit's roof. He'd fixed most of the thatching as he daydreamed, which surprised him. He had no memory of actually completing the work. And while he'd repaired roofs before, he didn't do it every week, like braiding twine or casting his net.

Bran slept in the eaves of the roundhouse, but Brigit had disappeared. He must have been concentrating so hard, he'd lost time. He checked the spots he'd worked on, but the ties seemed sound.

"This is a place of dreams, young man."

He whirled to find Brigit behind him, looking even younger than she had before, and she gave him a bright smile. "Yours have been most nourishing, I assure you. I wouldn't do you such a bad turn as to make you fall when you gave with such a generous heart."

She helped him down off the ladder. "Do finish the story. What happened after you woke at the stone circle?"

His words wouldn't come, as his mind went blank. He had no memory of what had happened after he'd woken.

"Come, now! You must have woken. Otherwise, you'd still be asleep. I haven't got all day, now. The evening will be upon us in a short time. You've places to go on the morrow."

Finally, memory crept back in. He cleared his throat. "I woke, wet and alone, in my own bed. She took everything, leaving nothing for me, not even the brooch." He stopped to swallow down a sob. "She took my working voice and gave me a broken one."

Brigit cocked her head and spoke in a kind tone. "That's when you discovered the ability to speak with animals?"

He nodded, remembering the joy and apprehension when he first realized his gift. And how much he mourned what he'd lost.

"She has something of yours, you know."

"My voice?"

The goddess waved that away. "Well, the brooch took that, not her, but the brooch itself, young man. That belongs to *you,* not her. She gifted it, then took it back, and that's not permitted. You must retrieve it."

"Will it get my voice back?"

Her eyes softened. "No, my lad. I'm afraid not, until you gift the brooch yourself. That must be to someone in your family, and you've no one but yourself at the moment. So, you have several quests." She ticked them off on her fingers. "You must find your grandmother, retrieve the brooch, and then find yourself a lovely woman and have a family."

He dropped his gaze to the ground, pushing some grass aside with his toe. "I tried to find her when she left."

"Aye, so you have. You were young, though, and unsuited to cross-country travel. However, you're a man grown now, capable of caring for yourself on the open road. You made it here readily enough, with Bran's help. And with this fine hound by your side to protect you, how can you fail?"

The next morning dawned with foggy humidity. Fingin could barely see his hand in front of his face, but he was rested and eager to travel.

However, Brigit regarded him, tapping her finger on her lower lip. "I've a few things for you."

She led him outside and gestured over a pile of things. This bounty loomed as a dark mass in the mist.

As Fingin sorted through the items, he tried to figure out how in the name of the Good God he would carry it all. She'd given him cooking ware, several changes of clothing, hunting weapons, as if he knew how to hunt, food for several weeks, plus some odds and ends he couldn't begin to identify. His back ached at the thought of carrying everything.

Brigit kept returning to her roundhouse and rustling around, coming out with a new treasure or find. She added it to the growing pile and returned for more, without stopping for questions from the erstwhile travelers.

When she emerged with nothing in her hands, Fingin let out a sigh of relief. Bran gave a breathy woof.

The goddess stood with her arms crossed, frowning at the mound of supplies. "No, that won't do. It won't do at all." This time, she strode to the tree line and disappeared into the woods.

Fingin glanced at Bran, apprehension clear in his eyes. He'd just about convinced himself that she'd gone for good when crunching leaves heralded her return. When a donkey emerged first, Fingin heaved a sigh of relief. He should have trusted Brigit.

By the time they'd packed the items into pannikins and strapped them to the donkey's back, the sun had burned through the mists, allowing the heat to bake the dew-wet grass.

Fingin had no experience riding. He'd been on a horse once, but that only lasted a few seconds before he fell flat on his back on the dusty ground. He had no urge to repeat such an experience.

However, he didn't need to ride the donkey. Instead, the placid creature seemed content to carry their gear, which would be a nice break for him.

Once Brigit finished tying the packs down, he patted the donkey's neck. "What's your name, friend?"

"The woman calls me Donkey. Is that my name?"

"It's *what* you are, not *who* you are. Would you like me to give you a name?"

The beast nodded and brayed. "Yes!"

"How about Sean? Sean is a good, strong name. You're a good, strong beast. Does that suit?"

The new-named donkey nodded again with great vigor, almost knocking Fingin over. "I am Sean!"

With a laugh and a pat to Bran's head, Fingin turned to the goddess. "I think I'm ready to leave, but where do I go? How do I find my grandmother?"

She gave him a pat on the back. "Head west. There's an island with monks from the new religion. One knew your grandmother, and may direct you further."

"What's his name?"

"Ask for Maol Odhrán, an older monk. It's been many years since either of us has seen your grandmother."

Brigit placed her hands on his shoulders and stared into his eyes. The regard of her gaze grew heavy, and he wanted to turn away, but he didn't dare. "Do not fail in your quest, young man. Generations of your family depend upon your success. Each one has an important place within this land, and you're the linchpin that will keep that lineage in place."

With a frown, she placed an object in his hand. An iron pendant, shaped into a flame on a circle. The jewelry hung on a long, thin piece of fresh-cut fabric. "I made this for you, Fingin. It has the power to heal, but it takes time to work. Keep it close and use it when needed. You may feel ill afterwards, but all magic has a cost."

She turned to Bran and placed a hand on his head. He wagged his tail so hard it thumped against the ground. "For you, loyal hound, I give you my blessings. Take good care of your friend, Fingin, and protect him from harm. For that is the purpose of good hounds in the world of men."

With a final pat on Sean's flank, she handed Fingin the donkey's lead. But when Fingin turned to thank her, she'd disappeared. He turned in a full circle. Not only had she disappeared, so had the roundhouse.

Fingin hadn't imagined the place. He'd spent the good part of the day repairing the thatched roof. His fingers still bore tiny cuts from the straw. He rubbed his thumb over one cut and shook his head. He supposed if one dealt with goddesses, one must get used to magic.

Into the empty glade, surrounded by the fog still clinging to the underbrush in the trees, he shouted, "Thank you!"

The wind echoed the words of a faint response. "Blessings on your quest, young man."

The blessings of a goddess surely meant more than blessings from a mortal. Bolstered by this faith, he clucked his tongue at Sean the donkey and Bran the dog. Somehow, after winters of aching loneliness, he'd gained two companions. Better yet, companions who didn't judge him or his ability to speak.

Friends who make one forget self-loathing are treasures beyond that of gold or silver.

Fingin's optimistic faith flagged as he climbed his third steep hill. The first had been a challenge but a choice, as villages lay in the valleys to either side. The second had been a necessity, as rivers cut around the edge of the slope.

This third one ended in a short cliff on one side, and impassable bracken on the other. He glanced at Sean. "Are you feeling tired yet, Sean? Ready for a rest? Or shall we tackle this hill?"

Sean peered up the mound, then glanced back at the path behind him. "We can't go back to the woman's home? She fed me."

Brigit had supplied hay for Sean, but Fingin hadn't considered that he might not have eaten yet that day. "Are you hungry? How about you, Bran?"

He chuckled as the dog's head perked up. "Fish?"

"No fish, but I have bread and cheese. Stand still for a moment, Sean, and I'll get out some hay. Or do you prefer fresh grass?"

In response, Sean yanked a chunk of greenery from the ground near him and munched in contentment, a few purple clovers hanging from his mouth.

Fingin pulled out bread, cheese, and a waterskin. He quaffed deep of the cool, clear water from Brigit's well. He poured some for both Bran and Sean and shared his meal with the dog.

Once they finished eating, his flagging strength returned. He peered up the path, determined to conquer this hill. It was just another obstacle to surmount.

Fingin and his small band of friends climbed the third hill with renewed vigor. As they reached the top, the sun burst out from behind the clouds and illuminated the valley before him.

What a sight! Fingin had never traveled more than five leagues from his birthplace. Now, looking across the landscape before him, the land extended so much further than he'd ever imagined.

His grandmother told him that an ocean surrounded their island, and lands existed beyond that ocean, like the legendary city of Rome. What would a city be like? Thousands of people living on top of each other? Did they have enough space to turn around? How did they all eat? It took tracts of land to feed just one family.

A patchwork quilt of such tracts, green and black, lay before him. Low, rolling hills of emerald velvet dotted with dark forests and glittering lakes drew his gaze. A cloud to his left roiled with dark moisture, threatening to douse the bright sunshine, but a brisk breeze blew the shadow away to the south. Beams of sunshine played out along the ground, dancing between the white patches in the sky, shading in a merry frolic.

The wind now found him, and he shivered, rubbing the bumps from his arms. This hilltop was a place of power but also of exposure. He hugged Bran tight for a moment and closed his eyes, wishing they were home in front of a warm, flickering fire, rather than on this mad, goddess-driven quest.

How could he find someone after fifteen winters, someone who'd deliberately hidden herself, retrieve the brooch, and then find someone to make a family with? A lifetime's work, and he must complete the quest quickly.

In the far distance, where the horizon kissed the sky, the ocean reflected the sun. As the day waned, the sun would set the sky and water afire.

Brigit had said the monk lived on a western island, a rock jutting out of the ocean. First, he must reach that shore. As much as Fingin squinted into the soft mist, he saw no islands. Still, he just needed to go west, she'd said. West toward the setting sun.

The trip down the hill seemed easier, but dodging bracken and rocks tired them. Though the sun still burned in the sky, they stopped to rest.

Dark clouds returned with a vengeance, as if angry that the wind had blown them away. They darkened the sky with ominous speed and spitting hail, forcing Fingin to search for shelter.

Sean brayed, "Ow! Ow!"

Bran found the small cave on the hillside, a series of several along the ridgeline. They huddled within the nearest one as pellets pounded earth and stone in a violent cacophony. The hail became a raucous song, a hammering distraction to his own thoughts.

Fingin wondered if he might find a wagon, so they'd have shelter wherever they went. But wagons cost dearly, and people didn't abandon wagons on the side of the road.

His father once had a wagon, tall with a wooden cover. He took it into the larger village to trade farm produce. He'd stay away several days, times Fingin remembered as full of smiles and freedom.

The tiny cave had barely enough room for him, Sean, and Bran. The rain and hail bounced up and got them wet, despite their shelter.

Soon, the sun dipped toward the far shore, taking the hail with it. Twilight fell with sudden silence, loud in the absence of the constant drum of hail on stone. His ears rang with the emptiness of the evening. No birds sang and no breeze stirred.

Exhausted, Fingin curled up next to Bran. Sean stood guard as they slept.

Angry barks dragged Fingin from a deep sleep. A sneering voice filtered through Bran's alarms. "Oho! What have we here?"

Sean let out a nervous bray as Bran kept barking.

Another voice joined the first. "Looks like a kid with too much wealth. At least, too much for one lone boy."

Fingin sat up, rubbing sleep from his eyes and placing a hand on Bran's back. The dog stopped barking, but growled, his hackles raised and his fur bristling. Sean stood between them and the new arrivals.

Nine men, all dressed in warrior garb, stood along the thin ledge. They all seemed to be around Fingin's own age, if not younger. Their linen *léinte* with fine embroidery, peeking out from behind leather chest-plates and wolf-skin shoulder pauldrons, spoke of wealth and privilege. They wore their hair in braids, the distinctive badge of warrior status.

The closest man stood with his arms crossed, eyeing the packs next to the donkey. Sean brayed and bobbed his head, his eyes wide with alarm. He stamped his hoof several times.

Fingin was worried that Sean might get hurt. The poor donkey wouldn't be able to save himself if the warriors shoved him off the cliff. While it didn't seem too high, even a small drop could break the loyal beast's leg.

He clicked at Sean and pulled on his halter. "C-c-come over here, b-boy. It's… safer next to the wall."

The leader elbowed his nearest companion. "Listen to this one. He can't even talk."

Curse the crows, Fingin said under his breath. Bran bared his teeth with a snarl.

"How did you get such a fine wolfhound? Did you steal him, boy? And all these goods. Food, cooking pots. You're either a tinker or a thief. I'm betting thief. Tinkers need to talk to barter. What do you think, men? Do we judge this man a thief?"

General agreements came from each warrior. The second man frowned. "I'm not sure, Cailte. What if he's related to someone important? He might just be a scion looking for adventure in the hills."

Cailte raised his eyebrows and made a show of examining Fingin's *léine.* While he had newer ones in his pack, thanks to Brigit's generosity, he was still wearing his older, threadbare garb.

The warrior frowned when his gaze reached Fingin's feet. He wore the boots Brigit had gifted him. Cailte glanced to his companion. "Look at that, Fearghus. His boots are new. You may just be right. Is that who you are, boy? Some younger son of a noble, off to find your own adventure?"

Fingin hated lying. However, he also hated being killed.

Their leather armor and their stylized braids gave them away, marking them as the Fianna, legendary bands of warriors pledged to defend the island from all dangers. If they'd judged him a thief, they'd be within their rights to execute him on the spot. At least their justice would come swiftly.

Despite tales of past heroes, though, the Fianna had never been paragons of honor. They had a reputation for strength and might, but not for being kind or gentle.

During the winter, the Fianna were known for pillaging. But the summer offered enough game for them to support themselves as they roamed between each *túath*, keeping order.

The leader waited for his answer with increasing impatience. With a deep sigh, Fingin nodded. "I'm a younger son. I'm looking for a p-p-place I feel at home."

He spoke the truth, as far as it went, though he didn't mention his father was a farmer, rather than a nobleman. He let that implication float within his answer. If the leader took the wrong meaning from his truthful words, so be it.

After a few moments' consideration, Cailte gave a quick nod. "That's that, then. Care to come with us for a while? Which way are you headed?" He glanced at Bran, who still hadn't dropped his guard.

Bran's low growl grew, despite Fingin's hand on his back. "I don't like him. He wants something."

Fingin nodded, more for Bran's benefits than in answer to Cailte. Hoping the warriors travelled some in some other direction, he replied, "I travel west."

"Excellent. We shall walk with you."

Hiding his sigh, he gathered his pannikins and secured them to Sean's back with a few words of quiet encouragement. Bran calmed somewhat after the confrontation broke but remained on his guard. Fingin couldn't blame him, and hoped the dog would continue to keep his senses sharp.

As they made their way off the cliff, the silence was strained. Fingin didn't wish to talk and highlight his speech difficulties. The warriors eyed him with both curiosity and calculation. If they wished to overpower him and take Sean, Bran, and all their gear, they could do so at any moment. But if Fingin turned out to be the son of a powerful chieftain, even the Fianna could get in trouble for that.

On the other hand, if they discovered his father had not only been a farmer, but a tenant farmer at that, he wouldn't last another minute.

For a moment, Fingin entertained the outlandish notion that he could send to his own father and convince them Rumann was the thief, instead. But Fingin shook his head at the petty thought. While he had no love for his father, in the past or the present, he couldn't set a squad of killers on his trail, even if he knew where his father now lived. *If* his father lived. For all Fingin knew, he could have found a drunken grave in some brook by now. He'd been heading in that direction when Fingin ran away.

Would he mourn his father's death? It seemed disrespectful to not care. He simply never wanted to see the man again, ever in his life. His mother had been little better, inattentive and concerned with her own comforts over everything else. His brothers… well, his brothers had tormented, beaten, and bullied him, but their deaths would still cause him sadness.

One warrior murmured something to his companion, and both laughed with loud brays. Sean spoke in Fingin's mind, "They want to kill you. I can smell it. A nasty, sour smell."

Bran couldn't hear Sean's words but still glowered at each warrior with suspicion.

A village came into sight as they walked around a hill. Six farms huddled together around the path, with a muddy pond to one side. A drover passed them with six head of cattle, nodding cautiously at the troop. The leader, Cailte, nodded back.

When the drover disappeared over a hill and they'd gone through the village, his closest companion punched Cailte's shoulder. "Should we circle back tonight? I could devour one of those cows."

Cailte shook his head. "Too close to the last one. They'll track our route if we're too obvious. Wait a few days and quiet your demanding gut, aye?"

Fingin gritted his teeth and tried to think of a plan to break away. He needed to leave without arousing their curiosity. What would be a plausible excuse? If he said he needed to turn left at the next fork, they might follow, and then he'd be stuck. If he said he had a stop to make, they might join him. He must find some way to extract himself.

He'd make a mistake, eventually. Then they'd find out he had no noble birth. They'd take Bran and Sean and all the wonderful supplies Brigit had given him. At least the healing pendant was buried under his *léine*, well out of sight. Not that it looked valuable, being made of wrought iron, but anything jewelry-like was fair game.

Maybe he should pretend to be ill? A mere cough wouldn't be enough. He'd need something truly disgusting. Diarrhea would be too dangerous. Projectile vomiting repelled people but had its own dangers. Besides, he'd seen no herbs nearby that might induce such a reaction. But he'd noticed nettles at their last stop. If he rubbed nettle on his cheeks, the hives might convince them to abandon him.

Then again, they might turn noble and insist on escorting him to the nearest healer. In addition, any rash he gave himself might heal too quickly to be natural, due to Brigit's pendant.

Curse the crows. His head ached with the possibilities.

When they stopped to eat near a brook, Fingin wandered off nonchalantly to relieve himself. He found a small patch of nettles and harvested some, shoving them in his pouch. He'd thought of no better plan, so nettles would have to do.

Cailte nodded toward Fingin's packs on the donkey. "Have you any fresh bread? We ran out yesterday."

Swallowing hard, Fingin shrugged. "I think I have a loaf left, but I d-d-don't know how fresh it is."

With cautious movements, he found the bag he thought Brigit had packed with food. He snaked his hand inside to avoid unpacking everything, as that would show the entire company what he had. He'd rather keep their knowledge of his supplies to a minimum.

His hand found something soft, and he pulled it out, holding up the loaf of rosemary rye bread. Fingin handed the treat to Cailte, and the leader sliced it, doling out the bread to each person.

Fingin didn't get a slice.

That act alone told Fingin all he needed to know of their intentions. Basic rules of hospitality meant nothing to them. He must escape before they commandeered the rest of his possessions.

Cailte handed out the hard tack, this time giving Fingin a portion. The rough, preserved travel food took forever to chew, but it kept both the warriors and himself occupied while he considered his options.

One of the younger warriors let out a deep sigh. "I'm bored. Who has a story?"

Fearghus settled into a storyteller's pose. "So, I went patrolling near the end of the last season. I hadn't found anyone worth fighting in a moon and ached for a good battle. My company had already settled down in a coastal village for the winter, but I was restless, and went off on my own."

He stopped to take a swig from his waterskin. "I walked along the western shore, on some lonely spit of land. A rugged island jutted out of the sea, almost white with seabirds and their shit. I walked to the beach, hoping to find oysters when there, on the beach, stood a woman."

The hoots and howls of his companions filled the glade, along with suggestive gestures and a few pats on Fearghus' back.

He waved off his enthusiastic companions. "Settle down! It's a story, not a brag."

They chuckled but subsided as bidden.

"She wore a black cloak, shiny as the sea, and stood with it drawn around her shoulders, as if in the winter wind, though it was still summer. That's when I realized that though the sea breeze was strong, neither her cloak nor her long, ink-black hair stirred in the slightest."

A heavy silence crept over them all.

"I knew then that I beheld no ordinary woman. Besides the skin like milk and hair like night, she stood with one foot in this world and one foot in the other, without doubt. Her black eyes bore holes into my soul as I stared at her.

"She lifted one slim hand and beckoned me forth. No force on earth could have kept me from obeying her command."

Fearghus' jovial manner had turned grim. He took a deep sigh before continuing his tale. "When I got close enough to touch her cheek, she laughed."

Cailte furrowed his brow. "She laughed? Did you tell her a joke?"

Fearghus shook his head. "I'd said nothing at this point. Her laugh wasn't the sort you give for a joke. It scratched at my bones, harsh against my soul. Her cackle spoke of death, the hysterical laughter of tortured children and bloody heads rotting on the battlefield."

Fingin drew in his breath. He knew who this woman must have been.

One of the younger warriors sprang to his feet, anger in his eyes. "You saw the Morrigú? Liar! Why would she appear to you?"

Normally, an accusation of lying demanded a fight to settle the insult. However, Fearghus simply nodded, refusing to rise to the other man's words. "Aye, and I had no doubt. This creature came of the night, of the dark, of the dead."

Another warrior spoke in a voice a little too shrill. "Was she beautiful?"

With a half-smile, Fearghus closed his eyes. "Beautiful and terrible at the same time. She held the type of beauty you hope never to see in your lifetime, the type of beauty you'd sell your life for."

"What did she do next?"

Fearghus took another deep breath. "She touched my forehead and I shut my eyes, knowing I'd be dead in a moment. And yet nothing happened. I felt no touch. Instead, when I opened my eyes again, she'd disappeared. Not even a depression upon the sand where she'd been but a moment before."

A few nervous laughs from the other warriors died quickly into silence. One of the younger men coughed and another sneezed.

Fingin shivered. Having met a goddess himself, he could understand how unsettled Fearghus seemed. While Brigit had as much, if not more, power as the Morrigú, a goddess of healing, inspiration, and smithcraft was less terrifying than a goddess of magic and death. No one craved to meet the Morrigú. No one with any shred of sanity.

In the somber quiet following Fearghus' tale, several warriors drank from their skins. Fingin walked to a nearby bush to relieve himself, though he'd just gone before the story.

While he was out of sight from the rest of the company, he pulled the nettles from his bag and, with quick swipes, rubbed them on his cheeks, forehead, and hands. For good measure, he touched a few places on his arms.

The welts turned red quickly and burned. If that's the price he must pay for his own safety, then so be it.

He returned to the warriors and bent to help them clean the fire like nothing was wrong. Then he bent over, groaning and holding his stomach, as if in great gut pain.

Fearghus laughed. "Boy? What happened, boy? Is your belly too delicate for man's food? Would you like us to prepare some buttermilk and soften the bread for you? Maybe I should chew it up and spit it in your mouth like a bird?"

Fingin fell on his side, moaning and writhing. The warriors now had full view of the reddened welts on his face and hands. They backed up and exchanged nervous glances.

Bran barked, an assault on his ears. Fingin hadn't had time to tell Bran the plan, so he'd have to reassure him later. Besides, his plan might work better if the dog thought he'd truly fallen ill.

Cailte peered down at him. "What have you got all over your face, there? Did you find some raspberries? Do you not know how to aim for your mouth?"

Fingin shook his head and groaned again, pressing his palms into his belly. He curled further into a fetal position, praying to all the gods they'd just leave him here to die.

Fearghus poked him with his foot, prodding his shoulder. "This came on sudden. You looked fine earlier."

Cailte crossed his arms and scowled. "Do you think it's a trick?"

"Aye, I do. We ate the same things he did, and we're not covered in splotches."

One of the other men rushed up to Cailte and handed him something using his glove. Fingin couldn't see what he held, but he could guess. Some enterprising warrior had found his discarded nettles. *Curse the crows.*

The leader nodded. "Grab him."

Fingin tried to punch back, but one wiry young man against nine trained warriors would never be a fair fight. He struggled, pulling one arm free, but another man grabbed it a second later.

Bran jumped on one man, pushing him to the ground, and sunk his teeth into his arm. That warrior howled and another man kicked the dog. He kept kicking Bran as the dog tried to rise and bite again.

"Bran! Sean! Run!"

Startled, the donkey brayed and reared before galloping off into the woods. Bran hesitated, sent him a guilty look, then followed Sean.

Fearghus sent four of the men to fetch the animals, thinking they'd only been spooked. They'd have no way of knowing the beasts had understood Fingin. He prayed they both could escape. Bran could have broken bones from those kicks.

A dozen hard kicks to his ribs made something crack inside. Every part of him ached, and sharp kicks into his midriff made him groan and curl into a ball.

With a moment's consideration, Cailte took aim at his cheek, kicking him so hard, his neck snapped back, and he saw a flash of light. Three more blows, and darkness enfolded him.

Chapter Six

Fingin floated in clouds made of obsidian shards. Every twitch brought intense pain, but he had to move to avoid the spikes swimming around him. Something cold and wet fell on his face. He tried to push it away, but it returned, howling and snuffling.

Time meant nothing. His body was a separate thing, but it still shot agony to his mind. How could he escape the throbbing? The anguish? He couldn't even cry.

The wet returned. He reached up, though he couldn't see. Something hairy? Warm. The warmth moaned and whined.

"Fingin? Fingin, open your eyes. We're back. The bad men are gone. They didn't find us. Wake up."

Fingin tried to open his eyes, but they remained shut. He gingerly touched his face, but everything ached, swollen and tender. No wonder his eyes wouldn't open. The blows Cailte had rained upon his face must have blackened both eyes.

"Water. I need water."

He didn't know how either beast would get him water. The Fianna probably stole all his belongings. But something bumped his hand. He grasped it and felt a waterskin. It must have been on Sean's pannikins.

Through cracked and bloody lips, Fingin sipped with caution. After swished the water, he spit out iron-tasting blood. He clenched his jaw, but his teeth seemed sound through the aches. It would take a long time for his face and ribs to heal.

Heal. He remembered Brigit's charm and pulled it out of his shirt, sending thanks that the warriors hadn't found and stolen it. Fingin clutched it close to his heart, not knowing how it worked. With a vague memory of his parents' actions at their religious house, he passed it over his eyes and his ribs, grunting with pain as he moved his arm.

Nothing happened, but the goddess had warned him the healing would be slow. No matter. He had faith in her charm that he'd mend. For now, though, they needed to move in case the warriors returned to finish their work.

"Bran, are you hurt?"

The hound woofed once. "My side hurts, but not too bad. My former friend hurt me worse."

With a silent curse for the former *friend*, Fingin asked, "Sean, did they hurt you at all? Do you still have the packs?"

"I'm too fast for them. The packs aren't heavy."

He chuckled, and then groaned, because his ribs shifted again. "Oh, please don't make me laugh. But well done, both of you. Now, I need to get up. I can't see, and it hurts to move. Bran, can you stand next to me as I get on my feet? Sean, I may need to pull on your bridle."

With much grunting and grumbling, Fingin pulled himself to his knees, and after catching his breath, then to his feet. He almost passed out from the pain but gritted his teeth and persevered.

"In the pannikin, I have some cloth. I need to wrap it around my middle. I think it's in the left side. Can you move so I can get to it?"

Sean shuffled around as Fingin stood still, almost stumbling when the solid strength of the donkey shifted. He felt the pannikin and snaked his hand into the pack. He found one of the *léinte* and hoped it would reach all the way around him.

"I wish I had some rope. But Sean's bridle will have to do. You don't need it, do you? You're not planning on running off?"

"I'll stay with you. You feed me."

He chuckled, then winced. "I said stop making me laugh."

Bran woofed and Sean scraped his hoof in the dirt.

Fingin wrapped the fabric around his ribs, and after several tries, tied the bridle around that. It kept him from bending too much. "How late in the day is it? Is the sun setting?"

Bran let out a whine. "The dark is coming."

"We need to walk toward the sunset. Can you lead us, Bran? I have to stay next to Sean with my hand on his flank, so you need to pay attention to where I'm stepping. We can rest after a league, I think."

Bran yipped three times. Leaves rustled as he ran here and there. "I can't see the sun. The clouds are in the way."

"Do you remember which direction we came from?"

Another bark. "I can smell it."

"Then we should head in the opposite direction, continuing our journey. Oh, wait! The Fianna might have gone that way. Can you smell where they went?"

Snuffling the ground for a few moments, Bran barked. "Yes!"

"We don't want to go where they went. Let's head south, and we can turn west later. Bran, stand in front of me the direction we came from." The dog did so. "Now, which direction did the Fianna go?"

Bran barked from his other side. "This way."

Fingin turned about a quarter circle from that direction, which should be south. "We'll travel for a league and sleep for the night. In the morning, we can turn west."

He stumbled the first three steps, falling on his hands and knees. Pain shot through his whole body. "Curse the crows!"

With much muttering about his own clumsiness, he picked himself up with Sean and Bran's help. The palms of his hands burned with a raw rash from his fall. "Bran, you must be my eyes. I can't see stones, roots, or bushes. Choose the smoothest path you can find. Let me know if I need to lift my feet higher."

"I'll try."

After some refinement and adjustment, Bran learned how to lead him. They walked slower than normal, but at least they got away from that spot.

By the time they normally would have needed to stop because of the darkness, they hadn't gotten very far. However, Bran could see better than any human, so they continued until the last light of the setting sun faded. Fingin didn't even bother setting up camp. Instead, he curled up next to Sean's side, with Bran against his back.

Fingin's entire body ached and throbbed. He wasn't used to walking so far. All his leg muscles, unused to the strange method of walking, jumped and twitched. His face pulsed in a mass of agony, now that he had nothing else to concentrate on.

Fingin tried not to touch his swollen eyes or nose. He'd splashed it with cool water, but the burning skin stung worse than ever.

He needed rest, yet dreams wouldn't come. Perhaps no dreams would be a blessing.

As morning dawned, Bran roused, chasing after the birds singing in the bushes. Fingin rose, a glimmer of light filtering through his swollen eyes. He needed to greet the dawn. He'd missed the chance the last few mornings, but today the sky seemed clear. It almost felt like a betrayal of Brigit's help not to give a proper greeting.

Fingin sat cross-legged facing east and breathed deep. With each breath, he drew in the land's power, the rising sun, and the beauty of the dawn, what little he could see. The tonic suffused him with healing energy, and Brigit's pendant warmed.

He placed his hand on it, almost burning his already injured palm. It pulsed with tingling energy. The throbbing in his skin and bones faded.

When Fingin completed the morning ceremony, his muscles ached less than they had when he first rose. His skin was still tender, but not painful. He threw a thankful prayer to the goddess.

After a quick meal from his packs, with oats for Sean and dried fish for Bran, they headed west, away from the rising sun, and he reflected on the events of the day before.

His plan hadn't worked. While it had broken him free from the Fianna, he'd almost died with the process. He wouldn't have been able to forgive himself if Bran or Sean had been harmed or taken by the rough warriors.

How would he prevent something like that in the future? Fianna groups wandered all around the island. Some might be more honorable than that one, but some might be less. He couldn't risk another beating as he might not survive the next one.

The woods opened to a long, flat glade. No longer blind, he could walk almost normally now. He still had to step cautiously, as his eyes weren't all the way open yet, and the edges of his vision blurred.

As they reached the center of the glade, Fingin stopped to survey the view, noting a low cliff to the right and a gentle slope to the left. A glint of water in the bright sun drew his attention.

The glittering river grew wide around a bend. The forest line obscured the view past that. They should be able to follow the water to the ocean. That way, he could fish each day and the riverbank might offer a smoother path.

The group climbed down the slope, picking their way along a rocky field.

Fingin had grown up along *An Ruirthech* River. He'd always thought it broad and swift, filled with plenty of fish for his daily cast. But this river made the other seem like a trickling brook. He could barely see the other side through the roiling mist. The current flowed rough and fast, pulling debris along with alarming speed.

He glanced back at the trees, nervous in case anyone saw them in the open, exposed. Then his eyes returned to the river.

If he fashioned a raft for the three of them, they might be able to travel down the river, free from the danger of Fianna, bandits, or other evil men. They'd reach the western shore much more quickly, too.

"Bran, we need to find downed trees. At least… ten."

"Ten? Is that more than two?"

He'd forgotten Bran didn't understand numbers. "Just keep finding more until I say we have enough. Sean, I'll need your help in dragging them here. I want to build a raft. I have plenty of twine."

Bran ran into the woods and barked when he found a log. Fingin and Sean followed to assess what he'd discovered. The first two were too slim, while the third was so gnarled it looked like a knotted rope, and he tucked those away for kindling. The fourth, however, had once stood straight and tall.

Fingin used Sean's bridle and his twine and tied the log. Then he rifled through Brigit's supplies and shouted in triumph when he found a small hand-axe.

With lots of sweat and cursing, he chopped off the protruding branches. He hacked at the trunk for a long time and only made it halfway through before he had to stop, every muscle aching.

He grabbed his waterskin and gave some to both the dog and the donkey, then refilled it at the river. A wizened apple and some jerked meat, and his stomach quieted. A sharp snap made him jump up, axe in hand, but rather than Fianna, he only saw a squirrel. Bran chased off the intruder with furious barks.

After a great deal of work, he won through the thick trunk and trussed it to Sean's bridle. Several shouted orders later, and a few scary moments when he thought the trunk would slide down the slope, taking poor Sean with it, they carried it to a low beach where they'd assemble the raft.

Now they just had to do all that nine more times.

Maybe this wouldn't be faster than just walking. Still, it might be safer.

They got two more deadfall trees trimmed and down to the beach before he needed to stop for a longer break. Sweat streamed down Fingin's face and on Sean's flanks as he pulled out both oats and jerked fish. He gave some to Bran, who played with it before he ate it, flipping it into the air and pouncing on it several times.

The sun roasted the top of his head. He wished it was overcast, but he shouldn't complain. This task would be much more difficult in the rain. If he wanted to risk that current, he might cool off in the river.

After his meal, he brushed down Sean's coat, getting the worst of the wood chips and dust off, and sluiced some river water over his flanks to cool him down. Bran jumped into the water, finding a shallow pool protected by a rocky outcropping, and Fingin joined him, sighing with relief as the water cooled his skin and muscles.

He'd just dried off when Bran returned to shore, shaking his coat, covering both Fingin and Sean with a fresh splash of river water.

With a splutter, Fingin said, through a clenched jaw, "Thank you, Bran. That's exactly what I needed."

Bran's tongue hung out. "You're welcome!"

Fingin rolled his eyes at the dog's innocent answer and sent him to find a fourth log.

They only finished six logs the first day. His muscles hadn't ached nearly as much as they should. He gingerly tested his ribs, but they seemed sound. His face still stung, but the swelling around his eyes had retreated to almost normal. "Bran, what color is my face?"

"Color?"

"I mean, is my face bruised or is it normal?"

Bran cocked his head as if listening. "What's bruised?"

"Purple and black, as it must have been after those men beat me."

"Oh! It's still dark here and there. It's almost normal. Splotchy."

He grinned, the smile pulling on his aching skin. "That's what I wanted to know."

The welts from his misbegotten nettle plan had also faded from his hands. He sent a prayer of thanks to Brigit for such rapid healing.

As he lit a small fire for their evening meal, his muscle pain returned. But this was a normal ache for a day full of heavy activity, not the throbbing of a pummeled body.

He tossed fragrant herbs onto the flames in thanks for Brigit's forethought. Both the healing pendant and the axe had been invaluable.

He hoped he wouldn't need the pendant again soon.

The night was clear and cool, with stars twinkling above them in a magical dance. His body, exhausted from the day's efforts, didn't keep him awake with pulsing pain. Instead, he drifted into troubling dreams, his thudding heart waking him more than once. Despite his broken dreams, he slept through most of the night.

The morning dawned overcast, just as he'd wished for the day before, but no rain fell in the morning mist. Fingin didn't greet the sun, since he couldn't see it.

They pulled two more logs to the beach and dressed them, but Bran had difficulty finding two more. Each one he found was too gnarled, too thin, too thick, or too rotten. Farther and farther they searched, trying to find suitable logs.

Fingin considered using just the eight logs they had, but he didn't want to risk Sean falling into the river. He needed ten for both his friends to travel in safety.

In a clearing up the hill, he looked around, though the standing trees would hide any fallen logs. As he glanced back down to the river, something caught his eye.

A silver flash, a fish swimming against the current, jumped over the surface. The fish must have been enormous to be visible from so far. Frowning, Fingin started to climb back down to the shore.

He remembered the last time he'd encountered a huge salmon, when he'd almost drowned. And yet, if that fish hadn't destroyed his net, he might have missed Bran. Brigit had even hinted she'd sent the fish.

It couldn't be the same fish.

Still, he needed to check. Perhaps she was sending another message.

He slipped a few times, rushing down to the small beach. He made it just as the silver fish leapt again.

There couldn't be two salmon so large in Ireland, could there?

After he stared at the fish, disappearing upstream, he stared at the far shore. There, sticking out along the tree line, lay two more logs. They looked like they'd broken from their trunks at the exact length he needed for his raft.

Now, how to cross the river to get them?

Fingin considered building the raft with the logs he had, taking Bran and him across the river, and hauling the new logs back to finish the raft. Then he thought about having Sean pull him across the water to pull them back. Which would be less dangerous?

He pointed across the river. "Sean, do you see those two logs?"

The donkey nodded.

"I need to get them. If we swim across and tie them to your back, do you think we can drag them back here? We can do both at once or one at a time. Are you strong enough for that?"

"I don't know."

"Are you willing to try?"

Sean stared at the river for several moments before nodding.

Feeling guilty for relying so hard on his friend's help, Fingin said, "If you get too tired, we'll stop on the other side until we're rested enough to come back. Bran can even come across with us. Does that sound good?"

Sean nodded again, and Bran let out a woof.

"Let's eat first. Then we'll go over."

They ate in silence as Fingin watched the river, imagined the dangers, and thought about how his plan might go wrong.

When they'd rested, Fingin decided he'd first try with Sean, as the donkey had more stamina than the dog. "Are you sure you want to swim across, Sean? It doesn't matter how far down the other side we float, as long as we reach the other side. I'll hold on to your bridle, so we don't get separated. Can you do that?"

The donkey nodded a few times, but Fingin sensed the hesitation in the beast's answer.

With growing apprehension, he tied Sean's bridle around his wrist, and they entered the river.

As soon as they reached the center current, Fingin knew he'd underestimated its strength. The water tugged at them, pushing them downriver. The far shore looked leagues away now. He called to all the fish, asking for help, but they all ignored him. Even the big salmon had disappeared.

A large branch floated next to them and Fingin had to duck to keep from being hit on the head. It brushed Sean's flank, but Fingin pushed it away before the branches got entangled in Sean's ropes. It spun away on the water, cutting lazy circles as it sped along.

They swam hard for the other shore, but their goal seemed to get farther away with each stroke. Sean struggled to keep his head up while Fingin's arms ached and the pain from the prior days' work came back to haunt him. His eyes and nose stung, his healing not yet complete despite Brigit's pendant.

One more stroke. One more kick. If he hadn't tied Sean's bridle to his wrist, he would have drifted far from the donkey long ago. Together, they gained on the elusive shore.

Sean brayed when they'd almost reached ground. The donkey must have gotten a foothold on the riverbed. He climbed to dry land, dragging Fingin behind. They lay on the rocks, panting and exhausted, unable to move.

Distant barking echoed over the rush of the water. Fingin lifted himself to his elbows, spying the small gray blur on the other side that must be Bran. He must have followed them as they drifted down the river, trying to cross.

Once they stopped panting, they hiked back up along the river's shore to the two logs. Up close, Fingin worried about how large and heavy they were. They'd pull both him and Sean far downriver. Dragging them ashore would be hard, too. He'd need to rig a way to cut Sean loose if they got tangled.

Fingin cursed the fact that he'd left his knife on the other side. He'd tied his axe to his belt, though, in case he needed to cut small branches from the trunks. He bent to this task while he considered how he'd proceed.

Would they have enough energy to return for the second trunk? Or should they try to take both the first trip? Sean offered no opinion when asked, so the decision must be Fingin's.

Sean braced himself on the rocks as Fingin tied first one and then the second log to his bridle with twine. Once both logs bobbed in the river, sheltered by an outcropping of rock, he tied them together to minimize the water pulling them in different directions.

Once he'd set the tethers, he took a deep breath and told Sean to head for shore. Fingin swam with one hand on the logs, both to keep him afloat and to guide them.

At first, Sean swam easily across the current, only drifting down river a little. But a strong eddy formed beneath him, making him spin and flounder in the deeper water. He squealed and Fingin wished he'd stayed near the donkey, offering support and strength. "Stay strong, Sean! Just keep swimming! Push through the whirlpool!"

Sean pulled out of the eddy, but then the logs got caught in the same whirl. Fingin kept hold to keep some control on the dragging wood. The tied logs angled up, knocking his grip loose, and he sank beneath the surface.

The sunny day disappeared into the dark and swirling water. He didn't even get a chance to gulp air. Water burned in his lungs, and he struggled to the silver surface.

The logs floated above him, and he tried to shove them aside so he might breathe sweet air, but he had no leverage. His sight grayed around the edges. He needed to cough, but couldn't.

With growing desperation, Fingin waved his arms, trying to free himself from the whirling trap. His hand hit one of the logs, and it moved forward. He followed it and broke the surface. He drew in the fresh air, gasping and coughing. His vision returned to normal, though his lungs and eyes stung.

He searched for Sean and the logs, but he didn't see them. Fingin didn't even know on which shore Bran waited.

Silver water filled his sight, and he searched for any clue to which shore was the right one. With no clues to help, he chose one at random.

But now, his arms refused to obey his will. With enormous effort, he lifted one arm, and it dropped on the surface, making a loud smack. He drifted further downstream as he tried to lift the other. All his strength was gone.

With alarming fatalism, he decided the water would eventually throw him ashore at some bend in the river. Perhaps Bran might find him someday.

Adrift and unable to move, Fingin bobbed along the current, turning now and then with the motion of the water. He stayed afloat, but he couldn't muster the strength to swim ashore.

He hoped Sean had made it safely. How would the donkey untie the logs? Maybe Bran would bite through the twine. Then they'd be free.

They'd be better off away from him. He'd only brought them pain and danger. If the river swallowed him, his friends would live happier lives.

It seemed an eternity later that he heard the barking. He blinked several times to focus on land, but his vision swam. Only blurry water and colors danced in his sight, waterlogged with the wool of drowning daydreams.

Something pulled him and he fought with feeble struggles. He tried to bat away whatever attacked him, but his blows were useless. He just splashed around at nothing. Whatever bit at him ignored his actions.

Now he'd be dragged under, to some river monster's watery lair. Perhaps he'd been seized by a legendary *murdúchann*? A lovely woman who turned into a seal and lured men to their death. Fingin welcomed her sultry embrace.

Blackness engulfed him.

His grandmother's strident voice cut through the black. "Rumann, what are you doing to that child? Stop it! Immediately!"

Fingin ducked away into a corner as soon as his father was distracted. He huddled in the dark, hoping to stay hidden from his father's eyes. Or more importantly, from his father's leather strap.

"I'm teaching him a well-needed lesson, Mother. Leave me to my own child."

"I'll do no such thing! Drop that at once."

Rumann growled but didn't drop the strap. Fingin shuddered, knowing his anger would find a target, and that target would not be his grandmother.

"I'm tired of healing the welts and cuts you leave on the poor boy. He's doing his best, Rumann. Can't you see that? He can't work as hard as the older boys. Fingin weighs half as much."

"He's a slacking idiot. He doesn't do enough because he's lazy."

"The boy is barely eight winters! You didn't work as hard at eight. And before you protest that you did, may I remind you that I was there?"

He growled again, muttering under his breath. He slapped the strap into his hand in a rhythmic tattoo, an ominous warning that he itched to use it again.

His grandmother crossed her arms. Her shawl showed bright red in the dim light, a beacon from his misery. Fingin wished he could escape with her, to run away from his father, far away to another land. He'd even asked her once, but she'd laughed. She said she'd leave some day but had work yet to do here.

He didn't know what work she meant. His grandmother left for the village during the day and sometimes returned in the evenings. She wore bright, new clothing and always came back cheerful. Except that one time he'd found her crying, but she'd said they were happy tears. He didn't understand what she meant by happy tears.

His father barked, but that seemed strange. His father must have found it odd, for he furrowed his brow. When he opened his mouth, he barked again. Then something cold and wet touched Fingin's cheek.

Fingin blinked away grit and opened his eyes to Bran standing on his chest. It hurt.

"You're awake! You're awake! I didn't think you would wake but Sean said you hadn't been hurt. I found you and you're awake!"

Fingin had to fend off a fresh onslaught of licks as Sean brayed in the background. Once he gained control of his body and asked Bran to stop trying to drown him all over again, he sat up, trying to make sense of everything.

They landed nowhere near where he'd left the rest of the raft. However, both logs had made it to shore, despite the frayed string looking ready to break. Sean sat on the ground, exhausted and drained. They both deserved a long rest.

"Let's sleep here tonight, and then we'll head back to the rest of the raft in the morning. But I have no food, so we'll have a grand breakfast in the morning when we get back to our pack."

"I have fish!"

Fingin peered at Bran. Three trout lay at his feet.

"Wherever did you get those?"

"I got them from the river, after I caught you. They jumped into my mouth!"

He chuckled. "Then you're a real fisherman, like me! You should get first choice."

Bran's tongue lolled in joyful satisfaction at his new title. Sean laid his head down on the ground.

"Let me gather some kindling for a fire and grass for Sean before we rest. He did all the work today and deserves all the pampering I can give him."

Fingin's limbs felt like wood as he gathered sticks and searched for sweet sedge grass and cattails. He yanked them out to deposit near the brave donkey, but Sean had already closed his eyes in sleep as he started the fire.

"Bran?"

"Yes, Fingin?"

"Thank you for saving my life today. I would have died if you hadn't pulled me to shore."

"I had to."

Fingin crinkled his forehead. "You did?"

"Brigit told me. She warned me this would happen. She said to be ready. So, I knew."

He hugged the hound close. "You did well, my friend."

That night, he didn't dream of his father's violence, nor his grandmother's secret life. In fact, he dreamt of nothing at all, except the warm, fluffy body that curled up next to him as darkness fell.

Chapter Seven

It took the three of them a great deal of effort to haul the two logs back upriver. If he'd completed the rest of the raft first, he might have floated that downriver to where the new logs waited, but they weren't tied together yet.

They left the new logs floating in the river, and Fingin asked Sean to drag them along, while the donkey walked along the riverbank. Fingin stood by in case the new twine got tangled in bushes or rocks along the journey. With several rests and more than a few snags, they returned to the small beach with the other eight logs.

Now, Fingin began tying the logs together with the rest of his twine. Sean slept and Bran kept an eye out for any interruptions, bounding in the woods and chasing the curious ravens away. Once, he surprised a brace of rabbits, but caught nothing.

In and out, Fingin twined around each of the logs, pulling them tight and tying the string. The first two secure, he added a third, then the fourth, and so on. He built it on the edge of the beach, so all he'd need to do is shove it into the water.

Then he'd need to get Sean on board. He should persuade the donkey to sit down. Standing on the raft would be more dangerous and likely to capsize.

His twine supply had almost run out when he tied the last knot. With a grin, he tested the raft's sturdiness.

Just as he tugged on the last knot, he realized he needed one more thing. "Bran! I need you to find me a slender log, something I can use as a pole to steer the raft. As long as you can find, but strong enough so it won't bend. Can you find me one?"

Without answer, Bran bounded into the trees, disturbing a flock of robins who'd just settled down to dig for worms. They complained in a raucous chorus, both in Fingin's mind and in chirps. They had some choice words for the blundering dog who disturbed their meal, making Fingin smile.

Sean had woken again, but he still seemed off-color.

"Would you like some water, Sean?"

"I don't want any water ever again."

Fingin chuckled. "I don't blame you, my friend. But we need to drink water every day. I'll get you some."

With his cooking pot, he scooped water from the river. He also gathered more sweet sedge grass for a treat. Sean had well earned it. Fingin hoped the donkey wouldn't be too afraid to get on the raft. But he'd deal with that later. For now, he wanted to ensure his friend rested and fed.

Bran's barking in the distance made him rise. "I'll be back soon." He grabbed his axe and walked toward Bran's summons.

His dog had found a suitable tree, straight with only a few knots and those didn't bend the main trunk. With a few axe blows and some trimming, he had a serviceable raft pole.

Fingin dragged it back to the beach, where Sean was sleeping again. He began to worry that Sean had been hurt in the misadventure.

As Fingin squinted at the overcast sky, he judged the sun's height. Through the thin cloud cover, it was already well past midday. Today wouldn't be a good day to embark on their journey, anyhow. He should let Sean sleep and get some rest himself.

But first, he built a fire with the leftover branches he'd trimmed from his raft logs, tied the raft to a tree near the shore, and settled down to cook a meal. He'd been eating jerky and the last of the bread for several days and craved a hot supper.

Turnips, carrots, onions, garlic, and rosemary went into the pot. He soaked the dried fish before tossing it in with the rest. He let the stew simmer, his mouth watering as the aroma enveloped him.

A proper stew took all day, but he didn't have all day. At least he could let it cook for a few hours. The sun had almost set by the time he allowed himself to sample his supper. The fish was still tough, and he ought to cook it a half a day more, but his stomach gurgled.

Fingin scooped some into a bowl for Bran, who finished it in short order, despite the heat. Fingin forced himself to savor his. He wouldn't be able to cook on the raft, but they'd stop each night on the shore.

Fingin didn't have much practice guiding a raft, but he had to try. He'd steered one a couple times when he was younger and had learned how to make one from his older brother. They'd made smaller rafts and explored up and down the river.

Fingin drifted to sleep thinking of days past, but for once, he didn't dream of that. Instead, he drifted through a fantasy landscape, filled with fluttering insects in rainbow colors. His feet didn't touch the ground.

Instead, he floated on a musical note, riding it like a horse, as if he knew how to ride a horse. It rose up and down in a soaring scale. His ears almost burst with the pure sound as it spun and wheeled.

The note flew near the earth at the end of the song. When he dismounted, the ground felt spongy beneath his feet. He tried to pull himself from the quagmire, but it sucked him back and he couldn't escape.

When he woke, dripping nervous sweat, night had engulfed the world. A few stars poked through the clouds, but the moon hid, not even a faint glow through the overcast sky.

Bran snored next to him, his warm fur against Fingin's back. Sean lay on his other side. The chittering of night creatures crowded in his mind.

An owl wondered who was stirring, as a badger grumbled in his den about prey disappearing these last few days.

He felt sorry for the badger, as he must be the reason animals had run away. But the prey would return when they rode down the river the next day.

He whispered into the night, knowing the badger wouldn't hear him. "Rest easy, badger. You'll eat tomorrow."

Heavy rain woke Fingin, rather than sunlight or warmth. He lay in a soggy mudhole, steady drops pounding on his head. How had he even slept through this? He must have been more tired than he'd thought.

He didn't see either of his friends. Fingin stood, shaking the excess water from his *léine*, but it was covered in mud. He shrugged and waded into the river, as he might as well be clean since he was already soaked.

The raft bobbed on the surface as he waded into the water. At least it was still floating, proving out the soundness of his construction.

When he emerged, he sluiced the excess water, stamping his feet and shaking his hands. It made little difference. The downpour replaced any water he shook off, but at least the mud was gone.

He grabbed his pack and climbed up the hill to search for his companions. The oiled leather should keep things dry, though after almost a week on the road, their food was running thin. He could cast his net, but this river seemed too powerful for a fishing net from the shore. Maybe he'd find a smaller tributary as they traveled.

There, under a thick pine tree. Both Sean and Bran looked soaked and miserable, huddling together for warmth. He chuckled as he made his way through the soggy ground. "Lovely morning!"

Bran bowed his head. "It's not lovely. The rain wants to drown me."

He had to chuckle at the hound's misery. "The rain just falls. If we don't get out of its way, that's our own fault."

Sean nodded and brayed. "We found shelter, but it still wants to drown us."

Bran looked up, his scraggly hair dripping despite the cover. "Can you tell it to stop?"

"I have no power over the weather. My grandmother did, but not me. I'm as miserable as you."

The hound remained sullen. "You don't have fur. You can take your wet off."

"But I can't shake myself dry like you can."

Fingin realized Bran may take that as a suggestion, so he backed up, but he wasn't fast enough. Bran shook his body so hard, a drop flew into Fingin's eye. It stung, and he rubbed his face.

"Well, we can't go anywhere until this lets up. If the rain was soft and misty, we might make do, but this is too heavy. Getting on the raft would be dangerous. Let's find a better shelter than this tree, though. Bran, have you found any caves? Holes in rocks we can fit into? We stayed in one before the warriors found us that night."

Bran stood, dripping, while he thought back to his roaming, but then he shook his head, dislodging further droplets. "I found nothing like that place. I found lots of rocks, but no holes in rocks."

The wind rose with a whine, making the pine tree limbs shake, dripping more water. Some snaked down his back, making him shiver.

"I think we're stuck here until the rain stops. I wish we had a fire, but it would never burn in this."

He sat with his back against the trunk, his arms on his knees. The needles beneath squished. He tried to close his eyes to rest, but he'd just woken up from a full night's sleep. He'd never get more sleep in this.

Drops seeped through the pine boughs and fell less frequently than in the clearing but were still annoying. The damp air grew redolent with pine.

Fingin opened his pack and, careful to hold it sideways, pulled out his tiny remaining ball of twine.

He'd need to collect more materials, but having more twine was always useful. "Stay here, and I'll be back in a while."

Bran's ears perked up. "Are you going to get fish? I would like fish."

"No, I'm not going fishing. But wait, I will get you some food." He rummaged through the pack again and found the last of the cheese and more dried fish. He gave these to Bran and turned to Sean, but the donkey was already munching on the green grass peeking through the pine needles.

Bran let out a whine and nosed the fish. "I want the hot fish. The rain is cold."

Fingin shook his head. "I can't cook anything, Bran. The rain is too wet for a fire."

The hound poked at the dried fish with his paw and whuffed, unhappiness clear in his posture. After a few moments, he held it in his paws as he gnawed on it.

Fingin chewed on a piece of dried fish himself as he went in search of reeds.

The rain became a downpour, making him gasp as left the shelter. In a short time, a headache formed from the onslaught. But he collected reeds, grasses, and one small vine he found along the ground before hurrying back to the tree.

He didn't have horsehair, but he squinted at Sean. "Sean, can I brush your mane for you? It looks tangled."

The donkey raised his head but didn't say no.

After grabbing his bone comb, Fingin brushed out the donkey's mane and tail. The hair took a great deal of work to unmat and untangle, but soon, he had a good supply of donkey hair to add to his twine-making supplies.

Now he sat next to the trunk and lost himself in the braiding rhythm, the sound of the rain helping him keep time with the task. His mind drifted, as it often did, but he stayed well aware of the cold, wet mud, and the miserable, damp air.

Fingin's fingers chaffed since they'd started out wet. Thin layers of skin sloughed off as he formed twine from the rough materials, and he had to stop more often than normal. This helped to break his concentration and the task became a chore rather than a joy.

With a sigh, he put away his materials. He'd gotten some work done, but his fingers ached. Instead, he sat with his head on his hands, watching the rain fall.

Mist rose from the warm earth, making the atmosphere of the forest mysterious and beautiful. Sounds filtered through, birdsong, or animals rustling in the underbrush, perhaps displaced from their burrows by flooding.

Bran settled down after he finished gnawing on his fish and laid his head on Fingin's lap. Even Sean stopped munching grass and lay down beside them.

Surrounded by warmth and steady sounds, Fingin slept again.

When he startled awake, the silence almost pounded on his skull. No rain, no dripping, no rustling. He cracked one eye open and remembered to test his skin for tenderness. Thanks to Brigit's charm, the bruising had healed. No pain remained, even to his ribs. He breathed deep, thankful for the healing token.

Fingin rose, his clothing sticking in the mud as he stood. He grimaced at the mess and made his way back down to the beach. The humidity and heat had risen as the clouds scattered away in the brightening sky. Bran rumbled awake and followed him to the riverside.

He let out a breath of relief. The raft still bobbed, tied to its tree. In the back of his mind, he'd felt certain the raft would have somehow become unmoored and floated away on the current. *At least the logs have swollen to form a tighter seal.*

He waded into the water to clean the mud away again, shivering in the chilly river. Bran joined him, joyful in his playfulness now that the rain had gone away. The waterline had grown higher than the day before.

Sean joined them and Fingin made certain they had everything packed. He stowed the pannikins on the raft along with his pole.

Once the supplies were on board, he turned to the wolfhound. "Right. Bran, come on up."

Bran peered at the bobbing craft. "I have to get on that?"

"Yes. Not to worry. It's safe."

Bran shook his head. "I don't want to get on. I'll drown in the river."

Fingin crossed his arms. "Bran, it's not dangerous at all. See? I'm standing on it. It's sturdy. And it's been floating all night without sinking."

Bran retreated until he stood next to the hill and refused to budge.

With a sigh, Fingin turned to the donkey. He grasped the bridle and placed a gentle hand on his neck. "Sean? Will you show Bran there's nothing to worry about?"

He led the donkey to the edge of the raft. The animal put a tentative hoof on the first log, which bobbed. He pulled back and retreated to where Bran sat. Two immovable forces.

Fingin let out his breath and climbed onto the raft, jumping up and down. "See? It's stable! I can jump all over it and I won't fall off!"

He ran to one edge and then the other. He lay down on one side, trailing his hand in the water, then rolled all the way to the other side.

Neither animal seemed impressed with his escapades. With a firm set to his mouth, he climbed off the raft, back onto the beach. He had an idea.

After careful deliberation, he pulled some soaking branches into a pile and, taking out the flint Brigit had gifted him, started a fire. It took a great deal of work to build one with the wood so wet. Smoke billowed and stung his eyes, but soon he had a reluctant blaze.

He narrowed his eyes at the fire. It shouldn't have been so easy. Then he glanced at the flint and decided Brigit must have placed an enchantment on that, as well. Fingin got his cooking pot, filled it with water, and dropped in a chunk of dried fish. He waited in steaming silence as the fish soaked, getting soft and warm.

He refused to look at either of his companions as he stewed. When he judged the fish to be tender, he tested it with a nibble. *Perfect.*

Then, Fingin put out his fire, dumped out the excess water, and pulled out a sweet carrot from his pannikin. He placed the carrot and the lump of hot, cooked fish on the middle of the raft.

He turned to his two reluctant companions. "Now, will you come? I have hot fish and a sweet, tasty carrot for you."

Bran's head drooped, but he approached the raft with wary eyes, sniffing the edge. He craned his neck out as far as he could while standing on the ground, but the fish was still out of reach. Tiny waves from the raft lapped against his toes. The dog let out a low whine.

"Come on, Bran. Tasty fish?" He held the piece up and took a bite, exaggerating his enjoyment. "Mmm. Careful, I'll eat it all!"

With a whine and a yip, Bran jumped onto the raft. He stood, splayed, as the raft shifted, his eyes wide and darting back and forth. Then he took several careful steps toward the food.

"Well done! You earned your treat, Bran!" Fingin held his hand out and Bran ate the piece of cooked fish. Then he cuddled the hound's head in his arms and ruffled his ears.

Bran then looked over his shoulder at the shore, his body tensing as if he were about to move back to the beach.

"No, I need you to stay here. How about you, Sean? Wouldn't you like this sweet carrot? Bran showed you how to do it."

The donkey bobbed his head but tried the raft again. In a moment of inspiration, Fingin ran to the shore. Bran barked but didn't follow. Instead, he sat and put his head on his paws. Fingin, once he got onto the land, pulled the raft onto the beach with all his might. The edge came up onto the sand.

"Now, the edge is stable. Give it another try, Sean."

The donkey stepped on the closest log, but it just sank a little into the wet sand. When Sean put a second hoof on the raft, it moved a little more, but still not the bobbing target it had been before.

The animal climbed all the way onto the raft with slow steps. His legs were at awkward angles, but he stood in the middle, happily crunching his carrot.

"Try sitting down, Sean. It will feel more solid."

The donkey stared at him and then lowered himself with achingly slow movements. He didn't look at all comfortable, but he'd gotten on board. Fingin cheered inside and bent to shove the raft off the shore.

The logs sat deeper with both Bran and Sean. He grunted and sweated until he shifted it a few inches, and then a few inches more. By the time he had the craft all the way into the water, he'd just about run out of strength.

The raft bobbed in the water while both animals' eyes grew wide, the whites showing in alarm. Fingin grabbed the line, untied it from the tree, and jumped onto the raft himself. He lifted his steering pole and shoved it into the slope of the riverbed, pushing away from the land.

They twisted and swerved in the river current. Bran sang a mournful howl and Sean let out a terrified bray. To calm them, Fingin sang a song his grandmother had once taught him.

Aréir is mé téarnamh ar neoin

Ar ar dtaobh eile 'en teóra seo thiós

Last night and I wandering as you do,

On the other side of my lands, I was.

He shoved against the pole again, and they drifted further into the center of the river.

Do thaobhnaigh an spéirbhean im' chomhair

D'fhág taomanac breoite lag tinn

There a beautiful woman approached me,

Who left me sick and moody afterwards.

Bran still whimpered, but he'd calmed down since Fingin began singing, so he didn't stop, hoping it would distract the poor hound from his fear.

Le haon ghean dá méin is dá cló

Dá bréithre 's dá beol tanaí binn

With her lovely bearing and shape,

Her sweet words and slender lips.

Sean's eyes grew less frantic, and he swung in time with each stroke of the vessel.

Do léimeas fá dhéin dul 'na treo

Is ar Éirinn ní neosfainn cé hí

I hastened to be in her presence,

But for all of Éire, I'd not tell her name.

By the time he'd finished the song, both beasts seemed calmer. Fingin sang two more songs as they floated down the river. As they passed a bend in the river, he shoved his pole against the far shore, keeping them near the middle, almost losing his balance.

The rest of that afternoon, they drifted down the water. He'd never moved this fast and the land rushing by on either side of them made him dizzy if he peered at the details too hard.

Bran stopped whining but kept his head on his paws. He didn't look happy, but at least he no longer seemed miserable. Sean also seemed resigned to his current situation.

A few drops made Fingin glance up, surprised to see gloomy clouds roiling in. They didn't look like a storm front, but the day was fading. They should head toward the shore and find a place to spend the night.

The center of the river ran too deep for his pole to reach, but as they passed a bend, Fingin shoved the pole into the riverbed. At first, nothing happened. Poling a raft took skill Fingin had never learned. However, with some practice and a few mistakes, he steered the raft close enough to shore to jump into the shallows. With quick movements, he tied the raft to a large rock.

Bran bounded off in a moment, his thrill to be back on dry land apparent. Sean stepped with more caution, but once he stood on solid ground, he shook all over. "I'm glad that's done."

The rain dissipated as quickly as it had come, but Fingin didn't have the energy for getting back on the raft. With a clear sky, they slept on the beach. Fingin felt proud for how far they'd traveled, three times as fast as he would have done on foot. It almost made up for all the time making the raft.

The next morning shone bright and clear. Fingin greeted the dawn with excitement. Their vantage point, on a shallow cliff above their little beach, commanded a fantastic view of the rising sun along the river. Morning rays colored the water with delightful shades of orange and peach. He took in a deep breath with the promise and hope of the new day.

He convinced both animals to mount the raft again without having to beach it first or offer a bribe of food. Perhaps today they'd reach the ocean.

Once they got to the ocean, then what? Brigit had mentioned an island off the coast. Fingin's grandmother had taught him history, geography, numbers, and practical things like making twine and manners. He tried to pull up the memory of the map she'd drawn of the island.

She'd drawn a rough rectangle, tall rather than wide. She pointed almost in the middle. "That's where we live, Fingin."

He'd laughed. "We live over there, in our home. Not here, in the stable yard. I don't understand."

His grandmother had let out a deep sigh. "This is a drawing of what our land looks like, but much tinier than the real thing. Those Christian monks your parents love have drawings like this, in their scrolls and books. If you walked from side to side, east," she pointed toward where the sun rose, "to west," and she pointed to where the sun set, "you'd have to walk for about two days if you never stopped to rest, eat, or sleep. Four days if you traveled wisely."

She pointed to the two sides of the picture. "That would correspond with my map here and here."

He tried to get his head around the concept. "So, this is like when I make a tiny horse whittled out of wood?"

"Yes, just like that! A tiny model of our land. Now, I know you're familiar with our river, *An Ruirthech*. That's here." She drew a line near the right side of the map, about in the middle, top to bottom.

"That's fresh water, but if you go out to the edge of the island, the water that surrounds us is salt water, unfit to drink."

"Are there no fish in the ocean, then?"

"Oh, no! There are much bigger fish in the ocean! But they can breathe the salt water. Some of them are enormous, much bigger than the horses or cows."

He didn't quite believe her, but he'd never say so.

Now, as he rafted down a different river, on the opposite side of the island, he watched for this ocean, this mythical body of undrinkable water, which held gigantic fish. He wondered if they'd jump over the surface like that huge salmon had. Would he see them? Would they talk to him?

He quested out in his mind to find any local fish, and a few voices filtered through the water, but he found only trout, salmon, minnows, and other river denizens, voices he recognized. A few birds chattered about their passage, and a curious doe stared at them as they floated by. The deer bounded away as he glanced at her.

The river widened ahead, and he shoved the raft closer to the shore. He chose the south bank, as Brigit had told him the island lay to the south.

Should he try to raft along the ocean's edge? The water might be rougher, from what his grandmother had said. Great storms sometimes pounded the western edge of the island, furious weather which ate bits of the shore. He had no wish to be caught in such a storm.

Still, walking across land seemed so slow to him now, after this delightful swift mode of travel. He should wait to decide until they came to the ocean.

Bran howled, startling Fingin from his thoughts, and someone answered him. Frantically, he searched both shores for the source of the answering howl. After a moment, he saw three ragged dogs on the south shore. They pawed at the dirt, trying to get up enough nerve to jump into the river to get at them.

Bran kept howling, an unnerving sound which made Fingin's stomach feel hollow. "Bran, stop that! They can't get to us from here."

"But they're there! I have to talk to them!"

Fingin quested out in his mind, asking the dogs what they wanted. Their only response was a question *Who are you? What do you want? Don't come here, this is our place!*

"We'll be past them soon. They're just trying to figure out who we are."

The hound whimpered, but whimpering was better than unearthly howling.

Soon, the river opened into a great estuary, small islands dotting the wide expanse of the river mouth. Fingin had never seen so much water in one place in his entire life. Bran stared around with wide eyes, and even the usually laconic Sean seemed impressed.

"This is the ocean. My grandmother told me about it."

Bran let out a few curious yips as something bumped the raft. Then he barked several times, running from one corner to the next, peering into the water. "Something's there! It's a big fish! But it doesn't smell like a fish. It's huge!"

The craft lurched and Fingin sent his thoughts below the surface, searching for animal intelligence. The voice came strong and loud. "What are you? You don't look like the coracle boats."

Startled at such a cohesive response from a fish, he said, "I'm Fingin, and this is Bran and Sean. Who are you?" and then, with even more curiosity, "*What* are you?"

A large gray fish with smooth skin rather than scales popped her head up. She chittered, nodded a few times, and said, "I'm Tanni! I'm me, of course. What else would I be?"

The fish was larger than Sean. A sudden clutch of fear gripped Fingin's heart, but she'd spoken in a kind tone. He smiled at the creature. "Bran, this is Tanni. She has a name, just like you!"

Bran cocked his head and regarded the visitor. He barked again and sat with his head on his front paws. "Then we can't eat her? I bet she doesn't taste as good as salmon."

With a chuckle, Fingin turned to Tanni with an idea. "We are looking for an island full of religious men. It's covered in sea birds and lies to the south, a steep mountaintop jutting out of the water. Do you know the island I'm talking about?"

Tanni chittered a few more times, almost like a cat who sees a bird and wants to catch it. Then she dove under the waves, and Fingin worried he'd upset her. Then she burst up through the surface on the other side of the raft, causing Bran to bark again. "That was mean of her! She scared me!"

Fingin put out a hand. "Settle down, Bran. I'm asking her for help."

The dog let out a token growl and sat, keeping a wary eye on Tanni. He kept letting out little whines.

The fish leapt out of the water, splashing them as she landed. "There are many islands! Islands everywhere. What's *south?*"

Fingin searched for the sun, struggling to shine through thin clouds. First, he found west, where the sun would set over the ocean. Then, he turned to his left and pointed. "South is that way."

"South! I can lead you to south. Follow me!"

Tanni leapt away in the direction Fingin pointed, but returned when she realized they hadn't moved. He was trying to pull out his pole, stuck deep in the riverbed.

"I have little control over the raft, Tanni. It's difficult to move it when the current isn't pulling, and the current may not head south."

"No, the current twists and turns in delightful ways. I love playing in the currents. Some are warm and some are cold and they all have yummy fish."

Fingin glanced at Bran, but the dog couldn't hear Tanni's words. He held up the twine moorline. "I have a rope tied to our raft, for when we go ashore. If I tied this around you, could you pull us south? Would you be willing? In return, I can talk to fish to convince them to come closer, if you wanted to eat some."

Tanni regarded the twine rope and touched it with her nose. She chittered and touched it again. "It's rough, like coral."

Nodding, Fingin smiled. "It is. It might chafe your smooth skin. Why don't you have scales like other fish?"

"I'm not a fish!" Her tone turned indignant.

He cocked his head. "What are you, then?"

"I don't know what humans call me, but I'm not a fish. I breathe air. Fish breathe water."

Fingin furrowed his brow. "How do you breathe air underwater?"

She chittered again and ducked under water, only to burst forth again in a flip. "I don't stay underwater long."

Fingin knew fish didn't breathe the air, but perhaps Tanni was a magical creature, like a Fae fish. So far, she'd been pleasant and helpful, whether Fae or mortal. He couldn't turn down any help at this point.

Fingin fashioned a crude harness from the twine and looped it over Tanni's nose. Her fin kept the loop from slipping right off. "Are you sure the raft isn't too heavy for you to pull?"

"If it is, I'll stop."

"Fair enough."

"Which way do you want to go, again?"

With another glance at the sky, Fingin pointed south. After several trills and clicks, Tanni tugged on the rope in the chosen direction.

At first, the raft didn't move at all. Then, Tanni rocked forward a few times, and it shifted a little. Tanni strained and pulled, and the raft moved at an increasing pace. Eventually, they raced across the water almost as fast as they'd traveled in the river current.

After a while, Tanni slowed as she spoke. "Your strange boat is heavier than it looks. I think it's because of the others." She chittered directly at Bran, who growled back.

Fingin shushed him. "You're probably right. I understand if it's too heavy. Thank you for trying, though."

"Wait here."

They could hardly do anything but wait. Before Fingin could protest, Tanni had disappeared. He hoped the Fae fish would return soon. The raft was too far from shore for Fingin's pole to reach the ground.

While they waited, he doled out food to both Bran and Sean. Bran pouted but gnawed on his dried fish. Sean munched on the last of the hay from Brigit.

A chorus of chittering and barking made him look up. A half dozen Fae fish now surrounded the small raft. Bran went crazy, barking at each one. Even Sean's eyes grew wide and he let out a loud bray.

Tanni popped up beside him. "I'm back! I brought help. Do you have more scratchy things to loop my friends? We'll get you where you're going fast!"

Fingin looked from one Fae fish to the other, amazed at the assembled creatures. "Do they all have names, too?"

"Of course! This is Fetti, and Lonno, and Tas, and Stom, and Rassa."

Each Fae fish leapt backwards as Tanni recited their names, a coordinated dance of mischievous joy. He'd never be able to keep track of them all, but at least Tanni had a darker spot on her nose, and he could recognize her.

Fingin pulled out his twine, thankful he'd made plenty. Still, he only had enough for four Fae fish.

Tanni let out a chitter. "The other two will come along for the fish."

Fingin grinned. "Would you like to eat before the trip? I don't know how far away it is."

A chorus of agreements came from the Fae fish.

"What sort of fish do you want? I don't even know what type live around here."

"Eels!" "Salmon!" "Squid!"

Fingin had never heard of squid fish, but he knew salmon and eels. He closed his eyes and quested into the depths of the ocean, searching for any salmon or eels in the water below him. A few answered, curious to who might be calling them.

As they came close to the surface, the Fae fish squealed and dove. The salmon and eel voices ended with sudden silence. As always, he felt a twinge of guilt at using his power to kill the creatures who answered him, but as always, he reassured his conscience that his actions were for a greater purpose.

"We like you, human! Can you do that again when we get to where you're going?"

"Of course! And if it's a long distance away, we can do it several times."

Another chorus of chittering and several flips answered his offer. "We like him!"

Fingin secured the first squad of Fae fish to his four loops. Once they tested their harnesses, they surged forward, almost knocking Fingin off the raft. But he caught himself and gripped hard to the edge of the raft, and they went south.

After the initial surge, Fingin, Bran, and Sean settled down for a pleasant, if somewhat noisy, ride. They bounced along mild ocean waves, hugging the shore more or less, as the sun played hide and seek amongst the clouds.

Fingin started to sweat, and he removed his *léine*. The ocean breeze cooled him as their fishy friends dragged them along the surface.

A few times, startled fishermen in their round hide coracles stared as they passed. Fingin gave each a jaunty wave.

The land sped by on their left, much faster than when they floated down the river. The Fae fish raced each other, making it a game as to who swam faster.

Their game jerked the raft around until Fingin asked them to stop. They'd apologize, swim abreast for a while, and then get into an argument about who was faster and do it again.

Sea cliffs winked by, flanked by white-sand beaches. Rocks jutted out of the water, covered in seagulls. The raft threaded between tiny islands along the coast and around long peninsulas, fingers of land reaching toward the west. The brilliant sun sparkled on the ocean's surface, highlighting white-capped waves and an occasional cloud scudding across the sky.

Thus, as the first day waned, their journey had been a mix between delight, relaxation, and terror. The sun dipped into the fiery water, glittering across the waves, a few brilliant orange clouds painting the sky. Then the temperature dropped considerably in the pending gloom.

Fingin called out to Tanni. "Do you need rest? Night is coming."

Tanni barked and they all slowed. "We're tired, yes. And hungry. Will you call more fish? We can sleep and start again in the morning. You haven't seen your mountaintop yet?"

He shook his head. "Not as she described it. She made a drawing. Most of these islands look empty of men, and the one I'm searching for has lots of men on it."

One of the other dolphins piped up. "Oh! I know that place! That's stinky island!"

Fingin cocked his head. "Stinky island?"

"The men throw their waste into the water. All the water stinks of it. The fish there taste bad, so we avoid it."

As Fingin called for the evening meal, he decided that made sense. He grinned at the name. "How much farther to stinky island?"

"We can get you there by sunset tomorrow."

He had them shove the raft to shore for the evening and moored the craft to a tree. He didn't wish to wake up in the middle of the wide ocean.

Even before the sun had set, he saw nothing on the western horizon. No mountains, no hills, no trees. It was as if the world ended in a vast expanse of water. Fingin didn't care for the hollow sensation in his belly as he stared at it. He preferred lakes and rivers to the ocean.

He slept in fits, not used to the bobbing of the raft. Sean and Bran had refused to disembark, as they didn't want to risk getting on again, and he couldn't blame them.

The ocean was so different from the rivers he knew well. Vast and endless, filled with dangerous waves and strange, talkative fish. A strange god with unknown dangers and joys.

When morning came, there was no sunrise, only fog. The Fae fish woke him, their voices filtering through the thick mist. "Wake up! Wake up! Time for more fish!"

After their morning meals, and with many shouted directions and suggestions, he looped his twine around four of the Fae fish. Two who pulled yesterday would be escort today, and they all agreed to switch out at noon so a third pair might rest.

Their high voices filtered back to him as they pulled. "Hey, stop shoving! This is my spot!"

"Then stop swimming in front of me!"

"You stop swimming behind me!"

Fingin prayed the stinky island was the one he wanted. He'd never recognize it in this mist. He prayed for the fog to burn away as the sun rose higher, but as the day passed, the fog remained thick.

Everything was soggy. No amazing views of the coast caught their attention. Only gray greeted their gaze. Today's journey was much more boring than yesterday's.

Because they were already soaked, he didn't even notice the first raindrops. But when thunder boomed across the sea, and cracks of lightning cut through the fog to light it in a preternatural brilliance, Fingin realized they were in the heart of a storm.

Rising waves swamped the sides of the raft as he shouted out. "Tanni! Tanni, we need to seek shelter."

Chittering answered him. The shapes of the Fae fish disappeared in the mist, though they must have been only a few arms-lengths in front of the raft. He dug his fingers into the twine between the logs, desperate to hold on. Bran howled and Sean's eyes grew white with fear. "Tanni! Tanni, bring us to shore!"

A wave slapped the raft so hard, he almost slipped off, despite his death's grip on the twine. Sean slid toward the far edge.

"Tanni! Fetti! Lonno! Please! We won't survive if the raft tips!"

The trajectory of the raft shifted, heading to the left, toward land. Some of Fingin's abject terror faded, but he maintained his tight grip. He wished he'd thought to tie Sean or Bran down, but that might not have been a good idea, either. If the raft tipped too far, they'd get tangled or stuck underwater.

A dark shoreline hove in the distance, against the still-foggy horizon. Without warning, the bottom of the raft scraped and scratched against something, and the world flipped sideways.

His fingers were still stuck inside the twine knots, and now the raft floated above him. He panicked and breathed in water. He tried to yank his fingers out, looking around frantically for Sean and Bran, but seawater filled his vision.

One more mighty pull, and his bruised fingers came free. He launched himself to the edge of the bottom of the raft and broke the surface, pulling in the air with sweet relief, despite the pounding rain. He coughed, trying to clear his burning lungs.

Sean brayed next to him, floundering in the water. He listened for Bran's bark, but only heard the storm raging around him. Waves pounded his face as he tried not to swallow more bitter seawater.

One step at a time. He got hold of Sean's bridle and swam to shore, keeping the donkey's head above water. A rude bump to his bottom made him cry out, but his attacker was only one of the Fae fish, trying to help. Another bumped Sean, and then a third.

By the time he reached the rocky shore, he sucked in air, everything aching. His skin was soaked and his body scraped and bruised from the rocks, but Fingin and Sean stood safe on dry land.

With frantic desperation, he searched for his hound. "Bran? Bran! Bran, where are you!"

A rumble of thunder and the constant pounding of the rain against the rocks answered.

AGE OF SECRETS

Chapter Eight

The storm raged on for the rest of the afternoon. After Fingin found a small cliff overhang for Sean to rest under, he searched up and down the shoreline for any sign of Bran.

Fingin called through the torrent until his throat rasped hoarse. He examined every lump on the ground, searching for his beloved friend.

In frustration, he cried, but the tears washed away with the constant rain.

Soaked and exhausted, Fingin trudged back to where he'd left Sean. The donkey, miserable and alone, huddled against the bare stone ledge, trying to keep away from the steady dripping.

The raft had disappeared, as well as the pannikins and all their supplies. He didn't even have flint for a fire. He still had Brigit's pendant, safe around his neck, but nothing else.

And no Bran.

The Fae fish had all swum away, no longer interested in the strange boat and its inhabitants. At least they'd helped him and Sean to shore. Maybe they'd also helped Bran find dry land somewhere. Maybe the dog would find them if they stayed here for a little while.

Despite the rolling thunder, he curled up next to Sean and fell into a fitful, restless sleep.

He woke several times, certain he heard Bran's bark or voice on the whistling wind. Once, lightning struck the water just past the rocks where they sheltered, lighting up the entire shoreline in bright white light.

The storm eased as darkness enveloped them. While the rain didn't stop, it settled into a fine misty drizzle, enough to keep them sheltered until the sun rose again.

Fingin had no wish to greet the dawn this day, even if the sun showed its face. But this morning, the sun struggled to burn through the fog, revealing a waterlogged landscape with rocks, trees, and little else. His heart grew heavy with Bran's absence. No joy sang within him.

Sean didn't want to travel anywhere, either, but he was hungry. With their supplies drowned in the storm, he found a patch of grass to chew while Fingin searched for Bran.

They'd landed on some small spit of land sticking out into the sea. He'd have to travel east to continue south.

In his exploration, he came across a few scraps from his pack. A bowl. A spoon. A strip of ragged fabric that might have been from a *léine* he'd had. He found no twine, no knife, no flint, and no food.

Fingin perched on a rock, gazing out into the still-choppy ocean, silently begging for Bran to pop his head through the surface and bark. Even a whine would be great. Sean brayed behind him, and he let out a sigh.

Something broke the surface. For a moment, Fingin's hope soared, but fell as the trout swam away. As helpful as the Fae fish had been, he was relieved they'd parted company. The raft had been swift, but too dangerous.

He'd blame himself forever for drowning Bran. The poor dog had already almost drowned once, and now he'd done it again.

Fingin sent one last resentful glare at the greedy ocean. He cursed the water and, his hand on Sean's flank, walked east along the shore.

The sun disappeared behind the clouds as the morning passed. Sean and Fingin picked their way along the coast, scanning ahead and behind for their furry companion. They stopped for a rest just as the shore swung south again.

Fingin wished he had his fishing net. He'd have to make more twine and create a new one, but that was a lot of work.

In the meantime, he was ravenous. A strawberry bush halfway through the morning had relieved his worst hunger pangs, but they came back stronger than ever.

Fingin searched the rocks for clams. He found none, but he did find oysters. He'd never eaten oysters, though he'd heard of them. Using a sharp rock, he pried one open, at the cost of a sliced finger.

Squinting at the squishy insides, he wished he had a fire, even a small one. With eyes squeezed shut, he swallowed the slimy, salty thing. He almost gagged but clamped his mouth shut, refusing to vomit the scarce food.

He offered one to Sean, but the donkey refused, preferring sweet grass on the sand dunes. Fingin sat for several moments, willing his gut to settle down. Waves lapped against the rocks, forming hollow claps and clicks.

In the distance, he spied a few shapes on the rocks. One of them moved, and he stared, trying to figure out what it was. When it flopped into the water, he realized it must be a seal, another creature of the sea he'd heard of but never seen.

Legend had it some seals were *murdúchann*, magical creatures who shed their sealskins and took human form. These *murdúchann* would mate with a human man, but then return to the sea, leaving their children on the land.

Seal barks echoed along the waves, bouncing and breaking across the rocks where he sat, transfixed by the unusual sight.

He still heard barking, even after the last seal dove into the water. Fingin cocked his head, confused. The seals couldn't be barking underwater.

When the wet, shaggy form slammed into him, dragging him to the ground, he didn't believe his eyes. "Bran? Bran, you're alive!"

His hound slobbered wet kisses all over Fingin's face, knocking him down to the sand and holding him with his paws. Fingin didn't even bother to push him away, but pulled the hound into a big hug. Bran's fur felt gritty and matted with saltwater, but dry. He must have been somewhere further along the coast all this time.

Bran continued to lick Fingin's face, hands, and arms. He even ran over to Sean and licked the donkey's nose, much to Sean's disgust. "I looked everywhere for you both! I ran up and down the beach, but I didn't see you anywhere! Too much fog. I couldn't smell anything but wet. I found fish on the rocks, but they tasted bad. I'm hungry. Do you have better fish?"

Fingin hugged Bran again, sobbing in relief. He had his friend back again. Everything looked brighter. "I have no fish, Bran, I'm sorry. I lost my net in the storm, along with our packs."

Bran yipped, a grin on his face. "I found one! But I can't use the net."

"What? You found one of our packs?"

For an answer, Bran disappeared around one bush and returned, dragging the leather strap of the pannikin. It had broken in the middle, but one pack, waterlogged and heavy, survived.

With an exclamation of delight, Fingin rooted through it, taking stock of his newfound possessions. "My fishing net! My knife, another bowl. Oh, that dried fish is disgusting now." He tossed it on a rock.

Bran ambled over to sniff it, but even he wouldn't eat it, soaked with seawater. "Two *léinte*! I'll need fresh water to clean them. Aha!" He held up his fire-making kit, with flint and fool's gold. "This is more valuable than silver, Bran! Thank you so much for saving this. And for not drowning!"

Bran ducked his head. "It tangled around my leg. I didn't do it on purpose."

"It doesn't matter. With my net and flint, we can have cooked fish for supper."

Bran barked in delight three times as Fingin pulled his net out and hefted it, eyeing the now-calm inlet.

Their walk along the coast stayed pleasant and uneventful for the next two days. The three of them journeyed on at a steady pace, only stopping for rest and food.

They climbed rocky outcroppings, detoured around boggy estuaries, ran along flat white beaches, and sheltered under enormous oak trees as they made their way south. Fingin could make out land on the other side of the water, another peninsula jutting into the ocean. Was the island around the end of that one? The Fae fish had mentioned the stinky island sat off the end of the tip of land.

A long, flat, beautiful beach crossed almost to the other side of the waterway. Out of curiosity, they walked along the sand, hoping it would connect to the southern spit of land.

When the beach curved away, just short of their destination, he eyed the waterway. It looked deep and swift, but narrow. He spied a few roundhouses on the far side, clear enough that he could see a man walking.

"What do you think, Sean? Can we swim across this?"

Sean stared at the water but didn't answer.

Bran, however, whuffed and shook his head. "I don't want to try. The water looks deep. What if another storm comes?"

Fingin glanced at the clear, blue sky, just one white cloud low on the horizon. "I don't think we'll get any rain today, Bran. It shouldn't take us long to get across. Can you smell a storm?"

Bran sniffed the wind. "It doesn't smell like it did last time, but I still don't like it."

With a deep sigh, Fingin nodded. "Very well, Bran. We'll walk. Come along."

They wended their way back to the mainland, along the other side of the beach. Staying on the shore wouldn't add too much to their journey. Perhaps a half day extra to round the inlet.

Fingin kept his eye out for mountaintops sticking out of the ocean, covered in seabirds, but so far, none of the tiny islands along the coast fit that description. Plenty of rocky outcroppings jutted up, but not on islands. He'd probably have to walk along the next peninsula to find the Fae fish's *stinky island*.

Their trek on this portion took most of a day, and the way ahead looked even rougher, if those outcroppings reached to the shore.

When the shore curved again, from east to south to west, they had to cross a river. But unlike the last one, this river had a friendly ferryman who took them across on his raft.

Bran didn't want to board the raft at first, but with some fish for the ferryman and more for Bran, Fingin got them all across. The wind had died, leaving the day warm and the water calm.

Refreshed by their midday meal, Fingin sang as he walked. Inspired by the seals he noticed earlier, when he mistook their barks for Bran's own, he sang a song of *murdúchann*.

He sang of the first humans who came to the island, the sons of *Míl*, those who encountered the *Túatha Dé Danaan*. The *murdúchann* played around the ships of these invaders, distracting them and keeping them from landing for many days. Sirens lulled the sailors to sleep with their song.

One wise Druid amongst them, a man named *Caicher*, handed out wax with which to plug their ears, an effective shield against their magic.

Should a man ever heed the call of *murdúchann* and enter the water to be with her, the sea creature would tear them apart and eat them.

Once he finished his song, Bran yipped. "Were those fish who pulled our raft the same creatures?"

"No, of course not. The *murdúchann* have the upper half of a human woman, with the bottom of a fish. The Fae fish had no human parts."

Bran peered out into the water, as if trying to conjure the creatures again, to get a better look at them. "But they said they breathed air. You said fish only breathed water."

"That's why I call them Fae fish. They have some strange magic."

Sean let out a soft bray, as if laughing at the hound's confusion.

Bran swiveled to glare at the donkey. "What's funny?"

After smothering a laugh, Fingin passed the comment to Sean, who snorted. Bran pouted and let out a mock growl. "What's he laughing at?"

Fingin couldn't answer and keep his laugh in at the same time. Instead, he pointed ahead. "Look! There's a mountain range. Do you think we can get to it before evening falls?"

The distraction worked, and Bran bound ahead.

The mountains didn't quite reach the ocean, so walking along the coast didn't involve hiking up hills. Still, it took the rest of that day and all the next before they came close to the western end of the peninsula.

Out of the ocean loomed a large island, with more islands dotting the ocean beyond that. Perhaps they'd be lucky, and this would be the monk's island. A lumpy hill rose on the far end, but not like Brigit had described. Fingin let out a sigh, suspecting that they'd need to travel to that large island before they could see any others.

A long line of half-sunk stones allowed them to ford an inlet to the large island. They then climbed a steep hill on the western tip.

The sun had almost touched the horizon as they reached the top, breathless. The island Brigit had described hulked right in front of him.

Islands, in truth. Two mountaintops, one smaller than the other, rose from the waves. Birds wheeled and nested amongst the crags of both. This must be where the monks lived and where he needed to seek for word of his grandmother.

Then he eyed the vast expanse of choppy ocean between his vantage point on his island and the bare shore of the monk's island. In no lifetime would he ever even try to swim that distance. He doubted he even wanted to cross it on a raft, even if he hadn't almost drowned using one.

If men were living on the island, they must return to the mainland for supplies. They'd have a boat for such journeys, so he'd be able to secure passage the next time it crossed.

But when and where would he find it? He peered along the coast but saw no great mooring site. He'd passed a flat beachy area on the way to the hill. Perhaps that's where the monks landed. He'd just have to search.

They picked their way back down the mountain and scanned the flat areas for evidence of frequent boat use.

The day was dying and he was hungry, so Fingin cast his net in the growing gloom, catching several large salmon and a huge fish. This strange creature resembled the Fae fish, with smooth skin and a single fin, but with a pointy nose and several rows of very sharp teeth.

Amazed that this strong fish hadn't broken through his net, he asked the fish what it was. However, his only answer was, "Food. Swim. Food."

With a shrug, he hauled in the net and cleaned his catch, tossing the entrails and one of the fish to Bran while Sean grazed. He stoked the fire with a wary eye on the sky. The night looked clear so far, with stars twinkling in the east.

As the last of the dying light disappeared in the west, Fingin snuggled between the warm bodies of Sean and Bran, content with his life and his quest. While he missed the security of a sturdy roundhouse, for now he had a goal, a direction.

That was something he'd been missing most of his life, a reason for living other than just surviving. Brigit had given him a gift more valuable than any magical healing charm. She'd given him a purpose.

Sleeping near the sea was different from the river. Strange noises woke him in the night, and the water glowed with an odd light. Fingin wasn't sure he liked it better, but the sight was lovely.

When he woke in the morning, he stretched, stiff and creaking, in the cool morning air. After the stresses of the last few days, with the storm, the long hikes, and the terror of almost losing his best friend, Fingin had welcomed the deep, healing sleep.

Everything seemed still except the faint lapping of the water against the rocky shore. Somewhere in the distance, a seagull cried. A few songbirds answered the seagull, heralding a morning chorus to wake him.

Fingin wished the sun rose in the west, so he might witness the precise moment it crested the horizon. Perhaps someday he'd travel to the other side of the island and watch the sunrise across the water. For now, he sat cross-legged and closed his eyes to greet the sun.

Birds sang with his chants, matching his rhythm and delight. A practiced chorus to welcome the dawn, a waking of the life of the day and the power of brightness.

Fingin's blood buzzed with a resurgence of energy and strength. His skin tingled with the magic of rebirth as sunlight burned his eyes.

When he finished his ceremony, the power returned to the ground, his steps felt lighter, and his heart had lifted. No longer did he look upon the journey across the water with dread, but with determined purpose.

In that frame of mind, Fingin called out for the Fae fish, but none came close enough to answer his call. If he didn't find a Fae fish or a regular boatman, he would have to build a boat himself.

Not a raft this time, but a coracle, the hide-covered, wicker-spined round boat most men on the island used for sea travel. His father had shown him how to repair one, long ago.

After their experience with the storm, Bran would not be eager to board another craft, and Sean would be unhappy on that almost vertical island. He hoped his visit wouldn't take long, and they should both wait here.

To build a coracle, Fingin needed thin wood and hide. Wood was easy enough to find, as trees grew everywhere. However, the hide meant a cow, and he had no cows.

He also had no trade goods, nor any way to find a market to buy a tanned hide. A horse would do as well as a cow. He glanced at Sean, then swallowed, horrified at even considering hurting his friend.

As he plotted strategies, a motion caught his eye. He focused his gaze across the inlet, as two robed men jumped into a coracle and paddled west.

That must be where the monks embarked from. He'd just been on the wrong side of the inlet.

Fingin jumped up and waved his hands with mad abandon, yelling and screaming to get the men's attention. Bran watched his antics and barked, evidently confused but playing along. Even Sean brayed and bobbed his head.

Fingin shouted himself hoarse, but kept leaping and gesturing until finally, the little coracle veered in their direction. Panting and voiceless, Fingin pressed a hand in his side and took a drink from his waterskin.

As the craft crept closer, Fingin stared at the rowing men, with shaved foreheads and undyed robes of rough weave.

He turned to his friends. "I don't think I can take you both on the island. Would you rather stay here?"

Bran shook his head and sneezed. "I don't want to go on the water again."

Sean brayed his agreement.

"I promise, I'll come back here when I return. Wait for me?"

Sean answered for them both. "We will wait for you, Fingin."

As the coracle beached, one man stepped out. "Who hails the brothers of Fionán?"

Fingin gritted his teeth, remembering his speech difficulties with humans. "I… I… I need t-t-to t-travel to the island. Are you g-g-going… there?"

The monks peered at Bran and Sean, but Fingin shook his head. "Just me. My hound and… d-donkey will remain here. My mission shouldn't t-take long. I only seek… information."

He held out three packages of the large fish, wrapped in seaweed. The monk with darker hair peeked under the wrapping, then nodded.

"We shall take you to the monastery."

Fingin left the rest of his supplies and the remaining pack with Sean, after leaving out plenty of food for Bran.

The small coracle might be ideal for one person. Three made it crowded and uncomfortable. In addition, Fingin fretted about too much weight for the wicker braces. He spent the trip in silence, gripping the edge and doing his best not to rock the fragile craft. The monks offered neither conversation nor questions.

When they arrived at the mountaintop island, Fingin stared in wonder at the winding ribbon of stone steps carved into the side, curving to the top in dizzying vertical construction. Around bare mounds of stone, tufts of grass poked their way through the cracks, like a man losing his hair to mange.

Still silent, the monks stowed his fish into packs on their backs and began the climb. With a deep sigh and a prayer to Brigit for strength, he followed them.

After his initial determination flagged, each step seemed harder than the last. The rough-hewn stone steps rose into the mists which clad the pointed top of the island, as if he ascended into the sky itself.

Step by step. Fingin's legs were already aching, and they'd only climbed a third of the way. Step by step. He needed to stop and catch his breath, despite being young and fit.

The monks didn't wait for him.

Step by step. His skin burned with heat and sweat, and his lungs burned. Step by step. His escort disappeared into the clouds as he panted, sucking in air. Step by step. He drank more from his waterskin, the liquid hurting his throat as he tried to swallow past the dryness. Step by step.

The sun dimmed as he reached the cloud. Everything around him faded into white, surrounded by mist. His skin grew cool and moist, the chilly damp of the cloud mixing with the heat of his sweat. He wiped his face several times to no effect.

Step by step.

The final steps rose more steeply, and his leg muscles screamed in agony. When Fingin reached the top stair, he stumbled, so used to stepping up. Then he did a foolish thing. He looked down.

The world tilted and his vision swam. He fell backward, toward the grass and not the stone steps leading down, down, down, into the ocean.

Little black and white birds zipped below him, criss-crossing the stairs in speedy flight. One dipped straight toward the water and the world spun. Fingin dug his fingers into the sparse grass and waited for the earth to stop moving. When his mind finally stopped spinning, he opened his eyes and rubbed at his face.

Four young monks ringed him, staring as he lay sprawled on the ground. They said nothing, but three nodded and left, leaving the youngest.

This monk grinned and offered a hand to help him stand. His blond curls looked odd with a shaved forehead, but his smile seemed genuine. "Greetings to you, pilgrim. I understand you're in search of information. I'm Onchú and I've been assigned to assist you. What would you like to know?"

Fingin smiled in response to the young monk's cheerful manner. 'I'm… I'm F-fingin and I'm looking for s-someone who… might remember my g-grandmother."

The young monk blinked several times. "Oh, dear, oh, dear. You have some difficulty speaking, do you not? Never fear, we can help. Your grandmother, you say? There are no women here. We're all men, monks of the Christian faith. Why did you think you might find her on our isolated enclave?"

Fingin's heart pounded, and he hoped Brigit hadn't sent him to the wrong place. "I was t-told someone here might know her."

With a cock of his head, Onchú asked, "Told by whom?"

He swallowed, as telling a Christian monk that a non-Christian goddess had sent him seemed the height of folly. With a flash of inspiration, Fingin answered, "A wise old w-w-woman. She lived alone."

"Hm. Well, wise old women have a great deal of knowledge that we don't have. Perhaps she didn't send you on a wild chase, after all. I'll ask around for you. Some of us maintain silence, but I'm allowed to speak. I'm not yet vowed to our Lord, you see. That means I'm free to ask questions. Come, you must be tired after your climb. I shall get you refreshment and rest, and then I'll get some details from you."

Onchú led Fingin to his home, a hut made of stone, rounded like an upside-down bowl or a beehive. They crawled into the doorway. A sleeping pallet covered in straw and a wool blanket took up one side, with a stone table on the other. They both sat on the pallet while Onchú pulled several items from a stone shelf above the table. A loaf of barley bread, a jar of honey, and a drinking skin. He also grabbed plates and mugs, serving them both.

Fingin dipped the bread in the honey and savored the pure sweetness. When he drank, he tasted not water, but mead. His head had ceased to spin from his climb, but started again from the drink.

Once they'd finished their meal, Onchú turned to face him, still sitting on the pallet, his hands on his knees. "Now, tell me. What was your grandmother's name? When did you last see her? Can you describe her? Did she have any habits or traits?"

Fingin took a deep breath, trying hard to make his words work. "Her n-name is C- Clíodhna. She left over… fifteen winters past." He swallowed another sip of mead. It seemed to help. "She had thick, dark curls with streaks of white then. B-b-black eyes. Pale skin. Strong voice. She loved p-p-poetry. We lived in th-the east, near a river."

The monk tapped his chin, staring at the ceiling. "Hm. That might describe half the women in Hibernia, to be sure. I'll inquire amongst the older monks. However, if they've been here too long, they wouldn't have even seen a woman in dozens of winters. We do have one who's freshly arrived, so he might have seen her about in the world."

He rose and refilled Fingin's mug. "Why don't you bide here and rest? With your difficulty in speech, I might have more success on my own. If I have questions, I can always come fetch you. Will that suit?"

With some reservations, Fingin gave a nod. He'd expected to ask each monk himself, but now felt relief at not having to do that.

The young blond monk exited the beehive hut and disappeared into the ever-present mist. Silence pressed in on Fingin, making him at once comforted and nervous.

A white cloud blanket smothered all sound, all movement, almost as if he were in some ethereal afterlife, in Tír na nÓg, the land of the ever-living. At the same time, the silence disturbed him, as if at any moment, some primal scream or a raving madman might shatter it.

Fingin lay back on the pallet and closed his eyes, willing his body to relax. What could hurt him on this lonely mountain? Only religious men lived here. His parents would be thrilled to see him amongst their Christian people. His grandmother would be less thrilled.

Would he ever find her? Even if he did, would the brooch she held give him his normal voice back? Would it take away his ability to speak to animals? If he couldn't speak to them, would Bran and Sean still be his friends? He missed them already.

As these questions swirled in his mind like the mist on the mountaintop, sleep eluded him.

Murmurs of male voices drifted past him, too low for him to understand words, too far away for him to see them in the fog. Mist did strange things with sound, transporting it further than normal, or muting it.

A monk laughed somewhere. Fingin didn't like the laugh, but he couldn't say why. Then everything fell silent again.

The lack of sound pressed on his ears, and he covered them, trying to keep the pressure away. He hummed to himself, but that made his uneasiness worse. He sat up, shaking his head to dispel the odd sensation.

Maybe he needed to be outside. He had to crawl to get through the doorway, so he got to his knees and began scooting out.

He almost ran into Onchú, who was just returning. "Aha! There you are. Believe it or not, you might be in luck! I found not one, but two monks who may have met your grandmother! They might be thinking of different women, but this remote corner of Hibernia is not such a large place. Come with me, Fingin."

"You c-call the island Hibernia. Is th-that its name?"

Onchú shrugged. "It's a name. Ierne, Ériu, Hibernia, people call it many things. The Greeks used Ierne, and our people used Ériu before the Romans came. They call it Hibernia. Since we write in Latin, we use Hibernia."

As they walked down a narrow stone path, which wended through several more stone huts, Fingin asked, "'Write'? What is 'write'?"

The monk stopped, putting a finger to his lips in thought. "Writing is… well, a method of drawing words. We make marks that represent the sounds, and those sounds form words. That way, we can record events or ideas, and later on, someone else can read those drawings, and translate them back into speech."

Fingin couldn't make sense of this complicated thing. "Why not j-just tell the other p-person?"

"If they are many leagues away, or must read it next season, they can do so whenever they wish, instead of that moment. It helps to record mighty deeds."

"Isn't th-that what druí are for?"

The monk waved his hand. "Oh, certainly, the storytellers are important. But the druí are all pagan. We Christians need a way to pass their own stories on. Writing is much more useful."

Fingin shook his head as he followed the monk, unwilling to argue with someone helping him. The new religion did things its own way. He hoped the druí would never go away, though.

It was their duty to remember the histories of the ruling families, the battles and legends, the tales and adventures. They memorized hundreds of tales just to become druí. Some specialized in healing magic, or music, or the Brehon law, but each still memorized the stories and took pride in remembering every word precisely.

Ériu would no longer be the same without the druí.

Chapter Nine

First, they stopped at a beehive hut similar to Onchú's. However, rather than crowd three people inside, the resident met them outside. They sat on the grass, cross-legged in a circle.

This tall monk seemed about forty winters. The dark hair left from his tonsure had thinned and grayed around the edges, and frown lines around his eyes ran deep.

Onchú turned to Fingin. "Guaire, here, remembers a woman who passed through his village. He lived far to the east, didn't you say, Guaire? Would your grandmother have lived in the east?"

Fingin nodded. "Near a river c-called *An Ruirthech*. My f-f-father farmed there."

Guaire's brow furrowed. "Yes, yes, I lived right along that river for a few winters. I remember a woman who roused quite a rabble, many seasons ago. Perhaps twenty? More? I can't remember. Well, they ran her out of town. Some sort of wanton, you know, loose with the men."

Fingin didn't want to believe this description of his grandmother, but then he remembered his dream. The mob was clearly attacking her, and she'd been with a man. Had the man been her lover? Guaire and Onchú waited for an answer. "I d-don't know. I was only eight when she left. I don't remember a lot of men."

Onchú frowned. "Well, maybe our other brother will have better information. Thank you, Guaire."

The older monk scowled and crawled back into his hut as they left.

"The next monk remembers a great bit more detail, so perhaps you'll have more success. He's my mentor, Maol Odhrán. He used to be a warrior of the Fianna, long ago, in another lifetime, but now he lives in peace here. Once, he even met the great Pátraic, in his youth."

At the mention of the Fianna, Fingin tensed, but he forced his shoulders to relax as Onchú mentioned peace. Fingin remembered the name Brigit had given him. This man would be old now, and no longer vowed to the Fianna's violence.

He didn't know much about this new religion, but peace seemed to be one of its strongest traditions. As a lone traveler on the island, he drew comfort from that.

Maol Odhrán was already sitting outside his round hut. Though mist swirled around him like a whirlpool, he sat on an outcropping, studying the ocean through the fog.

He rose as they approached, his arms wide in welcome. His long, white beard almost reached his waist, but he had no hair on his head at all. "Come, come, young friend. Oh! Oh, I do say! Yes, you must indeed be Clíodhna's grandson. You have her dark eyes."

Startled, Fingin halted.

The monk ignored his surprise and hugged him. The older man held him by his shoulders, peering at his face. "Yes, definitely her eyes. Her smile as well. Perhaps, even a bit of her soul, though that's buried deep. Do you have her powers?"

Fingin gaped, unsure how to answer such a strange question. He glanced at the younger monk.

Onchú came to his rescue. "Father, be kind to him. This is all new and strange. May we sit and talk with you?"

"Oh, of course, of course. Sit, be well. I shall fetch drink."

Maol Odhrán ducked into his hut and returned with a waterskin, but no mugs. He swigged from the skin and passed it to Fingin. This time, he expected the sweet mead, and drank deep. The buzzing in his head soon reduced his confusion to mere happiness.

"Now, Clíodhna. I haven't seen her in, oh, so many winters. At least fifteen. She'd been a tricky one, no doubt, but she disappeared into the hills. No angry mob would catch her. Even if they grabbed her, she'd simply call up the storm winds and they'd scatter. A little thunder and lightning can do wonders to scare the masses, eh?"

Images from his dream crowded in his mind, fueled by the monk's words and the mead. "D-d-did you know her well?"

The older monk chuckled. "Well enough, well enough, my lad! We had many long, lovely conversations in the abbey gardens. I tried to convince her to become a nun. I tempted her with sacred texts and magical secrets, but she'd have none of the idea. The Abbot didn't like her in the slightest. Accused her as a witch and threatened to take her children away. Well, that certainly didn't work! She called down her pet thunderstorm. I only saw her once after that, here on the island. She just appeared, as if by magic! She told me she rode in on some dolphins." He waved his hand at the silly notion.

So much of his story confused Fingin, he didn't know where to start. He grasped the one unfamiliar word. "D-d-dolphins?"

"Dolphins. They look like fish but breathe air. You can see them off the coast from time to time. Helpful beasts. Sometimes they do save a shipwrecked fisherman. Quite personable."

The Fae fish. Those must be the dolphins. He felt foolish for assuming them to be magical. "Where d-did she go?"

"Oh, dear, I'm not sure. She lived nearby, somewhere along the coast, but I'd just made my vows here, so I didn't dare leave to visit her."

Fingin bowed his head. His only lead hadn't helped much. He'd have to search the entire coastline.

Then an idea occurred to him. Perhaps the Fae fish—the dolphins— remembered her.

Eager to test his theory, Fingin nodded to Maol Odhrán. "I th-thank you for your help."

The older man raised an eyebrow. "And what will you do now, young man? I noticed you never answered my question. Are you a weather-witch as well?"

Fingin shook his head. His grandmother had warned of telling others of his power, and been run out of town often enough to stay silent. Besides, he could truthfully say he had no command over the weather.

A small bird swooped in and landed on Maol Odhrán's shoulder. Fingin had glimpsed the birds in the fog, but this was the first time he'd the chance to study them. Its black and white feathers contrasted with a bright orange beak.

It cocked its head back and forth, studying him back. "What sort of b-b-bird is that? I've never seen one b-before."

"This? This, my dear boy, is a puffin. Delightful creatures. Quite playful. Excellent at finding tiny fish. See? He has a few in his beak."

Fingin hadn't noticed the thin minnows, but as Maol Odhrán spoke, the puffin gulped them down. In his head, the puffin said, "Sometimes they take my fish, but I can always catch more. Bye!"

Away the little bird flew, flapping his wings madly. It disappeared into the mist.

After the climb down the almost endless column of steps, Fingin stared at the empty landing area. The coracle was gone.

Onchú scratched his head. "Uh, one of the other monks must have gone to the mainland. You might have to wait until tomorrow to get back."

They both glanced back at the steps. Fingin shook his head. "I won't survive another… t-t-trip up those. If I c-c-can't find my way b-back today, I'll sleep down here. I should be safe, right?"

He worried about Sean and Bran back on the shore, and glanced across the water, but he could barely see the land in the mists, let alone his friends.

The monk frowned, glancing up. The cloud still clung to the top of the mountain, but now other clouds were rolling in. Darker clouds, full of rain and fury, swept across the sun and the temperature cooled, despite his sweat.

"I shouldn't leave you here, but I have duties I must tend to. Are you certain?"

Fingin patted the other man on the shoulder. "Go home, *Onchú*. Th-th-thank you for all your help."

With a brief embrace, the young monk climbed the steps to his mountaintop home.

Fingin waited until he disappeared from sight, swallowed by the white mists. Then, he cupped his hands around his mouth and shouted across the water. "I need help to get back to shore."

At first, nothing answered. Then a tiny puffin flittered near him. "You want my help with something?"

He grinned. "Not you, but some of the Fae fish… I mean dolphins. The big fish who breathe air like us. Do you know them?"

The bird dipped a few times, his version of a nod. "I do! There are some on the other side of the island."

"Can you lead them here?"

The bird hesitated. "They don't talk like you do."

"See if you can make them realize I need their help. I'd be grateful."

For an answer, the bird zipped away. Fingin hadn't realized how fast the little bird could fly, but he barely made out the speck of white against the far rocks before it disappeared.

Soon, the familiar chittering of the Fae fish filled the air. The little puffin swooped several times and then flew up toward the monk's enclave.

A Fae fish complained, "Those birds pecked our heads! We chased them here. Now they're gone!"

Fingin suppressed a chuckle. "I asked them to get your attention, but I'm sorry if they hurt you. Will you help me? I need to get to shore. Before the storm hits, if possible."

They held a disjointed conversation. Words floated across the water now and then, but they all spoke at once, and he had difficulty separating their voices. The largest one came forward, balancing in the water on his tail. "Why should we take you?"

"I can call fish from the depths, so you have a nice meal. I can talk to them the way I talk to you."

They consulted again before the largest one answered. "We can take you. Can you hold on to our fins?"

Fingin glanced up again and stepped into the water. He gasped at the chill and hooked his hand over that dolphin's fin. He held on as it burst forward with speed.

For a moment, he wondered if the fish was trying to knock him off, but he held on tight. Faster than he could imagine, faster even than the other Fae fish had hauled the raft, they skipped across the choppy water. He bounced on the dolphin's back, his stomach pounding on the curved body, but he gripped tight.

The sky grew ominously dark as they traveled, but he'd committed to his course. If he fell off now, he'd surely drown.

The water rose next to them in a strange bubble. The dolphins all scattered, except the one he rode. His heart started pounding. "What's that?"

"Oh, that's Grandfather. He's not dangerous. He only eats tiny fish."

The bubble rose higher and higher. Water sluiced from the top, almost swamping him and making him lose his grip on the fin. A huge form rose from the surface, white and blue, several times as big as the dolphin.

Fingin gasped his question, "Hello! What are you?"

A deep voice rumbled through the water. "I am me. What are you?"

The new creature rose and slapped down, causing a wave that once again threatened his grip. He dug his fingers in, trying to hold on.

"I am Fingin, and I'm trying to get safe on shore before the rain starts."

"Oh… I thought you were just playing with my friends."

"I suppose I am. I'll be calling fish when we're done, so they can eat. Would you like some fish?"

The creature dove again, disappearing under the waves, but his voice filtered back through the water, distorted. "I don't like big fish."

"I can try to call little ones!"

Fingin heard no response, his deep voice fading away. Then, without warning, the huge fish burst to the surface. This time, Fingin did lose his grip and, try as he might to get purchase on the dolphin's slick body, he dipped below the waves, his arms thrashing in panic.

He tried to suck in a breath, but only water came in. He had to cough, but couldn't.

A body bumped against his arm and he grabbed at it, but his hand slipped. Again, he scrabbled for something, anything to hold on to.

Desperate for something to grasp, he flailed his arms. Fingin felt smooth dolphin skin, but not the fin. His fingers slipped across the slick surface until he lost contact. Then his vision grew fuzzy, but he tried again. This time, the panicked swimmer found the fin and pulled himself to the surface.

After he spluttered and coughed, Fingin vowed never again to embark upon the ocean.

The shore came into close view, and through eyes burning with salt water, he squinted, trying to focus on the details. He searched for his friends but saw no animals.

They might be waiting for him where he left them, or might have wandered off. He didn't think the dolphins had brought him back to the same beach he'd left from.

Fingin just wanted to be on the ground and no longer in the water. He ought to have waited for the monks the next morning. This is what he got for his impatience, and his arrogance for believing his talent gave him an advantage.

The Fae fish deposited him, choking and spitting, on the sand. They waited in the shallows while the larger creature swam in the deeper water. With the last measure of his strength, Fingin called out for feeder fish, making them curious. They came to see who called, and his helpers had a feast.

Fingin finally regained his breath as he sat on the beach. Once the Fae fish and their companion ate their fill, they swam away.

However, one lingered. "You are a strange human."

He managed a weak smile. "It's not a bad thing to be strange. Sometimes it's better."

The dolphin chittered. "I'm Nuanni. Why do you swim in the ocean with us? Most humans die when they try that."

Heavy drops of rain splatted on his head. "I almost died once, too. We move better on land, because swimming is more difficult."

"I remember a female human swam with us, but not into the deep. She didn't talk to us, but she'd bring the storms and storms meant more fish. We fed well. We liked her."

Despite the growing wind, this caught Fingin's interest. "A female human? Did she have black hair with white streaks? Do you know where she lived?"

After a flip in the water, Nuanni replied, "Stripey hair, yes. She sang to us and lived in a land structure."

"She did? Do you know where?"

The Fae fish chittered and pointed her nose toward the south. He peered in that direction, but rain obscured everything. Still, hope rose in

Fingin's heart, and he scrambled to his feet. "Thank you, Nuanni. I hope we'll meet again!"

For an answer, she chittered again and balanced on her tail, moving away. Then she dove into the water and Fingin turned inland. He needed to find shelter from the rain. He was incredibly tired of the rain. In fact, he was incredibly tired of being wet.

Fingin didn't see anything that might be a cave. Stretching before him was a line of pine trees along the beach. He spied one with a thick canopy to cut the worst of the rain. Wishing he had dry clothing, he pelted toward the shelter, his boots squelching in the sand.

Even if he hadn't already been soaked from the ocean, the storm would have re-drenched him within moments. A headwind almost blew him off his feet before he reached the trees. He crawled the last part, hugging the rough bark of the tree trunk as the storm raged around him.

Tired, hungry, alone, and soaked, he held hope in his heart. Nuanni had given him a clue to finding his grandmother's home. Did she still live there? The Fae fish didn't seem to have a concept of time or seasons. Somewhere out there, he also had friends to help him. Those friends carried his net, clothing, and tools.

After seasons alone, he knew that those friends were more important than any of the material things.

Raindrops lulled Fingin to sleep. He huddled, cold and wet, but at least he felt safe, despite his precarious position on a spit of land in a raging summer storm. As darkness fell, he fell into a fitful sleep.

When he stretched awake, the world dripped with the sharp, earthy scent of wet pine needles filling his nostrils, along with the tang of the air and the musty odor of seaweed.

The rich smells reminded his stomach he hadn't eaten for far too long. He had no net, but Fingin walked to a cluster of rocks and peered into the hollows for clams or oysters. He had no knife to pry open their shells, nor fire to cook them, but he'd leapt this hurdle before.

This time, he didn't cut his finger on the sharp edges. Somehow, the oyster didn't seem as disgusting as it had been the first time he'd choked it down.

He shouted for Bran and Sean but couldn't find a trace of his friends. After going silent and listening for any sound they might make, he decided that he'd have to search for them.

Fixing his starting spot in his mind so he could find it again, he turned up the shore, toward where he'd left with the monks. His friends were probably waiting for him there.

Fingin took his time striding along the beach, enjoying the post-storm air. The metallic scent tickled his nose, and he sneezed a few times as he climbed over rocky outcroppings, seaweed piles, and pebble washes.

He imagined his grandmother living in this place, at the liminal border between the land and the water, a place of balance, danger, and magic. If she liked singing to the dolphins, had they make friends with her? Did she have any friends here? Or did she live on her own?

A faint bark broke his reverie, and he turned toward the sound. In the far distance, two dots moved toward him. His heart felt whole again, and he grinned, anticipating the reunion.

When Bran caught up to him, the hound covered him with slobbering licks, to the point that he had to fend off the enthusiasm or risk losing the top layer of his skin.

Sean greeted him with less energy, but still glad at having found him again. "Bran didn't wait patiently. He's been running up and down this coastline looking for you since the moment you left."

Bran jumped around him. "Did you find her? Did you find her? I don't see her. You didn't bring her back?"

He shook his head with a chuckle. "No, I didn't find her. I found those who knew her, though. And she might be living nearby. Our next goal is to find her home. It should be around that bend back there. At least, that's what the Fae fish said."

Bran peered into the water. "You had another raft?"

"No, no raft. But the Fae fish brought me back, until the storm hit."

Bran woofed and shook his head. "I don't like storms on the sea."

"No more do I, my friend."

"Do you have fish? I finished the ones you left me. I'm very hungry now."

He laughed, ruffling Bran's fur. "No, but we can get some."

After getting his net from Sean's pack, the actions of casting and drawing his net, cleaning the fish, and then setting up a fire helped him settle his thoughts. Now that he had his friends once again, he'd find his grandmother with a lighter heart.

They set off along the beach after the brief meal. Despite the mostly clear sky, a quick shower dampened their spirits. Nothing nearby offered cover, so they pushed on through. The sand turned to mud and was difficult to walk through, so they moved inland to the trees.

While the way didn't seem as clear, their feet had more purchase with thick ground cover. They could still glimpse the shoreline, so any house would be easy to see.

The sun rose high before they got too far. Surprised, Fingin tried to figure out how much time he'd spent that day. He must have slept on the beach longer than he'd thought, halfway through the morning.

The shore wasn't smooth, dipping in and out again. Hills and rocks made it difficult to see around the next bend, so it was a long slog in and out of small inlets. By the time they stopped for the evening, exhausted from all he'd been through the last few days, Fingin collapsed.

They camped on the shore with a cheerful fire to keep back the gloom. The sky had cleared, revealing a blanket of twinkling stars above them, and he swore the ocean glowed in the darkness.

For the first time in a long time, Fingin realized he'd found peace, despite still being on a mad quest. His heart felt happy. He'd only ever been content with his life. But with Bran and Sean, and his own dawning confidence in his ability to fend for himself in the wide world, he found something stronger, something deeper, than mere survival.

Fingin embraced this nugget of joy, tucking it into his memory. He'd take it out when he needed reassurance of his own worth, a recollection of when he'd made the right decisions to battle against his doubts when things careened out of control.

Lying between Bran and Sean, the warmth of their bodies guarding him against the cool sea breeze, he drifted into a sweet sleep.

But in the velvet dark of the night, Fingin leapt up, wide awake as a mournful sound drifted across the water.

The low, slow ululation made his skin prickle. Was his imagination playing tricks on him? Was it something from a dream?

The wail drifted across the beach again. This time, Bran's head popped up, ears alert.

"You hear it too, huh?"

Bran sneezed, shaking his head. "We heard it last night. We thought someone had hurt you."

"Not me, Bran. Something out there."

The song seemed lovely, but lonely, as if someone cried for lost love. It drifted in and out, punctuated by a series of clicks and whistles, reminiscent of the Fae fish chittering.

Fingin called out to the water. "Nuanni? Nuanni, is that you?"

The answer, deep in his mind, didn't sound like a Fae fish, but the lower voice of the larger creature. "That is me, small human. I sing to the stars."

"Are you hurt? Can we help?"

"I don't hurt. I am happy."

Fingin let out a sigh as he lay back down. "One of the big fish is singing, Bran. You can relax. He won't hurt us."

Bran snuffled and turned several times before settling back in his spot. His wiry fur scratched Fingin's neck, but he treasured feeling the dog's

warm body against his.

AGE OF SECRETS

Chapter Ten

Though his muscles ached the next morning, Fingin was glad to get up with the dawn. He greeted the sun, packed his supplies, and they started their journey again.

More rocks, more climbing, more weaving between trees and underbrush filled their morning, that afternoon, and much of the next morning. However, late the next afternoon, they approached the derelict stone hut.

Larger than the beehive structures on the monk's island, this one looked cozy enough for a single person. It was round but made of stacked stones and a roof made of slate. A stand of trees backed the hut, leading to a denser forest as the ground rose from the shore. Beyond that, a tall cliff jutted up to overlook the ocean.

Shells and barnacles decorated some of the stones, and moss grew thick on other spots. A few flowers stuck out of the top, and as they approached, Fingin listened for any sounds.

A few stones had rolled away from the base, resting in the sand below. The high tide mark reached about forty paces from the front steps. A heavy storm might swamp the place, despite being on a rise.

Bran sniffed the air. "I don't smell people."

No smoke filtered out through holes in the stone, but the day was mild.

He approached the entrance with trepidation and prepared himself for disappointment. His grandmother might have moved away long ago. This might not even be her house. This could be yet another a dead end and his quest would be over.

Fingin clenched his jaw and peered into the darkness within, but nothing remained inside. Not one piece of furniture, no half-burnt sticks in the hearth, not even a broken spoon. Only a faint cloud of dust disturbed by his entrance sparkled in a sunbeam. The interior looked utterly desolate.

He sat on the threshold with his head in his hands, elbows on his knees. He wanted to cry. Everything he'd gone through to find his grandmother, only to find nothing at the end of the quest.

Bran nosed in and licked his face several times. He batted away his friend, trying not to giggle. "Stop it! Stop!"

"You're sad. I don't want you to be sad."

He ruffled Bran's fur. "I'm not sad because of you, Bran."

Sean brayed, facing the forest. "Someone's coming."

Fingin jumped to his feet as Bran bristled and let out a low growl. "Hush, Bran. We need to see who's coming before we warn them off."

Rustling in the forest undergrowth grew louder as it came closer. A glimpse of brown flashed amongst the trees, and the branches shifted.

Those weren't branches, but antlers. An enormous stag poked his head out from the trees, the keen intelligence in his eyes moving from Bran, to Sean, then to Fingin.

He let out a breath of relief. "Greetings, honored stag. I apologize if we've intruded upon your wood."

The stag bowed his head once. "The donkey is welcome, as are all my distant relations. Your hound is tolerated, if the donkey speaks for him. You are more problematic. The sons of men have often brought evil to my kind."

With a nervous swallow, Fingin said, "I mean no harm to you or yours. I only seek information."

"What information do you seek?"

He let out a deep breath, thankful the stag would speak with him. Deer of all types didn't linger to chat, being flighty and nervous. He couldn't blame them, as men often hunted deer. "I'm seeking the woman who lived here. She is my kin, and I must find her. Do you remember where and when she left?"

The stag twitched his head, his magnificent antlers brushing the leaves. "She lived here for many seasons, but I'm uncertain when she left. Perhaps the sea eagle can help you. She often shared meals with him."

"Where can I find the sea eagle?"

The stag glanced to a promontory above them, a large nest tucked into the cliffside. "He resides up there, but you should be able to call him. If he can understand your words like I can, he might heed them. He's rather intelligent for a bird."

Fingin squinted, trying to make out details of the large nest, but only saw a smudge of brown against the gray rock. "Thank you, honored stag, for your suggestion."

With another bow of his head, he walked away, his brown coat and antlers faded into the trees.

Bran bounded up. "You need to find a sea eagle? That's a bird? Birds are hard to catch. They fly too fast."

"We don't want to catch him, Bran. We need to speak to him. He might remember my grandmother." Fingin shaded his eyes and pointed up to the cliff. "Can you see if there's an eagle in the next up there?"

"I only see the nest. Can't you see it? It's right there!"

"I can only see a brown splotch, Bran. Perhaps he'll come back when the sun sets." He squinted again, this time peering west. The sun hung close to the horizon. Dusk would be soon. "We'll sit under the cliff. Come on!"

They pushed through bracken and bushes, oak trees and pines, until they reached a glade at the foot of the cliff. Small fishbones and other debris littered the ground beneath the nest. Fingin glanced up until his neck hurt, trying to stare the eagle back to his nest.

As the sun dipped closer to its evening rest, they ate and rested from the day's journey. Sean chewed on sweet grasses while Bran and Fingin ate the last of the morning's catch. Glad he'd taken the time to fish and cook, he chewed on the last morsel, wishing he had some of the garlic-studded bread Aideen had given them. That part of his life seemed so long ago, another world away.

A screech above him drew his eyes up. A massive sea eagle banked and circled over the cliff before diving. However, the bird didn't land in the nest. Instead, it wheeled in lazy circles, dropping to a tree on the edge of the glade.

He stood and bowed his head to the huge raptor. "Greetings, noble sea eagle. We apologize for intruding upon your home."

The eagle cocked his head and regarded him with glittering eyes. "How do you speak my words?"

"I have magic that allows me to speak with animals. I'm honored that you allow me to converse with you. The stag suggested you might be able to help me."

The bird squawked. "What would that silly creature understand about me? I help no one."

He opened his wings to their full span and fear gripped Fingin's heart. This raptor could claw the life from his throat in an instant, or snap his arm in two, should he decide to. Bran stayed quiet but quivered beside him. Sean ignored the bird and kept eating.

"I'm seeking news of my grandmother. She lived in the house on the shore. The stag thought you might remember her."

"Yes, I remember her. She sometimes shared food with me. What do you wish of her?"

"I'd like to find her. Do you remember where she went? Or how long ago?"

The eagle screeched, flapping its wings. "I do not. She disappeared one day, many, many seasons past. I have since laid several eggs and the chicks grown and gone."

Fingin hung his head, his hope draining away.

The bird spoke again. "The salmon might know where she's gone. He spoke with her."

Startled, he glanced up. "Spoke to her? She didn't have the same magic I do. How could she speak with the salmon?"

Another screech echoed in the glade. "He is the Salmon of Wisdom. He decides who can hear him."

Without waiting for an answer, the eagle took flight, flapping so strong that dust flew around them. Fingin coughed and rubbed the dirt from his eyes. The eagle had gone.

With a deep sigh, Fingin sank back to the ground. Where would he find the salmon? The only thing he could think to do was stick his head in the ocean and call for him. He'd probably drown before he could find a particular salmon in the wide ocean.

For now, he needed sleep. Perhaps a better solution would come to him in the morning.

After honoring the dawn, he paced along the beach in front of the abandoned stone hut, trying to think of a way to find the salmon.

Bran barked each time he walked in front of the dog. "Why do you walk like that? You aren't going anywhere."

"I'm trying to think. I have to find a salmon."

"Are you going fishing? I'm hungry."

He glanced out to the ocean, the waves choppy in the gray morning light. "I should. But I need to speak to a particular salmon. A smart salmon who made friends with my grandmother. Possibly the same one that got me started in this whole mess."

"A smart fish? Like the Fae fish?"

"Maybe. Oh! Maybe the Fae fish can find him for me! Bran, thank you!" He hugged the hound so tightly, the dog let out a yip. "Thank you! What a brilliant idea."

After a quick morning cast for fish, he waited impatiently for the fire to cook their meal. In the meantime, he called out for the Fae fish. "Nuanni! Nuanni, are you out there? Tanni? Anyone? Come to shore, I have questions to ask!"

They ate their morning meal and rested on the beach in the overcast morning. Time passed with no answer, but he kept asking every now and then. He even stuck his head under the water a few times, spluttering as sand and seawater got up his nose.

One school of smaller fish came to his call, but flitted away as a larger fish chased them. He tried to talk to the larger fish, but it swam away almost as fast. It seemed only the larger fish had enough sense to carry on a conversation.

Fingin sat back on the beach hard enough to jar his spine. He stared out at the islands peeking through the ocean mist. They danced among the wind, winking in and out of view as the breeze played with their white shrouds. He grew entranced by them, almost as if they were moving in the waves, disappearing and reappearing like *Hy Brasil* every seventh winter.

His grandmother might have been gone too long for the Salmon to stay near. Fingin was probably wasting his time searching for this intelligent salmon. Maybe it was time to admit that his quest had truly failed.

His entire life had been a failure until this quest. He'd had no family, worked no farm, and created no stories. He'd survived from day to day, scraping by, without contributing to his world in any way. If he'd never existed, would anything change? Would anyone be the better or worse?

Fingin squeezed his eyes shut, willing tears to stay away. If he'd drowned in the ocean, no one would have cared or noticed.

Bran nosed up against his hand, the warm, wet tongue interrupting his misery. He smiled and ruffled the wolfhound's fur. Perhaps he *had* lived a worthless life, but he'd saved Bran's life. That must be worth something. Perhaps he could still complete his quest, with his friends' help. Maybe, just maybe, he hadn't yet failed.

"There is no failure while there is life."

He leapt to his feet, spinning toward the owner of the deep, resonant voice. It flowed through his feet and into his bones, but he saw no one.

A low chuckle bubbled into his mind. "You see no one. I am no one, but I am also everyone. You may glimpse me, however, under the surface. You must look if you wish to see."

A glint of silver flashed in the ocean before him. An enormous salmon head popped above the water, black and silver spotted, with a hint of pink near the gills.

He'd found his salmon.

"In truth, I have found you, Fingin. Again."

A dawning realization made his eyes go wide. "So, you *are* the salmon in the river, the one who broke my net?"

Fingin imagined a smile playing on the salmon's mouth. "Indeed. I needed to distract you, so you could find your loyal companion. If I hadn't broken your net, you would not have seen the branch. If you hadn't seen the branch, you would not have rescued the dog."

Fingin set his jaw. "I would have seen that half tree coming down my river without you breaking my net!"

The menace in the salmon's mental voice brooked no argument. "Do you doubt my words, human?"

Fingin wondered at his own temerity. The salmon had an honored place in legends, a harbinger of wisdom. To ignore its words would be foolish. He hung his head in shame. "I do not."

"Excellent. Clíodhna has chosen well."

He raised his head, his eyes wide. Bran yipped once. "Clíodhna? Then you *do* remember my grandmother?"

"You already knew this. Why do you waste my time with foolish questions?"

Foolish questions. Very well, he'd ask what he needed to know. "Where is my grandmother now?"

"That is not the correct question."

He glanced at Bran, but the dog just cocked his head. "Can you hear the salmon, too?"

Bran whined. "Yes. I don't like him. His voice hurts."

He flashed the dog a sympathetic smile and turned back to the fish. "How can I get to where my grandmother is?"

"A much better question. I shall show you."

Images swam in his mind. Back the way he came, to the north edge of the large inlet, to a bog near the coast. Hills hung in the distance, across the flat marshlands and a strip of water. A sacred well surrounded by a throne of flat stones.

"The new religion will someday steal the well on *Imleach* Bog, dedicating it to one of their own holy men who travels the ocean. However, the old gods are still strong in this place. That is where you will begin your journey."

Sitting back on the ground, Fingin held his aching head. "My journey to where?"

"To where your grandmother lives."

Fingin bowed his head. "Thank you."

"My information comes at a price, young human."

He swallowed against a surge of worry. "What price do you ask?"

The salmon didn't respond right away. Fingin sweated as the fish remained silent. Perhaps the salmon only waited to make him nervous. Either way, it worked.

"I shall ask for a future favor." And the salmon disappeared.

Curse the crows. Fingin leapt to his feet again, scanning the distance for a sign of the fish, but nothing moved in the gentle ocean waves.

Bran glanced at him. "Is he gone?"

"He is. But he told me where to find my grandmother. At least, a way to get to her."

162

Bran barked three times. "Will there be food?"

For once, their journey to the sacred well had been relatively easy. No storms battered the coast, nor did any rogue warriors harass them. Instead, the sun beat on their backs as they slogged through a marsh. The land was flat here, vast and empty of trees. Tall, green grass swayed in the faint breeze, the wind a welcome relief to the heat.

In the distance, low hills rose against the ocean, just as they had in the salmon's vision.

A dark pile of rocks in the distance was their beacon. As they drew closer, the pile resolved into the stones he'd seen in his mind's eye. Arranged almost like a throne around the deep well, they looked stark against the green grass. Stone steps led into the dark depths.

Fingin dipped his hands into the water, taking a cautious sip. The clear, sweet liquid ran down his throat and his skin cooled, despite the humid day. Brigit's charm around his neck grew warm and he grasped it with his hand. The cloth it hung upon grew icy.

"It looks like we need to enter the well itself." Fingin glanced to his animal companions. "I don't insist either of you come with me. You're free to come or stay as you like. If you stay, you can go your own way, or you can wait for me. Bran, I'll fish for you before I go if you decide to stay, so you'll have plenty of food. Sean, there should be lots of grass for you."

In his heart, he ached for Bran to stay with him, but he doubted Sean would fit into the well.

The donkey peered at the steps. "I don't want to go down there. I'll wait here."

Fingin expected it, but still swallowed away his sadness. "We might not return this way, and I don't know how long we'll be. I don't want you to wait forever."

Sean bobbed his head. "I shall wait here for a few days, then."

Fingin removed his packs from Sean's back and gave his flank a final pat. "What about you, Bran?"

The dog whined and swiveled his head between Fingin and the water. "I don't want to stay. I don't want to go in there, either."

He hugged the big hound tightly. "I don't blame you. But I have to go down there."

Bran whined again and then woofed. "Then so do I."

He hugged Sean and patted his flank. "You've been a good friend and valuable help. Leave, if we don't come back soon. There should be plenty of people around happy to have your help on their farm."

The donkey nodded, his eyes sorrowful.

Fingin took in a deep breath and stared at the water. The way wouldn't look any easier if he waited. He stepped into the well, the cold water seeping over his boot. With the second step, it reached his knees. The third step made him suck in his breath with the chill.

Bran stepped beside him. "This is cold!"

"I know, Bran, I know. Remember to hold your breath when we get beneath the surface. I hope the passage isn't far."

"I can't breathe water. I don't like water. I really don't like water!"

"Neither do I. But from what my grandmother taught me, this is a sacred well. For the salmon to send us here, it must be a magical portal. We shouldn't have to hold our breath for long. If we don't come out soon, we turn around, I promise."

Bran didn't answer as they took another step.

By the time the water reached to his neck, his doubts rushed back. Were they descending into their own death by drowning? He reached under the stone, looking for some air space he could use to breathe, but found nothing except water and slimy stone. He glanced at Bran, took in a deep breath, and ducked under water, just as his friend did the same.

Chapter Eleven

Fingin had expected to continue down the steps, keeping his body under the water by pushing against the stone. However, as soon as his head dipped under the water, he was standing in a field. He glanced around wildly for Bran, and found his loyal hound at his feet, swiveling his head in understandable confusion.

Gone was the lonely bog, surrounded by tall grass with seagulls crying in the distance. Gone was the warm summer sun beating down on his sweaty skin. Gone was the patient donkey, the moss-slick stones, and the sacred well.

Instead, they stood in a dream glade. Trees grew along the side of their path, but different from any Fingin had ever seen. Purple, blue, and green leaves fluttered in a nonexistent breeze. Bright sparkling insects that looked almost like butterflies flitted amongst the vivid flowers. Even the gravel path sparkled.

Fingin searched for a source of light, but no sun hung in the sky. Instead, each living thing glowed with its own gleam.

Bran whined. "This is a strange place."

"That's true. But at least you can breathe!"

The dog's tail whipped back and forth twice, but he stopped whining.

Was he in Faerie, land of the *Túatha Dé Danaan*? *Tír na nÓg*? *Hy Brasil*? Whichever mythical place they'd traveled to, he had a mission to find his grandmother.

Fingin asked the butterfly creatures where he might find humans like himself, but they ignored him and flitted away on to the treetops. He frowned, unused to being snubbed. Even fish who declined to come when he asked usually answered back.

In one direction, rolling hills disappeared into a hazy yellow glow. In the other, land flattened out to a darker green mist. He didn't know which direction he should choose, or if he should even remain on the path.

Fingin knelt to his dog. "Bran, what do you sense here? Do you smell danger? Anything else? I don't know which direction to go."

Bran sniffed both the air and the ground in several directions, sneezed, and tried again. "I don't know these smells."

"Can you find people? Or animals? Something other than these weird butterflies. Someone I can talk to."

Bran yipped and sniffed again toward the green mist. "There's something that way."

He placed a hand on Bran's head, and they resumed their journey. The path didn't crunch under his feet as he'd expected. Instead, it rustled, like dried leaves in the autumn.

Fingin stooped to examine the rocks and found them to be lighter than he'd expected. He could crumble them with his hands, turning them into powder. As he poured the powder from his hand back to the gravel, it sparkled and floated, forming a beautiful swirl around them both.

Bran sneezed again, backing away from the whirling silver dust. He backed into a tree, which waved its branches, apparently angry at the affront. Bran whuffed and retreated to Fingin's side, his gaze scanning the surrounding plants for further threats. His eyes stayed wide and his hackles high.

Fingin had no idea how long they walked, as no sun moved to gauge the passage of time, no shadows grew, and no darkness crept in to herald the night. It seemed like days, and yet no time at all.

The landscape changed from rolling hills to a sparse forest of the colorful trees, to dense woods, and back again. They passed a sparkling pool, but with pink or orange water, rather than green or blue.

Bran stayed close to his side, occasionally exploring a rustle in the undergrowth or a flicker of movement, but not as boldly as he would have in the mortal realm. He seemed spooked, cautious, and Fingin couldn't blame him.

Though the air was warm, he didn't sweat. The water sparkled, but he couldn't find a light source. Creatures abounded in the hills, but none came close except the butterflies. They ignored both man and dog as they journeyed along the silver path.

Green mist retreated as they approached, always the same distance away. However, a spot appeared in the distance upon the path. This spot grew larger, and Bran said, "That's what I smell, I think. They're coming closer."

The form resolved into the shape of a man. Dark brown skin, gnarled and rough like the bark of an ancient oak tree, covered him. His lack of clothing revealed him to be male. Green leafy hair cascaded down his back, rustling with his movement.

As they grew closer, Fingin waited for the stranger to approach them. He held his hands open in a sign of welcome, praying the creature wouldn't destroy them on the spot.

The newcomer examined them for several moments before speaking. "And what manner of creature do I see before me? A human and a hound? For what reason have you tread upon our lands?"

His throat dry, Fingin stammered, "I am searching f-for my k-kin."

The Fae, for so he must be, circled them, studying them from head to toe, making clicks with his tongue, as if assessing them for danger…

or dessert. "How intriguing. And for what reason do you search for them here?"

He swallowed. "Someone told me they lived here."

In an instant, the Fae appeared before him, a mere handspan from Fingin's face. He jerked back, startled by the sudden movement as Bran growled. "Told by whom?"

"B-brigit."

After a moment of dead silence, the creature threw his head back and laughed. "Brigit! Brigit sent *you?* Oh, that must be the funniest thing I've heard in ages."

He bent over in his hilarity as Fingin and Bran exchanged glances. The laughter went on so long, Fingin clenched his fists. His purpose didn't seem so funny to him.

Eventually, his merriment subsided, and he resumed examining the pair. Without warning, he stood close, his earthy-smelling breath misting on Fingin's skin.

Fingin gasped and took a step backward, but the Fae walked forward. "So, sent by Brigit into the land of the Fae. What assistance can you expect here, mortal? You cannot hope to complete such a vague purpose."

He opened his mouth and shut it again. Fingin had no idea how to answer that.

The Fae cocked his head, making his leafy hair rustle again. "Still, I might have use for mortal servants." He snapped his fingers and a blue light formed at his woody fingertips. Fingin stared at the glowing spot as it fascinated him, drawing his attention despite him trying to look away.

Bran whined and pawed the ground. The scent of burning leaves and lavender swept around him. Fingin's feet moved against his volition. First one step, then the other, toward the Fae. That creature took several steps backwards, still holding his fingers up with the blue light, leading them down the path toward the yellow haze.

Bran barked and the blue light disappeared. The hound growled, his hackles raised, and he bared his teeth at the Fae. Fingin, now free from the beguiling light, shook his head to dispel the fog that held his mind.

The Fae frowned and snapped again, but though the blue light reappeared, it no longer held the compulsion it had before. Fingin stayed in place and crossed his arms. Bran growled again.

A scowl came across the newcomer's face. "How are you breaking my magic? You are a mere mortal. You should have no such ability!"

Fingin glared at the creature who would have enslaved them both. "I don't know. But I'm glad we can."

This time, the brown Fae growled back, stepping forward with menace and anger clear on his bark face. Fingin's blood ran to ice, but Bran returned his menace threefold.

With a great roar, the Fae shoved both hands forward, and a massive force slammed into Fingin's chest, throwing him back. He skidded along the silver gravel path, the wind knocked from him. Bran suffered similarly, his yip turning into a mournful whine.

Fingin scrambled to regain his feet, but the Fae moved too fast. Without touching him at all, the Fae pummeled him with unseen blows, connecting to his face, his chest, his legs, and his arms. With no way to fight back, Fingin curled into a ball, covering his face and stomach.

Bran's barks grew more frantic, and he snarled at the Fae, but couldn't get close, either. The same force that had knocked into Fingin must be keeping the hound from attacking their assailant.

Through his agony, Fingin croaked, "Bran, leave him! He's too strong."

Pounding punches and kicks rained on his body until everything throbbed in pain.

An eternity later, the Fae must have tired of his sport. Silence fell upon them, and Fingin opened one eye. They were alone again.

His muscles and skin blistered as if he'd come too close to a hearth fire. He tried to move, but his body screamed in protest. He forced one hand to lie on Bran's flank, checking to see if his hound breathed. When the warm body shifted, drawing breath in and out, Fingin sighed in relief. This Fae had already angered him beyond belief, but if he'd harmed Bran…

Fingin wanted to crawl off the path and shelter amongst the trees, in case some other murderous Fae traveled by, but his body wouldn't obey him. Even if it did, he mustn't move Bran in case he hurt the wolfhound more.

With careful motions, he pulled his waterskin from his pack and dribbled some in Bran's mouth, then his own. He had no stomach for food but offered dried fish to Bran.

"I'm not hungry. I hurt."

With a painful swallow, he nodded. "So do I, friend. So do I."

Brigit's charm worked better here in Faerie, with the metal burning so hot, it turned his skin red. The fabric it hung upon turned ice cold. Fingin made Bran wear it to ensure they both got the healing magic, but it seemed to make little difference. Both healed well enough within three meals.

Fingin judged this to be a day's time in the mortal world, judging from when his stomach rumbled. Judging by Bran's stomach would be useless, as the dog always wanted more food. That is, except for when Fae creatures beat them into quivering piles of pain.

Since the angry Fae had headed toward the yellow glow, Fingin turned in the opposite direction, toward the green mist. Once Bran felt up to traveling again, they resumed their journey.

This time, they travelled with more caution. They examined every movement in the trees, every butterfly or rodent-like creature that made noise as they passed. He wanted no more chance encounters like the last one, despite his obvious inability to prevent it.

Sometime later, something large loomed within the green mist. A building, or perhaps a ringfort.

Fingin had seen a ringfort once, tall upon a hill. The local chief and his warriors lived there, but Fingin had never been inside. His grandmother had told him a hundred people lived inside, but he had a hard time imagining so many in one place. They must sleep on top of each other. And how did they feed so many? Ringforts guarded the surrounding land, which included farmland, but it still didn't seem possible.

As they came closer, the shape resolved into thin, soaring towers, connected by gossamer walkways. When the green mist faded to the surrounding hills, it revealed shimmering pearl-like walls radiating with their own light, a beacon of burnished beauty.

Fingin halted to take in the structure's wonder. Bran glanced up, puzzled. "Why did you stop?"

Unable to tear his gaze from the palace, Fingin pointed. "Do you see that? Look how beautiful it is."

Bran glanced at the structure and back to Fingin, his head cocked. "It's shiny, like fish. Do you think it's made of fish?"

Fingin stared at the dog, then burst out in laughter. He bent to hug the hound and Bran jumped around him, licking his face. "I don't think it's made of fish, Bran. In fact," he took the dog's head in his hands, his tone serious, "I should warn you now. Eat nothing they give you. All the tales tell of how people get trapped in Faerie forever if they eat the food. Do you understand me?"

Bran let out a whine. "But what if I'm hungry?"

Fingin reached into his pack and pulled out two pieces of dried fish. He wished he had something else, but nothing else remained. At least it lasted a long time. "Here, eat this. I'll eat some, too. That way we won't enter with empty stomachs. Remember."

Thus fortified, they resumed their journey. As the towers loomed closer, their shine grew ominous, with shadows dancing in the corners. Webs of gossamer silk flickered in and out of sight, disappearing whenever Fingin tried to focus on them.

A crack behind him made him whirl. Bran woofed as a tall, thin Fae strode by, ignoring them. The creature had white skin with a similar pearlescent sheen to the palace walls, with bright orange fur on his head and all the way down his spine, like a horse's mane. Fingin wanted to ask him about the castle, but he also didn't want another beating.

When he'd passed, another creature approached, a shorter Fae with squat legs, almost like a toadstool. His greenish-gray skin had a mottled texture. He stood half Fingin's height. This one *hrumphed* as he approached, evidently disgruntled by his own thoughts.

He halted when he came to Bran, who cocked his head at the Fae. "What's this? What's this? A mortal hound, here? Well, that's a different thing, indeed. And a lovely human you have, dear hound. Wherever did you find him?"

The toadstool Fae held out his gray-green hand to Fingin, as one might to a strange dog. He resisted the urge to sniff the hand. "Greetings to you, honored Fae. We're strangers here. Might we beg your help?"

"What? We? Oh, the human can speak! You've taught him well, mortal hound."

Fingin didn't know whether he should laugh or get angry. Either way, he might insult the tiny Fae.

Bran cocked his head. "I understand you. I understood the other Fae, too. Before, I only understood my friend."

The toadstool Fae glanced between hound and human a few times before he burst out into laughter. Wheezy mirth took over his entire body. A third Fae passed them as the laughter continued, a woman with ebony skin and pure white furry stripes. She glared at the shorter Fae but ignored both Bran and Fingin.

He stared at her, fascinated by her grace. She wore no clothing but the fur. Fingin couldn't take his eyes from her undulating muscles.

"Now, now, let's see. You must be new here, mortal hound. What shall I call you?"

"My name is Bran."

"Did I ask your name? No, I most definitely did not. I asked what I should call you. Not the same thing in the slightest!"

Bran shook his head. "Call me Bran."

"Very well, if that's the way you wish it. And what have you named your human?"

Fingin's anger grew stronger than his amusement. He clenched his jaw so tight his teeth ached, and Bran answered for him. "He's called Fingin. He is a true friend."

All of Fingin's annoyance melted away and he smiled at Bran.

The Fae nodded in Fingin's direction in vague approval. "I'm called Grimnaugh, and I have charge of the Silver Path. I understand someone has destroyed several pieces of the Path. Do you know anything of this?"

After remembering the dust when he had crumpled the gravel into silver dust, Fingin surreptitiously wiped his hands. He'd opened his mouth to confess when Bran said, "They sparkled like fish scales. I bit into a few, to see if they were tasty. They weren't."

Fingin clenched his jaw to keep from laughing. Or crying. He hadn't decided which.

"Hmm. Well, for a newcomer, curiosity is natural enough. I shall allow it to pass this time. Be aware, however, that in Faerie, everything belongs to the Queens. As servants of the Queen, we are charged with the care of all things. We take our responsibilities seriously."

The Fae peered up at Fingin, studying his face. Fingin stared back, noting the details of the Fae's enormous spotted nose, his flat head, and his squat toes.

"He *is* a tall one. Have you brought him as a gift for the Queen?"

Fingin let out a deep sigh. "I am here for myself, Grimnaugh. My loyal friend, Bran, is my companion. I come in search for my grandmother. Someone told me she's in Faerie, but I don't know where to start my search. I saw the castle and thought it might be a good place to ask."

Grimnaugh stared at him as if he'd sprouted a second head, but he still wore his pleasant smile. Then Fingin blinked a few times. He'd lost his stutter. Sure, he'd stuttered with the cruel Fae, but maybe that had been sheer nerves and not his normal habit. He sent a prayer of thanks to Brigit for the small favor, or Faerie, or whatever might be responsible.

The Fae continued to stare until Bran spoke up. "It's true! This is his quest. I'm just helping. He feeds me fish."

"Well, well. I suppose I should help you. No, don't fear," he held up both hands, "I won't ask payment. It's part of my duty, being in charge of the Silver Path. Since you've trod upon it, you fall within my domain. Your grandmother, eh? And who is she?"

"She'd be much older than me, with silver streaks in her black hair. She has black eyes and stands about this tall." He held his hand to his neck, measuring her height. "Her name is Clíodhna."

Grimnaugh puffed his chest and glowered. "You're having some weak jest at me, human?"

Fingin's budding confidence drained away, and he took a step back from the sudden menace in the Fae's expression, remembering his beating. "What? No, this isn't a jest. Why do you think so?"

Bran didn't growl this time, but he moved to Fingin's side. The fur on his back rose.

"Can you be unaware that Clíodhna is the name of our beloved Queen?"

Fingin sat hard on the Silver Path, possibilities and impossibilities spinning in his mind. "This must be some sort of strange coincidence. My grandmother can't be the Faerie Queen."

Grimnaugh's angry expression melted, and he placed a gnarled finger on his lips. "Indeed, indeed. She must have lived for a long time in your world. Once, the Queen went to visit her sister Queen in the north, but… no, no, she wouldn't have. Might our Queen be…human?"

Fingin remembered her power over the weather. In a dull voice, Fingin said, "Or she was Fae, pretending to be human."

With several nervous glances around them, Grimnaugh let out a sigh. "We must find out. Come along. I'll take you in."

Another Fae approached them, this one a tall, older human-looking male with ink-black hair and a long beard. Fingin felt comforted by this Fae's appearance, rather than the stranger creatures he'd thus encountered.

Rather than walking by, this Fae squinted his eyes at Fingin. "Grimnaugh, what have you done here? Why have you obtained this human?"

"I did no obtaining, Adhna. I discovered them on the Silver Path. The hound claims his human is on a quest, so I'm helping him."

The new Fae clapped his hands. "A quest? Oh, I love a good quest! I want to help. Human child, you wouldn't possess any mortal food in that pack, would you? I have a particular love of cheese. Do you have any cheese? Hmm?"

In a daze, Fingin shook his head. "No cheese, no. I have dried fish, but not much left. I wouldn't recommend it. It's old and nasty. I'm sorry."

"Ah, fair enough, then. Then it seems I must provide the food instead." He rummaged in his own pack and pulled out a round yellow fruit.

Fingin hesitated, and Adhna noticed his reticence, rolling his eyes. "Don't believe all the tales, human. I hereby declare that you… oh, what's your name?"

"Fingin."

"Right! That you, Fingin, are under no obligation for my food, drink, or hospitality until you leave this realm. Will that suffice?"

Startled, Fingin nodded and took the fruit, his mouth watering. He didn't know if that negated any debt, but he had no other ideas. As he sank his teeth into the sweet flesh, a burst of tart-sweet flavor almost overwhelmed him. Sticky juices dripped down his chin. He hastened to mop them with his fingers and then sucked the last drop from each one.

Adhna turned to the other Fae. "Come, Grimnaugh, share your wealth. What is this burning quest the human must complete?"

In a quiet, bland voice, the toadstool Fae replied, "he's looking for his grandmother. Her name is Clíodhna."

Adhna's face turned ashen, paler than the white fur of the striped Fae. He sat on the verge next to the path and stared at Grimnaugh. "Truly?"

"So it seems. We have to go to the palace to discover the truth."

Adhna shook his head, visibly agitated. "Oh, you mustn't do that, not without preparation! Come, all of you. My home isn't far. We must make certain this young human is presentable before confronting the Queen with such a claim."

The shorter Fae planted his feet and scowled. "I disagree. To keep this information from her would be more dangerous."

Adhna let out a mirthless chuckle. "You don't know her like I do, Grimnaugh. You must admit that."

Grimnaugh crossed his arms. "Oh, that's how it is, is it, beekeeper?"

With a roll of his eyes, Adhna groaned. "I'm not Bodach. This isn't a power play. But we must clean him up, at the very least. We shan't tarry long, but the fewer insults he offers to her presence, the better."

With a grumble, Grimnaugh, Fingin, and Bran followed Adhna to his home.

After a pleasant walk down the Silver Path, they took a turn at a small offshoot. Fingin hadn't noticed any offshoots or smaller paths before.

Once they turned a bend through the trees, a small roundhouse stood next to a clear pond, and buzzing bees filled the glade with song. Even without a sun, this place seemed brighter than the Silver Path.

"Wash well, human child. Scrub all your parts. I'll find you something much more appropriate to wear. An audience with the Queen must be perfect. You, too, hound. Into the water! No, it's not deep. You won't drown here. Go on, play if you like!"

He gave them both a grin and Fingin peeled off his clothing as Adhna led him to the water, all caution seeping away.

Bran bounded into the pond, splattering them with warm waves. Fingin laughed and held his hands out, but the water washed over him anyhow.

He ducked under the surface and scrubbed at his hair. He felt his chin, wondering at the scant beard he'd begun. It was thin and meager, not like Adhna's long growth. Still, he reveled in washing the remnants of sea salt from his itchy skin. And he sighed as his bruises and aching muscles relaxed in the warm water.

While he washed, Grimnaugh and Adhna had an intense discussion on the shore, but Fingin couldn't hear their words. And since the Fae heard Bran's voice, he didn't dare ask the dog to listen for him.

Should he trust these two Fae? They seemed innocuous enough and had offered to help. But if he'd learned anything from tales, he shouldn't accept a gift from them without caution.

Every gift came with a price. However true that may be, he still must look his best for any Faerie Queen, whether or not she was his grandmother. He'd do his best to balance his obligations to these helpful Fae. To turn down their help might insult them, and then he'd be in worse straits than now.

He didn't wish a second or a third Fae beating. One had been plenty, despite Brigit's healing charm.

When he emerged from the pond, dripping wet and sparkling clean, Adhna laid out a clean blue *léine*. The simple tunic came to his knees, and he tied it with a braided reed belt. He tucked Brigit's charm beneath the fabric and tied his bedraggled pack to the belt. He should wash that as well, but he didn't want to wear wet leather to this important meeting. Better grubby than soaked.

Adhna frowned at the pack, then at the place beneath his *léine* where the charm lay hidden, but gave a knowing half-smile. "Well enough. Let's attend the court and satisfy Grimnaugh's concerns."

The Silver Path sparkled again as they crunched toward the glittering castle. Shadows grew as they approached until darkness overtook the bright. Fingin's neck strained to see details in the arches they walked underneath.

Coolness enveloped him, and the height of the ceiling made him feel tiny, insignificant, even worthless. The way he felt when his father had beaten him, a filthy insect on the back of a mangy dog. Fingin shrank into himself, unwilling to let any vulnerable part of himself be exposed.

Adhna grabbed his shoulders and yanked him straight. "Stand tall, human. She won't appreciate groveling. However, never speak against her or argue. Don't turn your back on her. Eat nothing. Drink nothing. That goes for you as well, Bran."

Fingin swallowed his growing fear and tried to calm his racing heart.

The darkness increased as they walked through several hallways, each one turning and twisting upon itself. The maze seemed eternal, impossible, and several times, Fingin felt certain they must be going in circles, but the delicate, curvilinear carvings on the arches never repeated.

A light shone at the end of their tunnel, growing into painful brightness. When they arrived at the audience hall, he had to squint against the glare.

The hall teemed with beings, Fae creatures of all shapes, sizes, and colors. Some so tall they almost touched the arching translucent ceiling, with clouds rolling across a fantasy sky. Others stood no taller than Fingin's knee, and a few even smaller. Some looked like tree trunks or stone carvings, but they moved as he passed, betraying their true nature.

An aisle formed as they approached the center dais. As Fae pulled away from their progress, the figure perched upon a chair made from a living tree came into view. The chair had several tiny wrens flitting between the branches and one rested on a large apple.

Long black hair cascaded around her shoulders and down her back. Her skin shone like marble in the striking light, and her black eyes glittered.

Though she appeared much younger than he'd ever seen her, Fingin recognized his grandmother. She looked precisely as she had in his dream, when he slept in Brigit's home.

Beside her, almost as an afterthought, sat a familiar form. The bullying Fae who'd first greeted him stared from the smaller throne. His eyes fixed upon some imaginary point above their heads, as if they did not deserve the honor of his regard.

Behind them stood a young Fae, almost a boy, with snow-white skin and ink-black hair. This young Fae studied Fingin with eager delight.

The Queen spoke in frozen tones. "Adhna? What do you bring me? And Grimnaugh. I thought I sent you on a task."

Her voice resonated in Fingin's bones, but he remembered it well. That voice haunted his dreams. The happiest memories of his childhood, and sometimes the scariest, had that voice.

Fingin wanted to step forward, to make certain she saw him, recognized him, but Adhna's hand kept a firm grip on his shoulder. Instead, the tall Fae stepped forward. "We have brought a traveler, your grace. A mortal man, here on a quest to find lost kin. We would like to request leave to assist him in his quest. Do we have your permission for us to commit our time for this purpose?"

His grandmother, Queen Clíodhna of the Faerie Court, now deigned to notice him. He searched her eyes but found no recognition within them. His heart dropped, but he knew he must say nothing. She held his life in her hands.

She gave a wintry smile. "Dear Adhna. You bring me the most intriguing gifts. But this lowly creature? Why should I allow you to waste time on this? The hound is handsome, though. I might keep him."

Fingin clenched his shoulders, unwilling to let her steal Bran.

"We believe someone quite powerful sent the human, my Queen. Notice the charm."

Her eyes narrowed in sharp suspicion and the fabric around his neck grew ice cold. Fingin clapped his hand on the charm, and the entire assemblage gasped. Transfixed by her attention, he couldn't move a muscle.

"Yes, so I see. Powerful protector indeed. You may assist him, my dear Adhna. However, you know the law. He must pay for this assistance. I shall consider the wage. Perhaps I shall ask for his hound. Bring him back to me after the ball."

With a final cryptic stare at Adhna, she lifted a delicate hand. Her paralyzing regard shifted to the next petitioner, a spotted Fae with feline ears.

Once her attention moved away, the rictus in his body drained. Fingin almost slumped to the floor in relief, but Grimnaugh and Adhna hustled him through the milling Fae and out of the hall. Bran followed on their heels, almost tripping the taller Fae in his eagerness to escape.

Once outside, Bran barked several times. "What did she mean? Is she going to take me? I don't want to live in there. It smells too flowery."

Fingin focused on Bran to settle his own mind, petting his head. "Shh, Bran. No one is taking you against your will."

Grimnaugh made a noncommittal sound and Adhna frowned. The shorter Fae said, "I don't believe we can stop her if she wishes to keep the wolfhound. However, we can offer something else instead if she makes that her price."

Fingin shook his head, trying to make sense of the situation. "Can't I just leave? That was without doubt my grandmother, but she didn't even recognize me. I may have succeeded in my quest, but I don't know what to do now."

Both Adhna and Grimnaugh shook their heads with vigor. The toadstool Fae made a rude noise. "She's commanded us to return you after the ball. That's a command you dare not disobey, nor may we. We must deliver you upon pain of punishment."

Adhna nodded. "You don't want to incur the Queen's wrath. We must avoid her fury at all costs. Only once did I brave her displeasure, and never again shall I risk such a strait."

"What did you do?"

The older Fae pursed his lips. "That, young man, is something I cannot tell you."

Chapter Twelve

From that point on, Adhna took Fingin under his wing, to teach him how to act, speak, and dance in the Fae court. Grimnaugh took his leave, having his own preparations to make.

As he stumbled a fifth time, Fingin whined. "Must I dance, Adhna?"

"This is the Faerie Queen's ball. Not only must you dance, you must dance well."

"How do we know I have to be there? She said after the ball, didn't she?"

Adhna narrowed his gaze. "We don't. However, not to attend would be an insult. Do you wish to insult her?"

Fingin let out a deep breath. "Show me the steps again. I'll try not to step on your feet."

The complex interaction of dancers hadn't been easy to learn with only two, so after he taught Fingin the basic moves, Adhna recruited help. Six more Fae arrived to complete their set.

"Please greet Gnathnad, Tomnat, Uasal, and Airiu." Four females nodded in unison, their hair varying from white-blond to midnight dark, and their skin in various shades of brown and green. The last one, a young woman with a mischievous grin, winked at him. Fingin flushed and looked away.

"And here we have Cúan and Némán." The two dark-haired Fae men also nodded, but with grimmer expressions.

They paired into four sets. Adhna assigned Fingin with Airiu, and she flashed him another smile before they began. With slow claps, Adhna called out their movements.

To Fingin's relief, he barely fumbled the complex steps in the first pass. However, just as they finished, he tripped over Airiu's feet and fell on his side with a surprised grunt. Bran, who'd been watching from the sides, let out a yip which Fingin could swear sounded more like a laugh.

Airiu helped him to his feet. "Just let me guide you where you need to move. I know this dance well."

Fingin shook his head. "I don't doubt you are an expert, but you might not be with me at the ball. I must learn this for myself."

Her blue eyes flashed. "Would you deny my help, then?"

He caught his breath, terrified of insulting yet another Fae. "By no means! I welcome your teaching, fair Airiu."

The Fae woman's smile returned, and his heart raced. Suddenly, he wanted to keep her smiling more than anything.

Fingin's world narrowed to the two of them, stepping through the complex dance once, twice, six times.

Finally, Adhna declared victory. "This dance is done! We shall meet again for the next one after a meal and a rest."

Flush from both his success and Airiu standing next to him, Fingin now gaped at Adhna's comment. "The next one? There are more?"

All the Fae laughed, a cascade from a trickling brook across his ears. Tomnat said, "There are countless dances, human. We could teach you a new dance after every meal for a turn of the seasons in the mortal world, and you'd still never learn them all. No human can hope to learn all the Faerie dances."

This set off another round of laughter, and Fingin's cheeks burned. Airiu held his hand. "Pay no mind to Tomnat. She enjoys tormenting humans." She sent a sidelong glance to the other Fae, who grinned back.

"Sometimes she goes out to the mortal world just to ruin their lives for fun."

Ruined their lives. Would this quest ruin his life? Before all this, his life had been empty. He'd fished, eaten, sold his goods, and slept. At least Bran had provided companionship, someone to work toward supporting.

Since he'd embarked on this journey, he'd nearly died several times, mourned the loss of Bran at least once, and angered several Fae. He couldn't tell if this was an improvement over a listless life or not.

Despite all that, at the moment, sitting next to a lovely Fae woman with a kind heart and a quick smile, eating fruit and honey, he thought life might just have improved.

Némán cleared his throat, and he launched into a song as they ate, a mournful tune of love lost. Fingin had never heard such a splendid voice, the warmth of the notes caressing him like a warm wool blanket on an icy night. Tears pricked behind his eyes, and he surreptitiously wiped them away, horrified that Airiu might notice them.

She smiled and touched his tear with a gentle finger, bringing it to her lips with a kiss.

Fingin had never understood the tales of mad love, love that started with first sight, love that burned so bright within the heart it obliterated all concerns.

Now, however, he had a glimmer. He swallowed, trying to think of something to say, anything at all. But he forgot how words worked.

Airiu bit into a red berry that might have been a strawberry, if it had grown in his world. "Will you be in Faerie for long, Fingin?"

Still unable to speak, he shrugged. She took another bite, and said, "I hope so. Dancing with you has been lovely. I never danced with a mortal man before. You make funny faces when you make a mistake." She giggled, her eyes dancing.

He wanted to repeat all the mistakes he'd ever made, just to make funny faces for her.

Némán finished singing, and in the silence, Fingin felt like he'd lost something precious. After several moments, Tomnat stood, gathering attention. "I would tell the story of tragic love, the only kind that lasts."

Airiu let out a snort, increasing Fingin's regard for her. Tomnat seemed jaded toward the glorious possibilities of love. Of course, Fingin had been of the same opinion just the day before.

Tomnat's voice carried across the clearing, strident with confidence. Curly dark hair tipped with green framed her face, and her skin glowed with the same color. Her eyes flashed with intelligence and a good dose of cynicism. She reminded Fingin of his grandmother when he knew her as a human.

The reminder of his grandmother as a Faerie Queen made his blood grow cold again.

He needed to escape after the Faerie Queen settled her payment for Grimnaugh's and Adhna's help. How ironic that their help had been for naught, as the person he wanted them to find was the Queen herself.

Why had Brigit sent him on this quest? She must have known his grandmother was the Queen. The tales told of at least five different Queens across the land of Faerie, perhaps more, but not so many that Brigit would miss one.

The other part of the quest was to retrieve the magical brooch, the one that gave him the ability to speak with Bran and other animals. His skin crawled with the notion he must take something from the Faerie Queen. He'd be lucky to escape Faerie with his life, much less with a magical artifact she surely kept close.

He glanced at Adhna, munching on a large yellow fruit. Grimnaugh had returned and was speaking in low whispers to Tomnat. The Fae woman frowned and glanced toward Fingin. When she noticed him watching her, she flashed him a seductive smile and then let out a cruel laugh. His cheeks burned again.

How could he complete that part of his quest? He grasped Brigit's charm, hoping for some inspiration.

Airiu cocked her head. "Why do you clutch at your chest, Fingin? Have you pain?"

He released the pendant and shook his head. "No, but I have some decisions to make. I don't know what to do. I was praying for an answer."

"Why do you touch your chest for answers?"

He chuckled, charmed by her question. "I have a token, given to me by someone I respect. I wished her wisdom might help me with my decision."

She gave him a knowing smile and touched his arm. "Perhaps I can help you in her stead."

Asking a subject of the Faerie Queen to help him steal an object from the same Queen didn't sound wise to him. That's why he hadn't told Adhna or Grimnaugh of this portion of his quest.

Fingin shook his head. "I need to figure this out for myself, but I thank you for offering. That's kind of you."

However, once he completed his mission and satisfied Brigit's quest, he meant to speak to Airiu at some length about her plans. Maybe he could convince her to include him in whatever she planned. Perhaps he'd found someone he'd be happy with.

As the others left the glade to get ready, Fingin watched Airiu leave. She gave one last look over her shoulder, her eyes inviting. The not-quite-butterflies that swarmed outside Adhna's cottage had taken residence within Fingin's stomach.

Bran whined. "Are you certain I can't come to the ball? I'd rather stay with you. I don't like some of those Fae. They smelled strange."

He patted the hound's back. "I'm certain. Grimnaugh thinks if the Faerie Queen doesn't see you again, she'll forget her desire to keep you. You're much safer in Adhna's home. Promise me you'll stay here?"

Bran shifted from foot to foot. A bee buzzed around his head and he snapped at it, but the bee flew away too fast to catch.

Fingin picked at the edge of his new clothing, a length of fabric which wrapped around his hips and over his shoulder. Despite the brass pins which held it in place, he was terrified it would fall off if he moved. The warm sunset colors blended into his skin. Airiu had told him he looked lovely, though.

Grimnaugh examined him from head to bare feet, making clicking noises as he went. "She has an idea, I can feel it. She will ask you for something big, and you must accept. If no, well, I'm not sure what she'll do. I *am* sure you won't like it."

The walk to the palace seemed much shorter than the first time. Fingin's nervousness grew as the towers loomed closer, the shadows growing more ominous. Even the glittering pearlescence seemed to be a warning, a flicker of certain doom.

What would the Queen ask him for? In the back of his mind, he harbored the idea that his grandmother might recognize him at the last minute and draw him into her arms for a warm hug. Another, more rational part of his mind scoffed at this idea. His grandmother had never been the nurturing type, given to long hugs and sentimental gestures.

The Fae they passed made no secret of staring at him. A mortal man amongst the ethereal Fae was a true novelty, even without his hound by his side. Each one dressed in superb finery, impossible costumes of shifting colors, translucent material, or soaring sculptures.

The Fae with black skin and white fur stripes had donned an outfit with opposite stripes in varying shades of gray, from pale eggshell to deep stormcloud. Each shade swirled within its stripe, making Fingin dizzy.

The summer scent of flowers grew intense, almost overpowering. Flowers, fresh-cut grass, cloves, and ginger.

Another Fae appeared, and Fingin recognized the bark-skinned bully who'd beaten him. This one glared at him, but Adhna kept a firm grip on Fingin's shoulder and sent a warning glance at the other. With a disgusted noise, the bully stomped away behind a group of chatting on-lookers.

The center dais housed the thrones, but no Faerie Queen or Consort sat upon them yet. Fingin let out a breath of relief, though his fate was merely delayed. Adhna nodded to several Fae as they passed but didn't mingle. Grimnaugh disappeared amongst the crowd.

The general buzz of conversation shifted as Fingin passed, the questioning tones increasing with the laughter. He did his best to ignore the obvious mocking tones. With every giggle or chuckle, he remembered his brothers' taunting voices and the physical pain which always followed. He wished he'd been able to bring Bran. The charm around his neck felt icy against his skin, and he resisted the urge to grasp it for comfort.

Silence flowed across the hall and all eyes turned to the far end, where the Queen stood. She was resplendent in what appeared to be a structure of white ice and icicles, sparkling snow, and gossamer webs.

Her Consort, the bark-skinned bully Fae, held her arm and escorted her across the translucent floor.

How she moved without breaking the fine threads, Fingin couldn't tell. She glimmered and glistened as she sauntered to her throne. Her midnight-black curls stood out in sharp contrast to the pure white, and her black eyes glittered against her pale skin.

As her gaze cast around the room, it halted when it fell upon Fingin. A half-smile played across her berry-red lips. The bully Fae sat next to her on the second throne and glared at him, menace clear in his gaze.

She clapped her hands twice, and all Fae backed away, forming an empty aisle before her. Somewhere, musicians played ethereal music, sweet and compelling. Several Fae stepped forward to make their sets. Adhna shoved him forward. "Go. You must dance in the first dance. See, there is Tomnat. She'll be your partner."

The brown-haired Fae woman matched him in height. As he placed his hands on hers for the opening set, she smiled. "Airiu said she liked you, human. Such a pity."

Before he could ask her to explain, they launched into the dance, swirling and twirling to the melody. He mostly kept up, only stumbling once or twice between the graceful Fae. The flowing fabric of his outfit merged with others as they turned, the swish of contact a pleasant counterpoint to the Fae music.

Out of the corner of his eye, he spied Airiu's ebony hair, flowing against her back as she danced with a tall, thin Fae with spots. She winked at him as they passed, an ephemeral promise he kept close to his heart. Perhaps, after the ball, after the Queen made her payment known, he'd be permitted to talk with Airiu more. She might even be interested in talking to him.

His cheeks grew warm again, and Tomnat laughed.

The Queen clapped again, and the dance ended with a graceful flourish. Another aisle formed as every being watched for her next command.

The Queen's escort whispered in her ear, pointing at Fingin. She glanced at him, still standing next to Tomnat, and smiled.

Her smile chilled his bones. "Come forward, human."

Fingin could no more disobey her command than he could take wing and fly across the countryside. He stepped forward, his eyes glued to the floor. He didn't dare meet her gaze.

"You came to my land seeking something. You elicited help from my subjects. You have incurred a debt due to me. I will now name my price for the help you've received."

Fingin wanted to scream that he hadn't asked for help, Grimnaugh and Adhna had offered it freely. That he hadn't gotten what he came for, and his quest was a failure. But his mouth refused to form any words. His muscles would not obey his commands.

Instead, his knees buckled and an unseen force pushed him to the floor. He knelt, sweat dripping down his neck.

"In days past, I might send you back to your world with some ghastly disfigurement. Perhaps a hump upon your back, or blindness. However, there is one here who has begged me to spare you this punishment, and I have conceded to their wishes."

Someone spoke on his behalf? Had it been Adhna? Airiu? Perhaps Grimnaugh had put in a good word for him.

"Tomnat, step forward."

The tall Fae girl flashed him a sly smile and bowed before her Queen. She stood again, while Fingin remained kneeling.

"Tomnat, you have asked to mate with this human?"

She lowered her head once in agreement. "I have, your Grace."

The Queen peered at Fingin, the disdain plain on her face. "Why would you ask such a thing?"

"I crave children, your Grace. I've had none so far."

The Queen waved a hand toward him. "You think this…this pitiful creature will grant you a child?"

"I do. I see great potential in him. Humans are often more fertile than our kind."

The Queen made a sound that, in a less graceful creature, may have been termed as rude. "Very well. You shall be contracted this night."

Fingin's panic took over his mind. He froze, unable to process what the Queen had said. Mate? Tonight? To Tomnat? *No, no, that was all wrong. Airiu, yes, please, let me be with Airiu.* If he must be tied to a stranger, let it be someone who showed him kindness, not sarcasm and disdain.

A flurry of activity whirled around them as various Fae rushed to make the hall ready for the ceremony. Tomnat disappeared into this bustle. Fingin sought Airiu but she'd vanished. Adhna's firm grip on his shoulders moved him from his position, kneeling before the Queen, into the hallway.

Once the door shut upon the madness, the screaming in his mind calmed. Adhna said nothing until they were outside the palace itself.

Grimnaugh joined them, his expression grim. Adhna gave Grimnaugh a few urgent commands and the shorter Fae exited on his mission.

The tall Fae turned to Fingin. "Your present clothing will do, but we'll return to my home so I can teach you the ceremony. You must perform without error, do you understand?"

He nodded once, still numb with shock. As they traveled back to Adhna's home, his mind whirled with images, possibilities, and many fears.

Adhna pursed his lips. "Now, Grimnaugh thought something strange was afoot, but he didn't expect this. I suspect Bodach saw you eying Airiu. He's the Queen's companion tonight, and he seems to have developed a distinct dislike for you. That's not a good thing. However, Tomnat must have made her request after our dancing lesson."

Fingin pushed some words through his lips. "Why? I don't understand why. She doesn't even like me."

"She dislikes everyone, young man. You're no different. However, she's wanted children for an age. Fae don't reproduce easily, you see. Perhaps one, two children at most in all their long lifetimes. We live much longer than humans, but our lives are much less eventful, on the whole. Fae often seek humans for such stud duties. We visit women in the dark of the night, or spirit men away under the full moon. You had the singular misfortune of being the first human to come to our realm in a long time. Had I suspected... but I did not. I thought Airiu and you might enjoy each other's company. I am sorry. My own meddling might have made this happen."

Fingin hung his head. "I have no way to refuse this, do I?"

"I'm afraid not. Oh, I could lead you back through to your own realm, but you'd forever be on the run from the Queen, and Tomnat besides. Neither one appreciates rejection, and both are powerful in the mortal world."

Fingin glanced up at the older Fae. "Have you lived in the mortal world?"

He clapped Fingin's shoulder. "Many times, Fingin. Many times. In fact, I get the itch to return on a fairly regular basis. Your world provides many lovely luxuries we find difficult to get here in Faerie. Cheese is my particular favorite. Cows don't care for Faerie, and we have difficulty convincing them to produce milk if we bring them here. Also, most Fae are rather reluctant to put in the work required for creating things like cheese. They'd rather either do without or obtain it from elsewhere."

"Which are you?"

Adhna let out a rueful chuckle. "The latter. Though I prepare my own when I live there. I find it satisfying to eat the product of my own hands. A pleasure, alas, many of my kind don't understand." He let out a deep sigh and stared into space. "Now, back to the matter at hand. We must prepare you for your wedding."

His stomach started flipping. "Wedding? I thought it was just a mating?"

Adhna waved his hand. "It comes to the same thing for the Fae. A contract is a sacred vow."

"Wait, can I speak to Airiu? I want to make sure she knows… that she knows I'd much rather have…"

The Fae placed a hand on his shoulder. "She knows, young man. She knows. I saw her face when the Queen made her proclamation. She left shortly thereafter."

Pain clenched at Fingin's heart. He'd received his reward for hoping to be happy, for grasping that glimmer of possibility. When would he remember not to wish for things outside his grasp? He should have learned from his past that happiness was forever out of reach.

They came into sight of Adhna's home, and Bran bounded out to meet them. Fingin gave him a hug, but said, "I can't play just yet. I have more lessons to learn, Bran."

Adhna drilled him on where he must stand, what he must say, what he must not do, under any circumstances. He made Fingin practice his moves and his words. The Queen might send for them to attend the ceremony at any moment, so they had no luxury to rest or relax.

Bran watched all these preparations with a mixture of interest and boredom. When he grew bored, he chased the almost-butterflies or romped in the pond, startling several aquatic creatures to the point they complained loudly, at least to Fingin's mind. He called the hound to task and chastised him for chasing the wildlife. Then he dove back into his own lessons.

After what seemed like an interminable time and still not enough, a messenger Fae arrived.

Fingin crouched in front of Bran. "You must remain here again, understand? Will you leave the fish alone?"

Bran let out a yip. "They're not like other fish. Do they taste different?"

"I don't know, and you shouldn't find out. They're in Adhna's pond, and they've asked you not to chase them. You need to be a courteous guest."

Bran pouted but didn't argue. Fingin narrowed his gaze at the hound, then turned back to the Fae.

Adhna gave him a final examination on his duties, and they were about to leave for the palace when a laugh behind them made them turn.

The bark-skinned Fae stood next to Bran, who growled and snarled at the sudden visitor. "So, you are off to your wedding. What a felicitous day. I shall watch after your lovely hound, shall I?"

Fingin clenched his fists until his knuckles ached, wanting to punch the smug smile from the Fae's face. "Bran can watch after himself."

Adhna stepped forward, his hands out. "Now, now, no need for all that. Bodach, we don't need your assistance here. Thank you for the offer, but we're prepared. Will you accompany us to the ceremony? I assume the Queen expects you to attend as Consort."

Bodach frowned, the bark around his mouth crinkling and creaking. He glanced down at Bran, whose hackles were high, and then at Fingin, whose fists ached. "Very well. I shall escort you to your sentence. I mean, your nuptials."

With a nasty grin, he patted Bran's head with condescending care, while the dog gave a low growl. "The hound might want to visit later, when you're tending to your bride. He might grow lonely for lack of attention."

Fingin didn't trust leaving Bran alone. He turned to Adhna. "Can Grimnaugh stay with Bran during this?"

The older Fae shook his head and crossed his arms. "I'm afraid not. He must attend. The hound should be safe enough until we're done."

As a child, Fingin had imagined he would someday grow up, find a wife, raise a family, and work a farm. Everyone else he knew had done this, except the neighbor's eldest son, who'd gone off to study with the druí.

But when his grandmother had left and stolen his voice, that dream changed, shifting to a more solitary life. But he still thought if he could find a girl to marry him anyhow, their wedding would be a joyful occasion attended by friends and family. Good food, dancing, singing, perhaps a few stories.

This wedding bore a poor resemblance to his fantasy. This was more like a contract, a business arrangement, rather than any pledge of undying love and loyalty. No romance or passion marred the ceremony.

Within a grove of strange trees, Fingin held both of his bride's hands, trying his best to avoid her eyes. Colorful bunting floating around him and the trees sang an ethereal descant. He fought the urge to run away, screaming.

Every second his legs and heart begged him to flee, to fight, to protest this marriage. At the same time, his entire body was rooted in place, unable to move a muscle.

Other than the bunting and the singing trees, little resembled a human wedding ceremony. While a few Fae courtiers attended as witnesses, no grand ball or procession marked the celebrants.

Adhna stood stiffly by his side, exchanging a curious, intimate glance with the Queen.

Fingin wore his sunset-colored draped clothing while Tomnat was clad in the shifting green and blue outfit she wore to the ball. The moving colors made him nauseous if he watched it too long.

Her hair hadn't changed from its dark curls tipped with green. She had worn a pendant, something swirling and silver, but he couldn't focus on it. His mind whirled as they stood before the Faerie Queen, his own grandmother, who didn't even recognize him.

Queen Clíodhna wore her sparkling snow-white dress and chanted in words he couldn't quite understand. Some ancient language, old words he almost recognized, a lyrical speech from another age.

Under his breath, Adhna translated for him. "This union is to last for the length of two live births. Until that time, the participants shall live together as the humans do in marriage, avowing all others, and care for any progeny resulting from their union."

Nothing about loving, cherishing, or honoring the other. Nothing about being bound for the rest of their lives. Nothing about vows or promises before any god. A business contract and nothing more.

Queen Clíodhna performed the ceremony with Bodach by her side. Adhna and Grimnaugh stood in for Fingin's family, while Airiu and Uasal stood with Tomnat. The patent misery in Airiu's eyes mirrored his own, but they couldn't even speak to each other.

Fingin gave up trying to connect with his bride and instead looked into Airiu's eyes. He fell into the blue sky of her desire. The world around him swirled into gray nothing. The wedding, the Faerie Queen, his bride-to-be, all vanished.

Airiu returned his gaze but moisture glistened in the corners of her eyes in sad surrender. He blinked to stem his own, and the surrounding world returned.

The Faerie Queen told each of them to agree to their contract. When Tomnat said, "I so vow," he repeated the words. Bodach clapped his hands twice, and the brief, brutal ceremony was complete.

The floating bunting disappeared. The trees silenced. Adhna hovered near his shoulder, but the Faerie Queen hadn't finished with them. She leaned in to hug Tomnat, holding her in a brief embrace. Then, to his intense surprise, she did the same to Fingin.

With a furious whisper, she said, "Be careful and quiet for now, my grandson. I'm not free to act as I wish. I will work to get you out of Faerie. Bide your time."

Chapter Thirteen

The small pavilion was open on all sides, except for sheer fabric draped on edge. A soft, round cushion lay inside, big enough to have filled his entire roundhouse back in the mortal realm.

Tomnat took his hand with cold detachment and led him to the cushion. She still hadn't spoken with him apart from their exchange of vows, or even glanced at him. He got the impression that this entire arrangement would be nothing but a task to achieve her desire for children.

She pushed aside one edge of the fabric and they both entered. Once the fabric fell again, the outside was awash with pale mystery. Their entire world narrowed to this intimate space.

Tomnat undressed, folding each item and placing them on the floor. He followed her actions, embarrassed at his nakedness in front of his new avowed mate.

Fingin couldn't call her his wife. The ceremony had been nothing but an exchange of contract terms. Any romance or beauty of a human marriage had been stripped down to bare bones.

The entire day had been unreal. The bare-bones ceremony, the contract, the words his grandmother had whispered in his ear. Those words rattled in his mind, but he had no time to think of that now.

His Fae mate sat cross-legged and naked across from him. They stared at each other, meeting eyes for the first time since they'd danced at Adhna's home.

She let out a sigh. "Very well. I don't imagine you have the needed experience. Lie on your back." She placed her hand on his chest and pushed him back. Exposed and vulnerable, he swallowed.

She climbed atop him and rubbed herself against his groin. His body reacted, despite his affection for Airiu. He hadn't expected this betrayal but was powerless to stop. She rubbed until she judged the time right, shifted, and inserted him into her warmth. He closed his eyes, unable to resist enjoying the incredible sensation.

It didn't last long. His reaction came quick and violent. When he'd finished, she dismounted and dressed. "You may return to Adhna's now. If required, we will try again. I will find you."

Tomnat left. Fingin lay in his own mess, aghast at both her methodical actions and his unintended reaction.

What had he expected from such an encounter? Relations between his parents had been no mystery. A small roundhouse hid few things. He'd witnessed animals mating all his life. But even animals had more complex courting than he'd just had with Tomnat. He was a means to an end and nothing else. She'd never even called him by his name.

After wiping his mess with leaves from the surrounding glade, he dressed and walked back down the path, his legs feeling odd.

The colorful trees seemed muted now. Without day or night, without weather or seasons, this land made him uneasy and off-balance. Time was difficult to measure by any familiar means.

Fingin walked toward his new home, the place he must live until Tomnat conceived his child. He felt like a prize bull, set out to stud against his own will. Did women feel this helpless when their fathers married them to a wealthy farmer? Most women he'd met at least had some say in their husbands, but arranged marriages happened all the time, especially for those with great wealth.

202

Adhna's roundhouse came into view. He glanced around for Bran but didn't see him. The hound might be inside sleeping the day away. Rest sounded wonderful. Fingin hoped Sean was safe in the mortal world, and that he'd given up on them returning to find his own way.

Adhna walked out his door just as Fingin arrived. "Ah, there you are, young man. I would ask if you enjoyed your nuptial bliss, but I can tell by the look on your face it was less than you'd hoped."

He nodded, peering inside. Nothing seemed to stir. "I never imagined such a wedding. Is Bran sleeping inside? Did he eat?"

Adhna glanced inside and turned back to Fingin, rubbing the back of his neck. "About that. Bran has, uh, found a temporary home. Just for a little while, mind you, until the first portion of your contract is complete."

"What?" His heart raced and he shoved the Fae aside. Fingin ran into the roundhouse, searching for any trace for his friend. "Bran? Bran, where are you? Bran!"

"Settle down, young man, settle down. He'll be well-cared for. Grimnaugh promised to keep an eye on him."

"He's with Grimnaugh? Where? Is he…is he safe?"

Adhna put his hands up. "He's not with Grimnaugh. He's with Bodach. But Grimnaugh promised me, a solemn vow, mind you, that he'd check on the hound regularly. You'll be permitted to see him occasionally."

"Permitted? Permitted?" Fingin's voice pitched higher with each word, touched with an edge of hysteria and a good dose of anger. "Who's permitting this? Who allowed Bodach to steal away my friend, my companion? This isn't right! I made the vow already. That vow should be enough to keep me here until my contract is complete. There's no need to hold my friend hostage!"

Adhna's eyes had turned sad, and he shook his head. "Bodach insisted, and so the Queen has commanded. Since you're a human unknown to us, he wanted surety of your obedience. This isn't an unusual demand. He wouldn't dare hurt Bran."

Fingin took a deep breath and tried to calm his heart. If he hadn't brought Bran to this place, he'd be free and happy in the mortal world, rather than a hostage to a cruel Fae lord. Why did he have to destroy everything he loved with his horrible decisions? Why had he acted so selfishly?

His hands curled into tight fists as he said, in a tight voice, "Adhna, I like and respect you, but let me tell you now. If Bodach, for whatever reason, harms Bran, I will make him pay for that hurt."

Adhna gave him a stern smile and clapped him on the shoulder. "Young man, if it comes to that eventuality, I vow you shall have my enthusiastic and wholehearted support."

Life became an odd mixture of domestic normality at Adhna's roundhouse and expectant anticipation for Tomnat's conception. Fingin helped Adhna around his home, learned more dances, and listened to stories about the Fae court.

He missed Bran sorely, but Grimnaugh visited every day with news of his hound's health, and a few pithy comments about how the dog did his best to make his host's life less convenient. Sometimes, the stories even made Fingin smile.

Other Fae came by for a visit, including Airiu. Fingin suspected she only came with other Fae to avoid any hint he might violate Tomnat's contract, but he didn't care.

The time he spent with her was the highlight of his life. They did nothing untoward but chatted about their lives and the things they loved. She taught him songs of the Fae and he taught her stories from his own world.

Airiu also taught him how to weave. Certainly, he'd woven and plaited things all his life. But Airiu had the ability to create lovely, lacey patterned mats and baskets from a variety of unusual materials. With patient hands, she showed him how to create such beauty for himself. He'd never have her level of talent, but she taught him basic patterns and techniques.

Each day, Bodach also visited. Sometimes, if he saw Fingin sitting with Airiu, he strode up with a deriding smirk and rude comments. "One Fae woman isn't enough for you, human boy? You must come and steal all our women?"

Fingin tried not to rise to the Fae Lord's bait. He'd bite his tongue and clench his jaw.

Bodach deepened his smile and traced his finger along Airiu's jaw. "Such a lovely young thing. I'd like to bed you myself. I wonder what sort of noises you would make with a real lover?"

The Fae woman looked away, obviously uncomfortable with Bodach's attentions.

Fingin's fists clenched, and his restraint flew away. "Leave her alone!"

"Oh, so the young pup has some baby teeth! Be cautious, youngling. Your hound is still in my care, did you forget? You must behave yourself or the cur might suffer. I still find it odd the Queen let you go with such a light contract. Do you have influence over her? Share your secrets, young human."

Airiu put a gentle hand on his upper arm. "Be still, Fingin. He only does this to rouse you, can't you see? He cannot harm Bran unless you give him a reason to. And teasing me is nothing. You forget I'm three times your mortal age. This is not the first time I've dealt with an unpleasant suitor."

Bodach placed his hands upon Airiu's cheek, leering with a wicked smile. "I can be most pleasant."

She hissed, her teeth now pointed with wicked sharpness. Her eyes had turned to cat-slits and her nails grew like talons. She raked said nails across Bodach's hand where it still touched her cheek. "Begone, foul creature. I do not want your touch, nor will I tolerate your taunts. Go crawl back to your Queen and pray she defends you from the consequences of your own actions."

Bodach's skin turned a paler brown, and his eyes grew wide. He took a few steps back, but Airiu's teeth, eyes, and nails had already reverted to their lovely form, as if nothing had happened.

Fingin glanced between the two Fae, remembering he was but a stranger in this land, a mere human amongst magical Fae, with no way to protect himself should any of them turn against him.

Once the bully left, Fingin no longer had a taste for company. He retreated to the roundhouse and curled up in his bed, unable to face anyone yet.

Fingin didn't have days and nights to regulate his sleep, so he took to his rest whenever he grew tired, overwhelmed, or bored. This seemed to be more and more often as time marched on. He didn't need to work to feed himself, as Adhna provided plenty of food. While he enjoyed learning the songs and dances from the Fae, the pursuit of knowledge had never been a particular joy for him, so it didn't drive him like it might a bard or druid.

He just needed to complete his contracted vows with Tomnat and retrieve Bran so they could return to their own world. Other than the brief physical encounter with the other Fae woman, he had no way to make that happen any faster. He must wait.

And he didn't like waiting.

Many sleeps later, Tomnat visited them, triumph clear upon her face. "I have conceived. Your contract is half done. As a reward for your success, I have brought your hound. You must now wait until the child is born alive, then we shall create the second one."

Fingin opened his mouth to say thank you, but she turned on her heel and walked away, her message delivered. His gaze flickered around wildly. "Bran? Bran, where are you?"

The woof behind him made him spin, and Bran jumped on his chest, knocking him to the ground.

He laughed as Bran licked his face, his hands, his neck, any place the dog found open skin. He hugged his friend so tight, the dog yipped. "I'm so glad to see you! Did he hurt you at all? Did he treat you well?"

"He fed me. He let me run. That's all. He never stayed with me. That's good, because he smelled bad. Like rotten trees. I don't like him. Don't make me go back to him, please?"

"I won't, Bran! If I can help it, I'll never let them take you away from me again."

Fingin was still bound to Faerie, but at least he had Bran for company. Airiu came almost every day now. She and Bran formed a strong friendship, though she couldn't hear his words. They developed a crude way of communicating through bodily actions and different sounds. With some work, they developed a basic level of understanding.

After a time, Fingin began to enjoy this lazy life. While he kept an underlying guilt for creating nothing, doing nothing to earn his keep, Adhna assured him that he had the status of a welcome guest, and he should treasure his respite from mortal life.

"I've lived in your world. I remember how difficult it is just to keep enough food to eat every day, much less to protect yourself from the weather, the people, and the dangerous ideas."

"Dangerous ideas?"

"Oh, yes, ideas can be dangerous. They can be quite exhilarating, but mostly they're dangerous. Ideas mean change, you see. While change itself can be good, reactions to change often results in much danger for both your people and mine."

Fingin recalled the new religion and his parents' feuds with those who still followed the old religion. Aideen, young Lorcan's mother, had also been contentious about this new idea. Maybe Adhna had a point.

Fingin didn't think he lived by any new ideas. He cast his net, cleaned his fish, and sold them at market. Nothing new about those actions. People had fished there for countless generations. However, Fingin created no art, no stories, no songs. He preached no ideas, no inventions, no religion.

He existed. Much as he did now, but in more comfort. Would that be enough?

He glanced at Airiu, working out the words to a new song with Uasal. She let out a laugh, a joyful sound that tickled his ears and made him smile, though he didn't know what she was laughing about. To create such joy by making something beautiful, that would be a great purpose, a goal to strive for.

To be fair, he'd created a child with Tomnat. Children often created joy, and they grew and created their own beauty in the world. Perhaps that would be his purpose, to create children of light, children with Fae blood to make the world a brighter place. He might have a son who sang beautiful songs, or a daughter who carved wooden figures.

For a moment, he felt grateful for his contrived vow as a chance to create children who would never have lived, but for the Faerie Queen's command.

He gazed at Airiu, wishing the command had been with her, rather than Tomnat. However, once his vow with Tomnat was over, perhaps Airiu would want to enter a similar vow with him, one with more romance and passion.

Airiu glanced up and caught his gaze. Fingin felt his cheeks burn and he glanced away, thankful that she couldn't read his thoughts.

He held this hope as a salve through the interminable wait for Tomnat's birthing. He still had to conceive a second child to complete the terms. In the meantime, he enjoyed Airiu's delightful company.

The image of her sharp teeth flashed into his memory, and he shivered. Even enchanting beauty had its dark side. He'd best keep that in mind with any of the Fae. Tomnat, Airiu, even Adhna must have a feral face.

He didn't doubt Tomnat had several. The taciturn, surly woman haunted his dreams, though he'd seen her but once since the ceremony.

More often, Airiu was in his dreams, where he fantasized about lying with her, instead of Tomnat, a loving embrace rather than a perfunctory one. During his slumber, they reveled in each other's bodies, exchanging joy.

Bodach sometimes interrupted his deep dreams with Airiu. The bark-skinned Fae would intrude upon their idyll and pull Airiu away with rough hands. Sometimes Fingin fought the other Fae. Sometimes he failed. Either way, he woke up in a cold sweat and short of breath.

Thus, more time passed. He had an amiable host, few duties, and the pleasure of Airiu's company. Who could ask for more?

Eventually, Tomnat returned, carrying a small bundle. Had she given birth already? He didn't think so much time had passed, but he had no way to tell. Perhaps she had spent time in the mortal world, which ran at a different rate than Faerie.

Her face showed the gentlest expression she'd yet worn. Her almost tender smile as she gazed upon her child made Fingin smile in response. "Is this our child?"

She nodded, offering the bundle to him. "We have a son."

He cradled the swathed baby in his arms and pushed aside the flap covering the child's face. Bright blue eyes blinked at him, then crinkled up as the child's face turned red. The babe fussed and burbled, working up to a proper cry.

Fingin held the baby against his chest, rocking and humming to it. The child quieted and made curious sounds, inquisitive gurgles. His son reached for a strand of his hair, pulling hard enough to make Fingin's eyes water.

This babe, this child, was his son. A shard of himself and of Tomnat, someone who would always carry a piece of his heart. His eyes were glued to the clear blue ones staring back. The skin on the child's fingers seemed translucent, too delicate to touch. Dark curling hair peeked out from under the swaddling fabric.

He glanced at Tomnat, delight still radiating from him. "Have you chosen a name?"

She gave a quick shake of her head. "That is your prerogative, as he's male. What would you like to call him?"

Fingin gazed into at his son's eyes. "He must be strong and fierce. I think 'Conall' would be a good name, which means fierce wolf."

Tomnat reached out for the baby, and reluctantly, Fingin released the child to her care. He still couldn't take his eyes from his son. The Fae woman flashed him a smile, gone as soon as it appeared. "Conall it shall be, then. I shall return another to time begin his sibling."

She turned and left with the babe, leaving Fingin agape and empty, yet strangely satisfied that he'd helped create something, even if that delight had been snatched from his care so quickly.

Fingin lay awake in Adhna's roundhouse, Bran a warmth against his side. Voices outside drifted in, some urgency in the sound making him strain to hear the words.

"I've heard of such ceremonies, Adhna. The humans celebrate the date they were born. The Queen told me that his is coming soon. We must do something to make him feel as comfortable as possible. We should create a celebration!"

"Grimnaugh, are you mad? We don't know what that even looks like."

"Me? I'm mad? You're the one always going about with bees in your beard."

Adhna huffed. "Is it a crime to like honey?"

"Regardless, we should have a celebration. Gifts. Decorations. Singing. Dancing."

"What sort of decorations?"

Grimnaugh snorted. "How in Danu's name should I know? Just something… festive. Colorful. Pretty."

"Colorful and pretty. Are you sure this isn't just a ploy to bring more females to my home? So you can dance the day away?"

Fingin could hear the grin in Grimnaugh's response. "I wouldn't be opposed to the idea, but no. That isn't my purpose."

With a low chuckle, Adhna walked away. Grimnaugh must have followed him, because when Fingin came outside, neither were in sight.

Bran joined him and gave a great yawn, shaking his head to dislodge the sleep.

When the two Fae returned, their arms were full of odds and ends, few of which Fingin could identify.

When he asked questions, though, Adhna shooed him away. "Just some things we need to prepare. Go see if Airiu will tell you a story. I'd heard she'd learned a new one."

With a narrow gaze at the two conspiring Fae, Fingin and Bran sought Airiu out. She had indeed learned a new story and smiled when he asked to hear it. Her smile lit up the surrounding air.

As the not-quite-butterflies alighted on her hair, Airiu told her tale, an intriguing story involving the Morrigú, goddess of war and death.

"When the battle had finished, she and her ravens fell upon the dead. She, in her form of Macha, collected the severed heads of the fallen warriors. One by one, she gathered their hair into her hands, like a harvest of acorns. She carried these heads with her, proud of her trophies, as the ravens picked the juicy meat from their eyes."

Bran lie down beside him, concentrating on her words. "You can eat acorns? I didn't know acorns were food."

"Not without picking out the inside and cooking it. It gives you an aching stomach. Squirrels can eat them, though."

Bran's head popped up, his ears alert. "Squirrels? Where?"

Fingin and Airiu both laughed. She said, "We have no squirrels here in Faerie, Bran. There are small scurrying creatures, but they aren't the same as squirrels. They can be a great deal more deadly than what you have in the mortal realm."

She took a piece of fruit from the dish between them, and savored the sweet flesh, juice dribbling down her chin. He reached forward to brush it away, but a sound made him turn.

Tomnat strode into the glade. Fingin let out a sigh. While he had a duty to fulfill, he was loath to extract himself from Airiu's company. Still, he dropped his hand as they stood to greet the new arrival.

His hesitation must have been obvious, for Tomnat scowled at the other Fae woman. "Play all you like, Airiu, but he has responsibilities. He is not yours to command."

Airiu narrowed her eyes. "You may have used your influence at court to get what you want from him, but his heart is mine, Tomnat. Go on, take him for your contract. He'll not surrender his soul to you."

Airiu's eyes had turned to cat-slits again, but her teeth were still human. Fingin feared that her feral self didn't lurk far from the surface.

Tomnat's eyes grew wide, but she returned Airiu's threat with a wicked smile. "You think you'll have your way with him when I'm finished, do you? Just you wait. You'll see. Now, human, we have business to complete."

She grabbed his arm, and as he shot an apologetic glance at Airiu, she led him away. Tomnat brought him back to the bower where they'd completed their first tryst. This time, his experience had even less romance, if possible.

He had no control over his body's reaction to her attentions, and she completed the act quickly. Tomnat hesitated when she'd finished, and then she raked her fingernails–which had turned into cat's claws–across his chest, leaving thin slashes which bled onto the gossamer fabric of the bower. Without another word, she let out a dreadful laugh and left him. He felt branded, like a farmer's kine.

Daubing at the scratches, he winced at the stinging pain. He dressed with care, trying not to get more blood on his clothing. He then returned to Adhna's home.

When the roundhouse came into view, Fingin noticed Airiu was waiting for him, but Bodach had joined her. She sat straight, doing her best to ignore his presence. The darker Fae moved his hand up her arm, caressed her shoulder, then ran his finger down between her breasts.

Her jaw clenched, and she refused to move or acknowledge his intrusions. When his efforts elicited no reaction, he moved closer, until his lips almost touched hers.

Fingin hurried, hoping to help Airiu. But as soon as Bodach's lips touched hers, Airiu bared her pointed teeth and, when that didn't make him draw back, she sank them into his cheek. His bark skin resisted more than bare skin would have, but they still broke the surface, making him cry out in pain and surprise.

He jumped back, holding his hand to his face. "Foul harridan! I will see you punished for this outrage!"

Airiu hissed at him. "Me? Punished? For your own outrages far surpass my own, Bodach, and well you know it!"

Bodach let out a hearty laugh, then winced from his wound. "The Queen won't listen to your side of the story, Airiu. Have no hope for that."

"She may not listen, but she will hear, nonetheless."

Another voice came from behind Fingin. He spun around to see the Queen. "What will I hear, Airiu?"

Both Fae fell silent, their heads bowed. Fingin's body froze. He wanted to run, to hide behind Adhna's roundhouse, but he had no control over his muscles. With great effort, he relaxed his knees, which let his body drop to the ground. He felt safer out of the line of the Faerie Queen's wrath.

The Queen's voice, even in this bucolic glade, far away from her imposing palace, bore through his bones. "Bodach, you will explain this situation."

The bark-skinned Fae sidled up to her, his head still bowed. However, his voice retained its customary arrogance. "My Queen, this Fae has been taunting the mortal, tempting him to break his vow with Tomnat. I'm only trying to convince her such activities aren't fair to a poor human, one unable to resist the lure of the Fae."

Airiu let out a harsh laugh, and the Queen turned to stare at her. "Is this the truth, Airiu?"

"Of course not, my Queen. Fingin and I had been chatting peacefully. I was telling a story when Tomnat arrived, and absconded with Fingin to complete the second half of his vow. During that time, Bodach arrived and pestered me."

The Queen didn't change her expression with either explanation. She crossed her arms and waited. "What else?"

Airiu glanced at Bodach, but he maintained his innocent façade. She glanced back to the Queen. "I may say nothing, your grace, in the current company."

The Queen narrowed her eyes and set her jaw. "Do you defy my command?"

Airiu stood straighter, the first glimmer of fear showing in her eyes. "Not at all, my Queen. However, the information I have is for your ears only."

The air grew colder, and the light dimmed. Fingin was still frozen, but it seemed as if everyone else was, too. Bran whined beside him, and he wanted to comfort the dog, but couldn't even move his hand to place on Bran's head.

The Queen's voice grew colder than an ice storm. "Bodach, you will leave."

"My Queen! But there is something you should hear—"

She held up a hand. "Leave. Now. Do not test my wrath, Consort."

The bark-skinned Fae gave Fingin and Airiu each a murderous look but slunk away with several glances over his shoulder.

As soon as he disappeared, the air warmed again. Queen Clíodhna sat on a log, a mundane action that removed some of the regal mystical quality from her stature. The freezing eased, and he placed his hand on Bran's flank, patting the dog in reassurance.

Again, the Queen spoke, but her manner had also thawed. She smiled, her berry-red lips in a beautiful curve which took Fingin's breath away. "Airiu, what have you to tell me? I suspect I already know your news, but I would hear it from you."

With a glance to Fingin, Airiu cleared her throat. "It's about your Consort. May I speak of him?"

"You may."

"Bodach is searching for information, trying to find something against you, your grace. I fear he's trying to undermine your power. He's interrogated me, Uasal, and even Tomnat."

"And have you told him anything to his advantage?"

Airiu's eyes grew wide. "Of course not! Even if I knew anything, I'd never tell his ilk."

The Queen nodded. "Good, good. You've done well, Airiu. I am aware of his machinations. I must find a way to reward you for your loyalty. Now I must speak with the human and his hound. Leave us."

The ice returned, but it had nothing to do with the Queen's magic and everything to do with Fingin's own fear.

As his love left, he sent her a beseeching glance, a wish and a prayer. She blew him a kiss as she disappeared down the path.

He steeled his spine and turned back to the Faerie Queen, his grandmother, Clíodhna.

She gave him a human-like half-smile. "You didn't think I recognized you at first, did you?"

He swallowed. "I didn't."

"Of course I recognized my own grandson! How could I not? But, for various reasons, most of them involving a certain consort, acknowledging you in front of my entire court would have been unwise."

"I… I understand. I think."

Some of the ice seeped back into her voice. "You don't understand, but your comprehension isn't necessary. Your cooperation is all I require."

He swallowed again. "What do you require of me?"

"I need you to leave."

He cocked his head and furrowed his brow. "Leave? But you've done everything you can to bind me here."

She let out a sigh and closed her eyes. "Yes, I am aware. That mess resulted from my conceit, my folly. I should have made you leave Faerie at once. However, external pressures kept me from doing so then. I needed to satisfy a favor, and that favor is now satisfied."

"A favor to Tomnat?"

"Indirectly, yes. She wanted a child, and none of her efforts with other Fae resulted in issue. Therefore, she made me promise the first human to arrive would be hers to do with as she liked. She insisted on two, in case of a sickly babe, as sometimes happens when our kinds mix."

"Our kind? So, you *are* Fae, then?"

She glanced around, nervous in case someone overheard. "Hush with that question, child!" She dropped her voice into a fierce whisper. It still held all the command of her speaking voice, but without the carrying power. "No, I am not pure Fae. But I have Fae blood, and therefore, so do you. However, this must remain secret. Do you understand? It's information Bodach could use to oust me from my throne. He must not, under any circumstances, discover the truth. This is one reason I didn't acknowledge you when I first saw you at court."

"But how can he take your throne? He can't be a Faerie Queen, can he?"

"He cannot, but he can raise one of the female Fae to that spot, if I were disposed of."

She spoke the words *disposed of* with no inflection or emotion. They sank into Fingin's bones with a chilling premonition.

"Now, I have a plan for you to leave. You must take Tomnat and your babe with you to keep them safe, but you must leave with stealth, lest Bodach stop you. Will you go?"

Fingin opened his mouth to agree, and to ask her about the brooch, when Bodach returned to the glade. He swallowed his words and resolved to ask her about it when they left.

The following day, when Fingin woke, he once again lay still, listening for voices. Grimnaugh grunted and Adhna laughed, but they said few words. When he got tired of waiting for something to happen, Fingin rose with a mighty stretch.

Maybe they hadn't prepared a celebration after all and had been distracted by something else. No matter. He'd rarely celebrated the day of his birth. His mother had usually given him some small token before he'd left home, but the gifts were practical in nature, like a new *léine* or a tool to help in the fields.

When he emerged from the roundhouse, though, a great shout rose up, and a dozen Fae yelled and screamed. Frantically searching for the threat, Fingin grabbed the doorframe, but then he realized they were all grinning.

Bits of leaves had been torn up and thrown in the air. Colorful vines draped every tree, radiating from the roundhouse roof like a giant wheel. A pile of wrapped things lay jumbled near the path.

Eager grins from Adhna, Grimnaugh, Airiu, Gnathnad, Uasal, Cúán, Némán, and several other Fae whose names he either didn't know or remember.

Flushed, Fingin sat on the ground, trying to make sense of everything. How could he have a day of birth when there were no days in Fae? His grandmother might remember such a day, but why tell Adhna? His own parents had never made such a fuss over days of birth.

Airiu sidled up next to him and hooked her hand around his elbow. "Come, Fingin! I'm told we must celebrate! Will you dance?"

Grimnaugh placed his hand on hers, stopping them from rising. "No, no, he must eat the food first. And open his gifts! Adhna said those are the rules."

Fingin stared at a table covered in food. His stomach growled audibly, and they all laughed. He grinned in genuine delight.

Adhna wouldn't let him go to the table, though. "We'll serve you, today only, young human! You sit, and we'll bring you samples. Then we'll bring you the gifts."

He caught his breath at the mention of gifts. Gifts from the Fae were dangerous and usually carried return obligations. His apprehension must have shown on his face, for Airiu giggled. "No, these gifts are free of *géis*, I vow to you."

With a lighter heart, he waited for the first plate of Faerie food.

When Gnathnad brought him a plate with sticky insects, rolled leaves, and red berries, his stomach rolled. He tried the berries first, their bitter taste making his lips pucker. The leaves, at least, tasted salty and savory, with some sort of nutty stuffing. The insect, however, remained on his plate until he could no longer politely ignore it.

With cautious fingers, he examined it from all sides before nibbling one edge. It crunched but sweet honey flooded his mouth. Bolder now, he took a bigger bite, finally finishing the delicacy with a satisfied grin.

Now, the first gift came, Némán holding it out with due ceremony. "I hope you like this. It was my brother's, long ago. Since he passed to *Tír na nÓg*, I can freely gift this elsewhere without requiring a gift in return."

The pale Fae smiled as Fingin accepted his gift, turning it around in his hand before unwrapping the broadleaf cover. Inside, a sparkling dewdrop shone in the light. Almost afraid to touch it, Fingin glanced up before doing so.

Némán nodded. "I found it on the pond near the Queen's palace."

"Thank you. I shall treasure it." He carefully re-wrapped the drop, having no idea what else he should do with it.

With a bow, Némán backed up, making way for Grimnaugh and his offering. Fingin opened his friend's gift. When he unwrapped the gossamer wrapping, he furrowed his brow, puzzled. "A leaf?"

"It floated on the wind near me when I thought of what I should get you. So, I decided it must want to be yours."

Fingin kept his grin strong. The Fae weren't to know what proper gifts should be, and he'd never let them know they hadn't gotten it quite right. They'd tried, and that was the most important part.

One by one, the Fae gave their gifts. Some, like Uasal, simply gave a tasty fruit or a filled mug. Others gave an odd bug, a twig, or a strange stone. However, when Airiu appeared before him, empty-handed, he waited.

"My gift to you is my voice, Fingin. My song, something to hold in your heart when we aren't together.

Fingin's throat closed, not trusting himself to speak. When she opened her mouth, the sweetest sound came forth, caressing him with power and love. He wanted to close his eyes to experience the song, but he also wanted to keep the memory of Airiu strong, to memorize every line of her body.

When she finished, he felt lighter, younger, and more vibrant than ever before. She squeezed his hand and said, "I wish you a delightful birth celebration."

Fingin melted into her eyes. "You've made it more wonderful than I could ever imagine."

Chapter Fourteen

Fingin wished night existed in Faerie. A cover of darkness would make their escape easier. However, with Adhna's help, he gathered a pack with food, supplies, and clothing. He didn't really want to leave Airiu, and the group of friends he'd made here, but knew that he must go, if he wanted to live. His grandmother had made that clear.

Tomnat arrived with a grim smile on her face. He tried to speak to her, but she stopped him with one hand. "I don't wish to go to your world, but circumstances have forced my decision. Don't make it pitiful with your groveling apologies."

He ached to say goodbye to Airiu, but his grandmother had forbidden it. "Adhna can pass on any message you like, but Bodach is watching her. He's convinced she knows something he can use. She'll act as a decoy for your escape."

He hated the thought of putting Airiu in danger for his benefit, but then he remembered her razor-sharp teeth and nails. She'd could protect herself much better than he would ever be able to.

With a silent curse, Fingin berated himself for forgetting to ask his grandmother for the brooch. Now, just before they left, he reminded himself to do so when she arrived.

His pack on his shoulder, he thanked Adhna for his hospitality. The Fae glanced at the Queen, arguing with Tomnat. "Think nothing of it, young man. I have obligations to your family for times past, and I'm certain we'll meet again. Perhaps even soon." A pensive expression passed over his face before he smiled. "Take care of Tomnat. She may seem prickly, but she is, at heart, a kind creature."

Fingin doubted this but wouldn't argue with a man in his own home. "Come, Bran. Time to say farewell to my grandmother."

Tomnat wore a pinched expression, as if someone had just stolen her puppy. She glared at him, but Queen Clíodhna waved her away. "You have your mission, Tomnat. Don't let me down."

With another scowl, the Fae woman stalked off to stand at the path, waiting for Fingin with transparent impatience.

His grandmother took him by both shoulders. "Fingin, you must do me proud. You are my last hope for the family, you know."

"What? I don't understand."

"Did you not know? Your brothers have all passed away. You're the only one left."

Fingin gasped and shook his head to clear the shock. "All four of them? What happened?"

She frowned, lines creasing around her mouth. "I suspect Bodach, as two of them went mad before they killed themselves. The others died alone by strange mischance. I cannot prove anything, but I have my suspicions."

"Killed themselves?"

"One jumped from a cliff onto the rocks. Another ate poisoned mushrooms, apparently on purpose. Cattle trampled the other two."

Fingin gritted his teeth. This Bodach had a lot to answer for. He would have to make him pay some day.

She shook his shoulders. "You will not be the one to exact this revenge, grandson. Do you understand?"

Had she heard his thoughts? "What?"

"Yes, your thoughts screamed so loud I'm surprised they can't hear in the palace. As I said, it's not your mission to bring revenge upon Bodach. He's much too powerful an adversary for you. I've tried in the past, and even my power isn't up to the task. You'll die if you try, just like your brothers."

Fingin's blood still boiled with rage. He'd never liked his brothers. In fact, they'd been the main reason he'd left home so young, to avoid their bullying. But they were still kin. Gaelic tradition demanded he seek revenge for their murder.

"Do not disobey me in this, Fingin. I need your vow."

He clenched his fists, unable to make such a vow, and yet unable to deny his grandmother. The conflict made his head ache, and he took a deep breath, trying to work out what he needed to do.

His grandmother's expression softened. "I will take care of the matter when I can, Fingin. This is not your retribution to visit. They were my grandsons, remember."

Fingin let out a sigh. He'd forgotten she had a better kin-claim than he did. All his family had been her descendants, her *dearbhfhine*, a kin group stretching across three generations.

A step behind them made Fingin jump, but it was only Adhna. "We must leave, my Queen. Your presence is attracting attention. I've seen three Fae pass already, peering around the trees. Bodach will learn of this gathering before long."

"Quite so. Tomnat, it is time."

The sullen Fae woman, their babe in her arms, gave a sharp nod. His grandmother led the way with Adhna bringing up the rear. The odd procession didn't take the Silver Path, but struck off across the countryside, with no idle chatter or conversation.

Once away from the Path, light dimmed as fewer trees glowed. They walked in silence in the ambient light.

Bran was subdued, forgoing his normal penchant for exploring every hillock and creature they passed. He still perked up at each sound but stayed close to Fingin's side.

The trees fell away into a small glade with a wide stone pool in the center. The circular wall had steps leading into the water. Once again, he'd have to walk down into a well. He didn't relish the prospect but knew he must escape to his own realm.

Maybe he'd be able to convince Tomnat to settle into her new life as his wife and raise their children in peace. He just hoped his speech wouldn't return to its halting habit when he left Faerie. He enjoyed being able to say what he wanted without difficulty. Such a freedom most people took for granted.

Queen Clíodhna turned to the Fae woman. "Tomnat, walk in first with the babe. The other side should be in a forest along the coast, far from any mortal village. You've visited that realm before, so at least it won't be too much of a shock. Wait for the human."

With a resentful look at Fingin, Tomnat took the first three steps into the pool. She glanced back just before the last step, which would take the babe below the surface, and her eyes grew wide.

Fingin turned to see what had made her react, and barely ducked in time to avoid the blow from Bodach's cudgel. He leapt to one side with a cry to escape a second blow. The look of murderous rage in the bark-skinned Fae's eyes spurred him away.

"You won't evade me forever, human! I know there's some secret here. It must have to do with you and the Queen. She wouldn't help just any mortal escape!"

A flicker of concern passed over the Queen's expression before she regained control. Bodach pounced on this clue. "I'm right! I knew it."

He glanced between each of them, searching their faces for more information. His eyes grew wide, staring at the Queen. "You've the look of that human! You're related to him!"

Fingin clamped his jaw shut, unwilling to say anything that might give away the truth. Tomnat still stood in the well, clutching her baby tight. Adhna's face fell in an almost comic expression of defeat.

The Queen, however, stood straighter, drawing around her an air of imperious strength, almost tangible in the low light. "How dare you, Bodach? How dare you accuse your Queen of such low blood?"

Glee bloomed across Bodach's bark face, almost cracking at the edges of his mouth. "Oh, I dare, all right! Imagine that! The Queen herself has mortal blood! This is interesting, very interesting indeed. Fascinating."

The Queen pursed her lips and lifted her arms. Intangible power shimmered before her as she gathered her strength.

Fingin remembered the whirlwind storm she'd called in his dreams. While Faerie had no storms to manipulate, his grandmother was shaping the air itself. A ball of glistening film rose, like a bubble, swirling with white wind inside.

Fingin stared into the whirling mass and grew dizzy. Then she flung her arms toward Bodach, sending her creation into his chest.

The bubble enveloped the Fae man, making him cough and sputter. The mist turned from white to a sickly yellow, swirling into an ominous brown.

He staggered back but didn't fall. Instead, he threw his arms out and broke the bubble, dispersing the menacing fog.

Then he laughed. Loud and long, a rasping saw against rotten wood, his laughter burrowed into Fingin's ears like a beetle in the dirt.

As his mirth died, Bodach raised his left hand and threw something at the Queen.

She took several steps back, surprise clear in her widened eyes. Whatever he'd thrown disappeared, and she scowled, forbidding determination taking over her face.

The Queen gathered her air power once again, now crackling with bits of lightning within the orb. The edges shimmered with rainbow reflection, an odd beauty masking the danger within. She flung this ball of sizzling energy at Bodach.

He ducked, but it swerved back and sought him out, like a dog on a rabbit's scent. Bodach dove away, plowing down to the earth, ripping up a grass divot. He growled with fierce rage.

With a feral smile, the Queen pulled upon her power again. This time, the well water rose in a thin spout. Tomnat scrambled back out of the water, her baby clutched close to her chest. She crawled to where Fingin huddled, behind the low stone wall.

The waterspout grew tall and long, arced overhead, and pounded into Bodach's body as he lay on the churned ground. Mud and water spurted in a furious clash around him.

Bran chose this moment to bark with furious volume at both the Queen and Bodach. Fingin whispered, "Bran! Hush, and get back over here. Stay out of this!"

He barked a few more times for good measure, but finally retreated to his side.

As Bran moved, the Queen's eyes flicked to the hound, and she lost control over the waterspout. Water splashed on the ground, no longer imbued with her spell.

Fatigue etched lines around the Queen's eyes, but she raised her hands again. This time, though, Bodach acted faster. He threw his invisible missile not at her, but at her feet. Dirt exploded beneath her, and she fell on her back, eliciting a surprisingly human "oof." Bran woofed in response.

The ground continued to churn, boiling like a thick stew, engulfing the Queen bit by bit. She scrambled to break free, but roiling dirt shot out strands and twists of gnarled roots, grabbing her clothing, her legs, her waist.

She let out an angry curse and raised her arms, once again calling a waterspout from the well. This time, she directed it at her own feet, pounding back the aggressive ground, beating it again and again until it retreated. She was covered in mud, but she stood free from Bodach's latest trap.

The Faerie Queen turned to her foe, grim determination clear on her face. Her lips compressed so hard, they'd faded from berry-red to white.

Tomnat took Fingin's hand and squeezed, the first human gesture she'd ever made toward him, despite their vows.

For a moment, his heart opened toward her. Fingin flashed her a quick, nervous smile and squeezed her hand back. He searched for Adhna but didn't see any sign of the older Fae.

Fingin glanced at the well, hoping they might make their escape. The stairs descended right next to where the Queen and Bodach battled.

A boom drew his attention back to the two Fae. Smoke wreathed them, obscuring who'd launched the latest attack, or how either fared. Cracking, hissing, and buzzing drowned out any details.

Bran stood restless next to him, his hackles raised, still barking at the combatants. The barking made his head pound.

Fingin couldn't figure out who had the upper hand. Sparks flew from inside the cloud of smoke, and a cry. Had that been a female voice? He held his breath, hoping to hear his grandmother's voice again.

He crept toward the edge of the well, but another boom from the cloud made him flatten against the ground. When it subsided, he tried again, gesturing to Tomnat to follow. He hissed a tight command. "Bran! Stop barking! We can't help them. All we can do is escape."

Bran ceased his barking, but only for a moment. He whined and growled as they crawled toward the steps.

Blue fire burst before them, making them all cringe back from the heat. The air burned with the cerulean blaze, and Fingin prayed to Brigit that his grandmother survived. Voices cried out from inside the battle zone.

Fingin burned to attack Bodach, but his grandmother had been crystal clear with her command. He must not pursue revenge for his brothers' deaths. Fingin must make his way to the mortal realm with Tomnat. Would the Queen's command still hold sway if she died in this battle?

Fingin peered into the smoke. The fire dimmed, but he saw no trace of his grandmother. He wished for wind to clear the air, but no such thing existed in Faerie, except by the Faerie Queen's power.

His eyes smarted with the smoke and ash filling the glade, floating like snow on a winter's day. He grabbed Tomnat's hand and helped her to her feet.

As the mist cleared, it revealed both his grandmother and Bodach lying on the ground. He rose without thought and ran to her, Brigit's charm in his hand.

Adhna cried out, "Fingin! Stop! She can take care of herself!"

"I can't, Adhna! I have to help her!"

If anything might heal a Faerie Queen, the magic of a goddess might. He skirted far around the bark-skinned Fae and slid to his knees at Clíodhna's side.

He struggled to move her head to his lap, draping the pendant around her neck. The cloth turned icy, burning his hands with hard frost. The mist enveloped them both with a sickly sweet odor, a mixture of lavender and burning peat.

Bran barked again, and bounded toward him, into the thick of the smoldering smoke.

"Bran! No! Stay back!"

The hound entered the thickest part of the cloud. A loud *yip* followed by a pitiful whine made Fingin call to his friend. He had to leave his grandmother and find Bran. He glanced at the charm, but after a moment's consideration, left it with her.

Fingin felt around for Bran. His hands found nothing in the darkness, but heat blistered his skin and air choked his breath.

Flames licked out in another blast, forcing Fingin back again. Something fell into his legs, and he fell under the onslaught. Painful, raking fingers gouged at his skin. He cried out, and frantic barking began. Bodach's face appeared a mere handspan from his own, a ghoulish grin on his face. The Fae gripped his head in bark-covered hands and squeezed.

The pressure grew so painful, Fingin screamed despite himself. His throat, already raw from breathing the smoke, grew hoarse and broken.

Bodach's weight upon him doubled as Bran's teeth sunk into the Fae's wooden shoulder, ripping with great strength. The Fae tumbled back, surprise on his face. His hands dug divots into the soft earth. He glanced behind him into the flames and let out an evil laugh.

The scent of burning, rotted carcasses filled the air. Parts of his skin glowed like embers as he batted at them with frantic desperation. He cast one last look filled with bitter hatred toward Fingin and escaped from the smoke-filled glade, disappearing into the trees.

Fingin searched again for Bran. "Bran! Bran, where are you? Grandmother? Are you there?"

He found something and gripped tight. The fur felt like Bran's, and he tried to pull him closer. The dog didn't move. With a grunt, he knelt and lifted Bran to carry him out.

He staggered under the weight of the enormous hound. Fingin stumbled out of the still-smoldering smoke, step by deliberate step. Once he fought clear, he took a deep lungful of sweet, clear air. He placed the dog on the ground and caught his breath again.

Tomnat knelt by the dog, Adhna by her side. Deep streaks of red matted the gray fur. With frantic fingers, Fingin searched for some sign the dog still breathed, but found nothing.

Then one shallow, ragged breath moved the dog's flank. Fingin fumbled at his *léine*, yanking at the cloth that held Brigit's charm, but it was still around the Faerie Queen's neck.

A hand on his shoulder made him look up, wiping his face with the back of his hand. His grandmother, scruffy and torn, stood behind him, Brigit's charm glowing around her neck. Soot covered half her face and her long, black hair had burned off in patches. Bodach's attacks had ripped and burnt her elegant gown to tatters, exposing sections of reddened skin. If he'd ever doubted her human heritage, he didn't now.

She took the charm off and handed it to Fingin with solemn dignity. "Have a care with this, Fingin. It might have killed me more easily than healed me. I'm thankful we're related."

Confused, he pressed the charm into the dog's fur, urging the magic to work faster than ever.

With a voice ragged with tears and smoke, he cried out. "Please, Brigit, listen to my prayer. Bran has been a loyal friend and a valuable help. Don't let him die, please!"

Grimnaugh came running, panting and sweating. He glanced at the carnage the battle had left, but Bodach had escaped.

Adhna knelt before his grandmother. "My Queen, how can we help?"

She took a deep breath and placed a hand upon his head with tender care. Her touch was almost a loving caress, as lovers might exchange. Then her icy dignity returned and she straightened.

Grimnaugh crossed his arms. "May I have permission to destroy Bodach, my Queen? I would derive considerable pleasure from such a boon."

Her eyes sparked with fury. "Nay, neither of you may touch him. He is mine to punish. I want him to suffer a long life as penance for his crimes."

The anger died and she turned to Adhna and Grimnaugh. "However, I do have favors to ask each of you. Adhna, I need you to travel to the mortal realm and guard Fingin and Tomnat. Ensure that Bodach doesn't harass either of them, nor the children."

Fingin glanced up, his hands still pressing the healing charm into Bran's flank. "Children?"

"Shush, Fingin. Yes, Tomnat is carrying another child. Now, Grimnaugh, you have another task." She knelt by Bran and put her hands on the dog's head. Bran twitched and let out a pitiful whimper. Fingin's heart leapt in his chest. Was the healing charm working?

His grandmother shook her head. "No, Brigit's charm is depleted, and must return to the mortal world to recover its strength, Fingin. Bran will not survive such a journey. However, he may yet live, with constant care. Grimnaugh, will you care for the hound?"

Fingin cried and cradled the dog's head in his lap as Tomnat pulled his arm, eager to escape. He couldn't tear his gaze off Bran's still-shut eyes as he cried. "I won't forget you, Bran! I promise!"

The Faerie Queen pushed him toward the steps. Tomnat and Adhna led him down into the water. Not until the surface engulfed his head did Fingin stop staring at Bran. Then he needed all his attention to keep from breathing through the passage to the human world.

Adhna led them out of the sacred well and into a dense forest, a different place from where he'd entered Faerie. Fingin wiped water from his face, but his tears for Bran made it wet again. "What about Sean? He'll be waiting f-f-for me at the other well."

The Fae shook his head. "Your loyal donkey has long since moved on, Fingin. It's been longer than you know."

His throat clenched. He'd lost both his friends. He hoped Sean had found a friendly farm and a happy life. Fingin glanced at Tomnat, holding his son, and realized he had a family now, one he must care for and support. Fingin swallowed back his grief and squared his shoulders for the next part of his life.

Adhna led them across the countryside, down a hill, and to a river. They followed the river until they spied a sheltered hilltop surrounded by pine trees.

Fingin stopped to look at the trees. "We're going th-there?"

The Fae nodded. "The people who lived there left some time ago. It's large enough for a family."

The roundhouse sat next to a gentle bend in the river with a lovely view of the valley beyond. Autumn colors painted the oak trees around them.

A large pen stood next to the roundhouse, large enough for several cows. An herb garden and a larger plot for other crops completed the property.

Weary from the battle and journey, both Tomnat and Fingin collapsed on the floor, their backs against the wall. The babe started fussing until Tomnat moved her clothing to feed him.

Now that he had a family to support, they couldn't survive by fish alone. He stared out at the empty stables until Adhna clapped him on the shoulder. "I'll find you some livestock and some supplies. You take care of yourself, your wife, and your son. I'll return in a few days."

With motions numbed by fatigue, he took stock of his new home. While some winter trash had blown into the corners, the place seemed too clean for an abandoned roundhouse. He spied no holes in the thatch, nor any rotten places in the daub and wattle walls.

A whistling wind whipped through the open door and slammed it shut, making all of them jump. The baby fussed again, though he'd finished feeding. Fingin turned to Tomnat and put his hands out for his son. "Rest. I'll take C-Conall and sit outside. I'm tired, but I don't think I can sleep yet."

Once outside, he glanced around for Bran, but then remembered his beloved friend was in Faerie, cared for by Grimnaugh. His heart ached for his friend, but the dog would be better off in the other world.

With a few deep breaths to stave off the tears, he fashioned a sling for his son to ride on his back. The child slept, content to hug his back. Fingin had to smile every time the child tightened his grip.

First, he gathered twigs and branches, as well as a few thicker logs, dragging these back to the house. Once he built a crackling hearthfire, he searched for other supplies. Grasses and fibers for making a new net, logs for carving into furniture and bowls, flat rocks for work surfaces.

Every now and then, he'd see something, like a rabbit warren, which brought Bran back to mind, and it would be a few moments before he could continue.

Odd how grief for losing his dog, his friend, his loyal companion, grew so much deeper than that of his own flesh and blood.

He'd mourned the loss of his brothers years ago, when he first left home. They'd never been kind to him, but he honored them as family. Still, it seemed odd not to feel upset about their deaths. Regardless of his feelings for his brothers, he had a score to settle with Bodach.

Perhaps he should find another dog, someone to be a companion, someone to help protect Conall. He didn't doubt Tomnat would be fierce enough for her own sake, but would a Fae mother be as strong protection for her half-human children?

Conall woke and began to fuss. He dropped the bag of stones he'd gathered and swung the child around, holding him on his knee. He bounced a few times and cooed at the child, giving him a bright smile. His son echoed his grin with a gurgling laugh, which made him laugh with delight.

The world fell away around him as he gazed into his son's eyes. All the burdens and responsibilities of being a father crept upon his shoulders. He could no longer live just for himself, surviving day by day to eat and sleep. Now he had a family he must care for and support, teach and nurture, keep from all danger and despair. And if the Queen was right, Tomnat had another child coming.

He'd dreamt of having a family, with children at his feet and a small farm to support them. Somehow, he hadn't imagined this. But he must enjoy this odd new life for as long as he had it.

When he returned to the roundhouse with his latest load of stones, Tomnat had wakened. She held her arms out for Conall and fed the fussy child. This elicited another smile from Fingin, who set the stones along the edge of the roundhouse floor, to cut down on winter drafts.

Tomnat had said few words to him since the battle in Faerie. Fingin wanted more than a silent wife. He wanted someone who would be a partner, someone to talk to. But what experience did she have in human relationships?

He cleared his throat. "We'll have to make bowls and c-cups, but I think we can make this a c-cozy enough home."

She glanced up as if surprised he spoke. "Why don't you look through the packs? The Queen might have given us some gifts."

He'd forgotten the packs. Fingin knelt by the largest flat stone he'd found, one that he might craft into a table top, and emptied his pack on the surface.

Amongst packets of salt, flour, cured bacon, several carved bone spoons, and a set of lovely carved wooden bowls, he also found a bronze cauldron and a leaf-shaped bronze knife. Another item peeked out from under the packet of bacon. He grabbed the shiny object to examine it and caught his breath as his skin tingled.

There, in his hands, lay the brooch. The intricately carved gold and silver brooch, with blood-red stones, that his grandmother had gifted him so many winters ago. This same brooch she'd taken when she stole his voice. The same brooch he'd vowed to ask her for, but never found a chance.

The same brooch that now grew so warm in his hands, he had to place it back on the stone.

A voice whispered in his mind, a voice he recognized. *Live your life, grandson. Raise your family. Keep the legacy.*

Tomnat narrowed her eyes. "What in the name of Danú is that?"

"That, T-tomnat, is my legacy."

They'd emerged from Faerie in the height of autumn, and through the bitter winter, Tomnat's belly grew.

Even the light tasks he used to love, like casting in the river several times a day, left him exhausted.

With grudging generosity, Tomnat offered to help. "If you only cast once a day, you won't be as tired. I can speak to the fish."

He rolled his eyes. "I c-c-can speak to the fish, too. Getting them t-to do what you ask is a different matter."

She flashed him a knowing smile, almost mischievous. "Just watch."

As he cast his net that morning, she waded in with him. Raising her arms, she sang out in a nonsensical chant, perhaps the same ancient language the Queen had used during their mating contract. When she finished, his nets grew heavy until the river current almost pulled him off balance.

Tomnat caught his shoulder before he fell into the water and then grabbed one edge of the net to help him pull it onto the beach.

Never in his entire life had he pulled in such an enormous catch. Scores of silver fish wiggled within his net, struggling to get free of the woven trap. A few broke away, but at least a hundred remained. Thankful he didn't have to haul it up a bank of steps, like at his last home, Fingin dragged the haul to his new workspace. Tomnat, despite her round belly, helped him clean them all.

In quiet companionship, they worked to skin, clean, and debone the fish. They'd need to dry most of them, or they'd go bad. He asked Tomnat to set up the drying rack, which quickly filled. He built a new one while she fed Conall, and then they both resumed cleaning.

Fingin used the bronze knife the Queen had gifted him to remove the thick skin, peeling back from head to tail. He cut a shallow incision along the bottom. With his fingers, he dug out the innards, dropping them in a pile. Scrape out the inner membrane. Chop off the head, fins, and tail.

Then he fileted the remaining flesh from the bones, cutting it into thin strips to hang over the drying rack.

After the first few fish, he no longer looked for Bran to come eat the innards.

The sun had long since set before they'd finished cleaning the massive catch. Tomnat had retired as twilight embraced them, holding her belly and complaining that her back hurt, but Fingin pressed on to finish his task before he slept.

By the dying firelight, he placed the final filet on the rack and stretched his back, his arms high over his head.

How far had he come, in truth? Fingin was still spending his days fishing, cleaning, and selling his catch. He still lived far from any village. While he had a wife and son, his wife held no love for him. He'd felt more companionship from Bran, despite being hound rather than human. And his body grew tired more easily than before. Maybe he just needed to rest more.

A moan from the roundhouse interrupted his musings. He ran inside to find Tomnat bent over double on their sleeping mat, curled up like a baby.

"Tomnat? What's wrong? Is the b-b-baby c-coming?"

She flashed him a look of pure frustration. "Of course, the baby's coming, you idiotic human! Ohh! I wish I stayed in Faerie! Your world is horrible." Her pain radiated through the house, moans shaking his bones.

He ran to boil water to make stew, but he had no other ideas. No midwives or healers lived nearby. When he'd broached the subject of moving closer to a village as she grew near her time, Tomnat had squashed the idea, declaring she wanted no human healers to touch her.

He grabbed Brigit's charm and held it close, praying for an idea. When it grew cool in his hand, he slipped the cloth over his head and placed it around Tomnat's neck.

She curled her lips at the charm and shrank away. "What's this? It burns! Take it off!"

He tried to get it back around her neck. "Burns? It's ice c-cold! You need t-to wear it. It's a healing charm. Brigit g-gave it to me."

She grabbed his forearm, her nails turning into wicked points. "That's cold iron, you prime idiot! I can't touch it!" Her eyes grew wide. "Brigit? She gave you a charm?"

Fingin furrowed his brow. "I thought you knew? The Queen knew."

"Since when has the Queen ever taken me into her confidence? Ohh!" She gripped her belly as a visible tremor spread across it.

Fingin swallowed and placed the charm back around his neck, at a loss. "How c-can I help?"

Tomnat waved him away, her nails back to normal. "Just stop bothering me."

He wasn't ready to abandon her in her state, though. "Maybe I should sing, t-to distract you? This isn't your first b-baby, so you should know how, right?"

Her face screwed up in a rictus of pain, and she let out a horrible moan. She panted after the latest contraction released its grip.

Fingin sent out another prayer to Brigit, anything to help the mother of his child. He didn't know what else to do. While he'd seen animals give birth, he'd never seen humans do so. Not even his brothers, as he was the youngest.

Fingin needed something to keep himself busy and not worrying, so he chopped onions, turnips, and garlic. He added burdock leaves and fish, then a sprinkle of precious salt. He'd heard somewhere that something warm and savory would be good for a new mother. Maybe it had been his grandmother, back before she'd disappeared. Back before she became the Faerie Queen.

Another moan rattled his nerves and Fingin gripped hard to the knife handle, wishing he could do something to make her pain go away.

A female voice outside shouted. "Sorry I'm late! I only just got the call. What in the name of Danú took you so long?"

He turned to see Brigit, looking even younger than when he'd left her hut. She bustled in and knelt next to Tomnat. "Oh, dear. Yes, I see. This is your first birth in the mortal realm, is it not? Indeed. I can help, my dear. Fingin, you should have known better than to use the charm on a Fae. Now, out with you. Neither of us need your help. Shoo!"

"B-b-but the stew—"

Brigit waved her hand. "Curse the stew. Leave. I'll take care of everything."

Fingin shuffled out, confused, relieved, and anxious. He didn't go far, hovering just outside the door, close enough to hear Tomnat's continued moaning, Brigit's terse commands, and the stew bubbling on the hearth. His stomach rumbled and he wished he'd scooped out a bowl of stew for himself before he went outside.

He didn't like Tomnat. They'd formed no friendship bond, much less affection. But she was the mother of his child, and her anguished cries still tore through his heart. Every screech and sob made him want to rush into the roundhouse and take her pain away.

Fingin paced back and forth, arguing with himself about braving Brigit's certain wrath, or waiting outside to suffer the wails of the mother of his child. Suffer? How could he consider what he went through suffering, when Tomnat's agonized screams ripped through the glade?

The long day caught up with him, and he curled up against the outside wall. He hadn't even remembered to bring a blanket, but the late spring evening was mild. He lost the battle with sleep while wishing Bran was there to curl up against his back.

Chapter Fifteen

A baby's squalling cry broke ripped him from slumber.

Fingin rubbed his face to wipe the sleep from his eyes. The cry didn't sound like Conall's. Realization that Tomnat must have given birth made him jump to his feet, and then grab the wall to keep himself from falling over. Despite a long sleep, he still felt exhausted.

Upon entering the roundhouse, he noticed several things. Brigit held a red-faced babe, Conall slept next to her, swaddled in a blanket, and Tomnat had vanished.

He bowed to Brigit, grateful for the goddess' attention to his prayer and his family. "Thank you f-for your help."

She clicked her tongue. "You're in well over your head with this lot. Now, would you like to hold your daughter? Tomnat has named her. Lainn, meet your father."

The goddess placed the tiny baby in his arms, but Lainn kept her eyes screwed closed, no matter how much cooing and tickling Fingin tried to open them. He contented himself by rocking her against his chest. A son and a daughter. Conall and Lainn. His own precious family. He glanced up, searching for Tomnat.

Brigit pursed her lips. "Ah yes, about that. Tomnat has already returned to Faerie."

He tried to make sense of that. "What? Did she f-forget something? She's been here for m-m-moons. Why did she need to go back now?"

"She's not coming back, Fingin. Tomnat's done what she set out to do."

Fingin's head swam with confusion. "But she wanted b-babies. Why would she abandon them?"

Brigit sighed and put her arms out for the babe. Fingin didn't want to give her up, so held her more closely. "Tomnat *thought* she wanted babies. She did everything in her power, pulled on all her favors, to make that happen. But sometimes what we want is not what we need."

Conall began to fuss, so the goddess picked him up. "Once she bore her child, a crying baby she must pay attention to every day, all day, then faced seasons doing the same in this mortal world with a creature she barely tolerates, she realized how much work they would be. She and I spoke before she left."

What woman would abandon her children without a backward glance? No human woman, of course. But Fae weren't human. He shouldn't ascribe human motives or needs to them.

Fingin shook his head and peered again into his daughter's face. Her eyelids seemed translucent, finer than any butterfly wing. A bee buzzed into the roundhouse and lit upon her forehead. She wrinkled her brow and he waved the bee away, lest it sting her perfect skin.

Conall struggled to get out of Brigit's grip now, and she placed him on the floor. "I've someone coming to help you, but you must find a human wife, someone willing to help you raise your children. I'll send a few prospects your way." Brigit rose, brushing some dried rushes from her skirts.

Fingin's panic rose. "Wait! D-don't leave yet! How do I f-f-feed her?"

"Adhna is on his way. He'll have milk, blankets, anything you need for the child. He's rather competent, for a male."

Fingin glanced at Conall, who had crawled next to the hearth and curled up next to the warmth, and at wee Lainn, burbling in his arms, her eyes shut tight.

Tomnat hadn't even bid him farewell. They'd been forced into a partnership, not one built out of love or even affection. She'd tolerated his presence as a necessity, and he stayed with her out of duty.

But it bothered him that she'd been able to abandon her children, the flesh of her flesh. Did Fae possess no maternal instincts at all? Or was Tomnat unusual? He wanted to imagine Airiu would be more tender-hearted.

Fingin caught his breath. "Airiu! I must let her know I'm f-free!"

But no one answered. Brigit had gone.

Before the darkness claimed the night, Adhna arrived. He carried a bundle over his back, which he swung to the floor as he smiled at Fingin's daughter, who was now fussing and grunting in his arms. "Greetings to you, young human! I've a gift and a message for you."

"A message? From Airiu?"

He chuckled. "No, Airiu couldn't send a message. Bodach is still watching her carefully. However, Bran sent you this." He reached into the bundle and held out his arms.

A squirming days-old puppy opened brown eyes, melting Fingin's heart. He wanted to cuddle the small dog, but his arms were filled with his daughter. "A p-p-puppy? Is he Bran's?"

Adhna's eyes crinkled with joy. "Indeed she is. Bran found a Faerie hound he is fond of. The puppy is called Brí. Bran asked if you would care for her as you cared for him."

Fingin placed Lainn in her cot and picked up the puppy. She immediately licked every bit of his face. "Tell me B-b-bran at least ate Bodach's clothing? P-peed in his shoes?"

With a chuckle, Adhna grinned. "As a Fae, I'd never lie directly to a mortal. Therefore, I cannot tell you Bran has refrained from such sabotage."

With a wide grin, Fingin looked around at his new family. In turns, he hugged Brí, his son, and his daughter. He'd subtracted two friends, added a wife and a son, then subtracted a wife, then added a daughter and a new puppy. His math had never been strong, but the results pleased him. He now only ached for one more person.

"You said Airiu c-can't send a message. Is she a p-prisoner?"

"Not a prisoner, but not free, either. She cannot risk a visit to the mortal realm now. The time difference is too great, young man. She'll have other duties now, with no leisure to gallivant off to your world whenever she wants. Bodach has seen to that." His expression grew pensive.

"What? What has Bodach d-d-done? He survived the battle, I suppose."

Adhna wrinkled his nose. "Oh, yes, he survived. The Queen has not been kind to him, but he lives. He takes his anger and frustration out on the lesser Fae, such as Airiu. The Queen protects her as much as she can, but she cannot leave."

Fingin squeezed the puppy too hard and she whined. "What can I d-do to help? This is all my fault. She shouldn't have to suffer for my own actions."

Adhna clenched his teeth. "You cannot return. Bodach would kill you as soon as you set foot in Faerie. He's set out sentries at all the entrances, in case you should try to sneak in. No, you must stay away from Faerie. Perhaps someday, seasons from now, he'll relax his vigil and you can find Airiu again. Now, Brigit told me of the task she gave you, and I've selected several options."

"Options?"

"For a human wife, of course."

Each young woman Adhna brought him seemed sweet enough. But none of them seemed to possess any sense of delight, any spark of the joy he'd found with Airiu.

He dreamt of Airiu's silken hair, her velvet skin, her musical voice. The stories she told, the conversations they shared. Their hopes and plans. None of the human women Adhna brought carried even a glimmer of that magic.

After a moon, Adhna threw his hands in the air. "Stop being so stubborn, Fingin. You'll never find a woman who compares to a Fae. Stop looking for true love and settle for true comfort. You have children to feed. Look at your daughter. The goat's milk isn't good for her. She should have grown more by now. And Conall was weaned too young. Have you no thought for their health?"

Ashamed, Fingin hung his head and sighed. "You're right. I'll t-take the next young woman you bring."

Adhna crossed his arms. "Oh, no. I've scoured the countryside for eligible brides, and you've turned them all down. Now it's up to you to find a mate. I'm done trying."

He'd never been any good at finding people, much less wooing women. But Adhna couldn't lie.

He'd squandered his chances, so now he must find his own. "C-can you at least fix my voice for a while? I c-c-can't woo a woman with this stutter."

Adhna scowl turned to a kinder expression. "I would if I could, young man. However, you'll just have to push through it. Magic isn't the answer for everything wrong in the world."

The next day, Fingin went to market, dried and fresh fish for trade. He'd also woven several mats using Airiu's exquisite patterns. Maybe his handiwork would attract the eye of a prospect. He brought both his children. Any woman would need to know what she's getting into right away.

Still, Fingin held out little hope. As Adhna mentioned, the local countryside held few options. But sometimes a relative would visit from another village.

The baker's daughter, a small round girl about his own age, had been one of Adhna's suggestions. She sent him a kind smile as he passed by, looking for a place to set out his goods.

He strolled by the tanner's stall, which shared a space with the cooper. They had no daughters, but he waved anyhow. Talking was still difficult, so he kept silent by default.

The blacksmith, a burly, dark man with curly hair, nodded as he settled in the next open spot. He had no daughters either, but a young woman was carrying a load of wood to his furnace. Wisps of dark brown hair had escaped her braid and a smudge of soot marred her face, but she flashed him a friendly smile.

Fingin set out his fish, his mats, and arranged the children so he could keep an eye on them. Lainn lay in a wide basket, while he kept Conall in his lap, the child occupied with a wooden puzzle game Fingin had carved last moon.

A few people wandered by, and by midday, he'd sold half his fish and two of his five mats. In return, he'd gotten an iron pot and two wool blankets, both green. The children would need them come winter.

The dark-haired blacksmith's helper stood behind him, hands on her hips. "So, what's your name?"

He gave her a nod but didn't stand. Conall gave him an excuse to remain sitting. "I'm c-c-called Fingin. What's your name?"

"Ligach. Do you live nearby?"

Epilogue

They married with little fuss. Ligach told him right away that she was barren. She'd married before, and gave birth to a misshapen monster. The druí told her she'd have no more children, and her husband left.

"So, when I saw you already had children, I thought you might take on a wife who'd bear no more."

He didn't fault her logic, and he enjoyed talking with her. She spoke her mind, even if she chattered more than he liked.

Sometimes, he even missed Tomnat's taciturn ways, but now he lived in a real home, with a real family, and a real life. He'd fathered two delightful children. When Conall got old enough to stand in the river, he'd teach the boy how to fish. Lainn grew into a bright child who loved to listen to the stories he'd learned in Faerie.

Ligach didn't seem as enchanted by the stories, but she didn't object when he entertained the children. He didn't have the undying passion for Ligach he'd felt for Airiu, but her company made him content.

Adhna stayed close by to help when he felt lost. His puppy grew strong and loyal, just like her father. He'd grown rich beyond his dreams.

Several years on, Fingin still hadn't recovered his full strength. Each day, he felt more tired than the last. Had he grown old so quickly? But he only had thirty winters. Even his morning ritual, welcoming the sun and the power of the earth through his body, did little to ease the growing fatigue that permeated every bone. He still delighted in the sunrise, but the delight didn't sink into his bones.

When he asked Adhna about being so tired, the Fae thought it might have to do with his time in Faerie. Sometimes that realm latched onto a human soul. It ached to have him back and pulled him every day.

Someday, when his children were older, he'd have to return. Hopefully, Bodach will have lost interest in hunting him down, and he could search for Airiu. They might go off together to some unknown corner of Faerie, or maybe even *Tír na nÓg*. However, he must wait until his children grew enough to care for themselves.

Soon.

A world shunning old beliefs. Can a pagan woman protect her family without falling prey to both Christians and power-hungry Fae?

Can this Fae-touched woman keep from becoming a forgotten relic in a society ensorcelled with a new religion?

Start reading *Age of Druids* to call the wind and the rain today!

www.GreenDragonArtist.com/Books

Thank You!

Thank you so much for enjoying Age of Secrets. If you've enjoyed the story, please consider leaving a review so other readers can discover Fingin's adventures!

If you would like to get updates, sneak previews, sales, and get a FREE short story and a FAMILY TREE, pease sign up for my newsletter.

www.GreenDragonArtist.com

Other Books by This Author

**See all the books available
through Green Dragon Publishing at
*www.GreenDragonArtist.com/Books***

Historical Note

Dear Readers,

As you embark on the enchanting odyssey of "Age of Secrets," I am delighted to offer you a glimpse into the historical inspirations that weave through this captivating narrative.

Set against the backdrop of Ireland in the year 500, this is another novel without much interaction with historical leaders. However, I delved deep into lore to pull out some gems. For instance, the salmon of knowledge is a strong legend within the Irish mythology.

The Fianna, bands of warriors who are pledged to protect Ireland from invaders, are the subject of an entire mythological cycle (Fenian cycle). These bands had lots of work in the summer, wandering around the land, but they were idle in the winter. And there were tales of these bands abusing their power, taking food and other resources whenever they wanted.

In this book, as in several others, I have some characters who are Christian and some who are pagan. Despite what the history books claim, no mass conversion is instant. Some places and people hold on to the old ways for centuries or more. That conflict between differing beliefs is eternal.

Fingin travels to Skellig Michael, a lonely, rocky island off the west coast of Ireland. It held a community of monks, who built stone, beehive-shaped huts that still stand to this day. He also encounters a trio of creatures; the stag, the sea eagle, and the salmon. Yes, there's that salmon again! Many quests and stories group things by threes.

Another divine entity shows up in this book, Brigid. She has been both goddess and saint, but there are certain things that are associated with her, such as creativity, blacksmithing, crafting, and red-eared cows.

When I was worldbuilding my version of Faerie, I researched the Queens associated with each area of Ireland. There are many different versions of these legends, but I tried to stick with the older sources. While Irish Fairies in the sources don't have 'courts' as is described in Scottish legends, I created one in my world, but that wasn't based on any lore.

"Age of Secrets" is an immersive adventure that explores themes of resilience, magic, and the indomitable human spirit. As Fingin navigates a landscape fraught with ruthless thugs, treacherous crossings, and enchanting faery magic, the narrative invites you to journey beyond the veil and embrace the wonder that awaits.

About the Author

Christy Nicholas writes under several pen names, including Rowan Dillon, CN Jackson, and Emeline Rhys. She's an author, artist, and accountant. After she failed to become an airline pilot, she quit her ceaseless pursuit of careers that began with the letter 'A' and decided to concentrate on her writing. Since she has Project Completion Compulsion, she is one of the few authors with no unfinished novels.

Christy has her hands in many crafts, including digital art, beaded jewelry, writing, and photography. In real life, she's a CPA, but having grown up with art all around her (her mother, grandmother, and great-grandmother are/were all artists), it sort of infected her, as it were. She wants to expose the incredible beauty in this world, hidden beneath the everyday grime of familiarity and habit, and share it with others. She uses characters out of time and places infused with magic and myth, writing magical realism stories in both historical fantasy and time travel flavors.

Social Media Links:
Blog: www.GreenDragonArtist.net
Website: www.GreenDragonArtist.com
Facebook: www.facebook.com/greendragonauthor
Instagram: www.instagram.com/greendragonartist9
TikTok: www.tiktok.com/@greendragonauthor